D1537061

THE DAY HE DROVE BY

HAWTHORNE HARBOR SECOND CHANCE
ROMANCE BOOK 1

ELANA JOHNSON

ISBN-13: 979-8648248175

"Aaron, you have to stop the car. We're not going to make it." Gretchen Samuels hated the weakness and panic in her voice, but the pain ripping through her lower back made it difficult to speak any other way.

"We're in the middle of nowhere," her husband said. "I can't stop." In fact, he accelerated to a speed their twelve-year-old sedan certainly couldn't handle.

As another labor pain tore through her, tears spilled from Gretchen's eyes. She didn't want to have her first child on the side of the road, miles from nurses and antiseptic and baby warmers. And medication. She really needed a fast-acting painkiller.

"I'm sorry," she sobbed. Aaron hated living out on her granddad's lavender farm, but the housing was cheap and he was almost done with his online securities degree. Their plans for a future in Seattle while he led the data security team at a top technology firm were months from coming to fruition.

"Don't be sorry." He glanced at her, and she disliked the panic in his eyes too, and the white-knuckle grip he had on the steering wheel certainly wasn't comforting.

Her breath caught in her throat as it seemed like this baby was going to claw its way out of her no matter how much she willed the little girl to hold on a little longer.

"Call 911," she said. "Please." She must've infused the right amount of emotion into her voice, because Aaron slowed the car and eased it onto the gravel shoulder. He leapt from behind the wheel, left his door open, and sprinted around the front of the car.

"Let's get you into the back." He supported her—the way he'd been doing for the four years they'd been together —and helped her into the backseat before pulling out his phone and making the emergency call.

Gretchen's pain eased with the new position, but it didn't go away. She wondered if it ever would, or if this degree of agony would hover in her muscles like a ghost forever. "Hang on," she whispered as she put her hand on her very pregnant belly. "Just a little while longer."

"They're on their way." Aaron poked his head back inside the car. "They said to get any blankets, towels, napkins, anything we have. You're supposed to stay lying down and try to relax."

Gretchen couldn't help the snort that escaped. "Relax?" She let her head fall back as she focused on the car's ceiling.

She hadn't been able to relax for months, not since her stomach had grown so large she couldn't see her toes. Simply getting up from the couch had grown increasingly difficult as the days had passed.

She hadn't minded, because she and Aaron had wanted this baby more than anything. The tears that heated her eyes this time were from desperation. A shiver ran over her body as the wind snaked its way into the car.

"Aaron, can you close the doors?" She lifted her head but couldn't see him anywhere. Fear flowed through her. "Aaron?"

The trunk slammed, and he came to the door closest to her head this time. "We don't have a blanket in the trunk. I found this jacket though." He balled it up and put it under her head before shrugging out of the one he was wearing too.

Gretchen steeled herself to deliver her baby and wrap it in her husband's polar fleece. Her range of emotions felt ridiculous as a wave of injustice slammed into her. "Close the doors, please," she said through tight teeth. "I'm cold." Should she be cold? What if she was going into shock or something?

Her jaw worked against the rising terror as he complied, going around the car—which had all four doors open—and shutting the wind out before sealing himself behind the wheel again. Gretchen thought the silence in the car might be worse than the wind, and she didn't want to bring her baby into the world under such a cloud of awkwardness.

"Remember when we first met?" she asked him, glad when his low, soft chuckle met her ears.

"You said my hair looked like a gorilla."

She giggled too, though the motion made her stomach muscles tighten uncomfortably. She hitched in a breath and held it. Aaron had been a freshman on campus though he was twenty-three years old. Gretchen had just finished her business management degree. His dark hair was swooped to the side, very much like the cartoon gorillas Gretchen had spent a lot of time watching while she nannied to pay for school.

He reached back and threaded his fingers through hers. "What if they don't make it?" he asked, his voice barely higher than a whisper. "I don't know how to deliver a baby."

And Gretchen knew there was more than just a baby that needed to come out. "They'll make it." She spoke with as much confidence as she could, the way she always did when Aaron confessed his worries to her.

You're the best in your class, she'd tell him. *You'll be able to find a good job.*

Don't worry about anything here, she said to him when he had to go to Seattle to take his tests, attend interviews, or deliver dissertations. *I'll be fine. Just watching the lavender grow.*

She closed her eyes and imagined herself in the fields of lavender now, the fragrant scent of the herbs wafting through the slow, blue sky. The same smile that had always accompanied her assurances when he left drifted across her face now.

Her next labor pain stole all the peace from her, and her eyes shot open and a moan ground through her whole body. Aaron's fingers on hers squeezed, and everything seemed clenched so tight, tight, tight.

The contraction seemed to last a long time before subsiding. Gretchen only got what felt like a moment's reprieve before the next one began. Time marched on, seemingly unaware of the pain she was in, the desperate way she cinched everything tight to keep the baby inside.

She wasn't sure how many labor pains she'd endured, or how much time had gone by, before Aaron said, "They're here," with a heavy dose of relief in his voice. He once again jumped from the car.

Moments later, the door by her feet opened and a gust of ocean air raced in. The scent of brine she normally loved only reminded her that this wasn't a hospital, there were no drugs, and she could do absolutely nothing about it.

"Ma'am, my name is Andrew Herrin, and I'm going to take good care of you."

She managed to look over her belly to a man who couldn't be older than twenty. A zing of alarm raced through her.

"Drew?" She couldn't believe she cared if the man whose family lived next door to her—who she'd walked with in lavender fields as a teen—delivered her baby. He had a bag of medical supplies. A faster ride to the hospital. And a kind face, with a calm smile.

"You're going to be fine, Gretchen." He snapped a pair of gloves on and touched her ankle. "So let's see what we've got."

1

Drew Herrin felt the morning sun warm his back as he worked. He'd already fed the chickens, the horses, the cows, and the goats. His mother and step-father had quite the little farm just north of Hawthorne Harbor, down the Lavender Highway. He glanced up and took a moment to just breathe, something he hadn't been able to do in Medina, though the town sat right on the water too.

The air simply tasted different here, and while Drew had hoped to make something of himself in Medina—do more, be better, actually help someone—he'd only realized the job was the same there as it was here. Just more stressful. Less fun. No room to run with his German shepherds and experiment with his ice cream flavors.

The wind picked up, but Drew was used to being windblown. Everyone on Hawthorne Harbor was. The long-time joke was that if you didn't like the wind, you should leave. Because it was always windy.

He looked across the water to the body of land he could just make out in the distance. He'd grown up on the harbor, but it still gave him a snip of surprise to remember he was looking at another country when he looked at that land.

For a fleeting moment, the same restlessness that had driven him to Medina three years ago squirreled through him again.

Then he put his head down and got back to work. He finished fixing the tractor his step-dad used to get the lavender fields properly built up for watering. He sharpened a few tools and whistled for his shepherds to come with him as he headed back to the house.

With a single bark, Blue announced his arrival from the huge flower garden adjacent to the farm. He brought the scent of roses with him, and even a white petal from a flower Drew would never know.

"You rascal." Drew grinned at the dog and flicked the petal to the ground. "You can't go over there." He glanced at the expansive garden, bearing row after row of flowers in all colors, shapes, and sizes. His family owned the land, but he'd learned that his mother rented it to a local florist in town, who apparently hand-grew everything she sold in her shop on Main Street.

Drew had never met the woman. She tended to the flowers when he wasn't there, obviously. And he had no need for flowers, as he'd sworn off women and all common dating practices when his last girlfriend had carved out his heart and then left town.

A text. That was what he'd gotten after a fifteen-month relationship where diamonds and children had been discussed.

I can't do this.

Drew thought the words his ex had sent now, though he tried to stuff all memories with Yvonne in them back into the box where he kept them.

Can't hadn't been in Drew's vocabulary growing up. His father had taught him to fix cars, tractors, lawn mowers, all of it. He worked the farm, rode horses, raised goats, planted lavender, and played a major role in the Hawthorne Harbor Lavender Festival. There was nothing Drew couldn't do.

He'd taken that attitude into adulthood, first finishing his emergency medical technician training and then going on to be a certified firefighter. He'd gone on to take cardiac life support classes, pediatric training, and tactical emergency care.

No, *can't* didn't exist in Drew's world. At least until Yvonne.

Something wet met his palm, and Drew danced away from his second German shepherd, the much more silent and sneaky Chief. A chuckle came from his throat, and Drew crouched to let his dogs lick his neck and face. His laughter grew, and he was reminded why this remote farm on the edge of Hawthorne Harbor felt more like home than anywhere else.

"Morning chores are done," he announced as he entered the wide, white farmhouse, his dogs right behind him. Their claws scratched against the hardwood, and he pointed to the utility room where he kept their food and water. "Go on, guys. I'll come let you out in a minute."

"Thanks, Drew," Joel said. His step-dad didn't mind the farm and the equipment upkeep, but his true love was with the lavender, and Drew figured they could both do what they liked best if he came out and tended to the animals.

Joel had spent the first thirty years of his life in trade carpentry, and he'd improved the inside and outside of the farmhouse until Drew barely recognized it. He stepped into the kitchen with the high, honey-colored wood beams slanting up to the vaulted ceiling to find his dark-haired mother standing at the stove.

"Morning, Ma." He swept a kiss along her hairline as she scrambled eggs. The smell made his stomach turn, and he opted for turning away and pouring himself a glass of orange juice. Funny how his father had passed nine years ago, and Drew still couldn't handle the sight and smell of his dad's favorite breakfast. How his mother continued making it every morning was a mystery to him. Thankfully, the grief that hit at unexpected times only tapped his heart today. Sometimes it could punch, leaving him breathless and confused.

"Are you working today?" she asked, switching her attention to a pan of sizzling bacon.

"Yep. Gonna shower and head in." He wondered what

today would bring behind the wheel of the ambulance. Probably another cat stuck in another tree. Or a kid with a scrape or two. Drew chastised himself that he shouldn't *want* anyone in Hawthorne Harbor to need emergency medical care. But that seething need to *do something worthwhile* wouldn't seem to quiet today.

"Can I leave Blue and Chief here?"

"Yeah." Joel exhaled as he stood and refilled his coffee. "I'll take 'em out to the lavender fields and then let them swim in the harbor."

Drew smiled at the man. "Thanks, Joel. I promise I'll come get them tonight. The raccoons out here get them barking at night."

"Maybe they'll finally scare them away from my chickens," he said with a grumbly note in his voice. Joel certainly did love his fresh eggs and those clucky chickens.

"Breakfast?" his mother asked when Drew attempted to leave the kitchen.

"I'll stop at Duality on the way in." Part gas station and part eatery, the chefs at Duality made the best breakfast burritos Drew had ever tasted. He softened his rejection of her food with the biggest smile he could pull off and hooked his thumb over his shoulder. "I'm going to use the bathroom upstairs. I'll hang up my towel."

She didn't protest, and Drew took the steps two at a time to the mostly unused second floor. His old bedroom was up here, completely redone with the same luxurious hardwood Joel had gotten for next to nothing when a client decided they wanted something different. He'd painted the room in a light blue-gray and wispy white curtains had been added.

But the bedspread his mother had quilted still draped the bed, and Drew took a moment to run his fingertips along it. His favorite colors were green and blue, and he loved everything about being outside. So she'd carefully pieced together pine green pieces to make trees, dark brown pieces to make mountains, and several shades of blue to make the sky and ocean that surrounded this town Drew loved.

How he'd thought he could ever leave it and be happy plagued him. "Doesn't matter," he muttered to himself. He was back now, and happy helping around the farm as his parents got older, happy to have his old job back at the emergency services company that contracted with the hospital in Hawthorne Harbor, nearby Olympic National Park, and four other towns in the surrounding area.

After he showered, dressed, and let his dogs back outside, he climbed behind the wheel of his truck for the fifteen-minute drive into town. He loved the commute from farm to civilization. Though he didn't make it every day, the straight road and country stillness allowed his mind to wander along new flavor combinations for his ice cream fetish.

He'd been circling something new for a few days now, something he hadn't quite been able to put his taste buds on. He'd tried lavender and honey—that combination was as old as the Lavender Festival in town. White chocolate and lavender had been well-received among his paramedic teams, but he didn't think it special enough to enter the Festival's contest.

No, he definitely needed something special, something with that added oomph to make the Festival judges give him the coveted Lavender King title this year. He knew Augustus Hammond would enter the competition, and he'd won with ice cream three times out of the last six years. If Drew was going to take on the three-time Lavender King, it wasn't going to be with lavender and honey.

And he wasn't just competing against other food artisans. Oh, no. The town hosted the largest lavender festival in the entire country, and they gave out awards for revolutionary and best-use way of utilizing the plant that brought a new twist to old lavender traditions. He needed something special, but so far, it had eluded him.

He'd nearly arrived at the flavor that seemed to skip in and out of his mind when he saw a big, brown van on the side of the road up ahead. The vehicle looked older than him, and it sunk low on one corner, indicating a flat tire.

A blonde girl stood in the middle of the road, waving both of her arms. Drew immediately slowed and pulled to the gravel shoulder, giving plenty of distance between his truck and the van.

"Thank goodness." The girl ran up to his truck before he could get fully out. She looked to be ten or eleven, with big front teeth she hadn't quite grown into yet. She had dark green eyes that had probably come half from her mother and half from her father. "You're the first car that's come along in an hour."

"Not much going on out here in the mornings," he said, glancing past her to the front driver's side, where the van leaned.

"My mom blew her tire, and we need help." The girl sized him up as if she could tell by looking alone if he could help or not. "Can you change a tire?"

"Sure I can." He gave her a smile, noting that all the windows on the van were glazed dark. His defenses went up, especially because her "mom" still hadn't made an appearance. Crime was low in Hawthorne Harbor—one reason he hadn't gone to the police academy to make his certifications a trifecta in public service.

But still. This non-moving van, with all those black windows, and a little girl in the middle of the road... Drew proceeded with caution.

She played with the end of her pale ponytail. "My mom will try to tell you she can do it herself." Her voice pitched lower with every word and her eyes rounded. "But don't believe her. We've been out here for over an hour, and she's cried twice. 'The flowers,' she keeps saying." The girl turned and skipped toward the van. "Come on."

Drew took out his phone and tapped out a message to his boss. *On my way in, I ran across a motorist on the side of the road. Flat tire. Just north of mile marker seventeen on the Lavender Highway. Going to check it out.*

That way, if something happened, someone knew where

he was. He'd been on the Lavender Highway hundreds of times, and he'd only stopped once—to deliver a baby almost ten years ago.

He glanced around. It had been right around here too, closer to the farm than the town, out in the middle of nowhere. He wondered what had happened to Aaron and Gretchen Samuels, and the baby girl he'd wrapped in a towel before delivering the afterbirth.

Let us know if you need help came back, and Drew pocketed his phone and shelved his memories of the last time he'd been out of a car on this stretch of the road so his senses could be on full alert.

2

T*he roses* ran through Gretchen's mind. They were never going to make it. They couldn't sit in a car for so long and still be fresh. Though she'd wrapped the stems in damp towels, the way she always did, the April sun had risen an hour ago, baking her dark brown van while she tried to get the lug nuts to work with her instead of against her.

"Mom, someone finally drove by." Dixie returned, her voice chipper as usual. Gretchen coached herself not to snap at her daughter. She'd been helpful that morning in the gardens while Gretchen had attended to the apiary.

She groaned as she thought about the honey sitting in the van too. It had probably oozed all over by now, and she didn't dare open the door to check. Instead, she straightened, very aware of the kink in her back. So she wasn't as young as she once was. She'd slept little the night before, thus prompting the pre-dawn trip out to the garden to gather the flowers she needed for the wedding that afternoon.

A scream gathered in the back of her throat, where she worked to tamp it down. She'd arranged so many weddings in the three years of owning and operating The Painted Daisy that a shriek was the only response she had left.

But weddings paid better than baptisms, than birthday parties, than first dates. The only things better were Valentine's Day and funerals, and one of those only came around once a year. So Gretchen took on every wedding that came her way—which was a lot, as Hawthorne Harbor seemed to be a popular place to tie the knot.

"Who drove by?" she asked her daughter as she braced one palm against her lower back and attempted to straighten further. The crunch of footsteps on gravel came closer, and finally a man appeared at the edge of the van.

Tall, with dark hair, a full beard that was salted with just the right amount of maturity, and deep, brown pools for eyes, Gretchen drank in the sight of the man like she hadn't tasted water in years.

"That man." Dixie pointed to him. "He said he can change a tire."

Gretchen pulled the girl to her side. "You talked to him?" The way the man watched her, curiosity almost in his expression, unnerved her. And why hadn't he spoken?

He stepped closer. "Looks like you really do have a flat." He said it like he hadn't believed Dixie. She did have the cutest, impish little face. A jokester, like her father. But Gretchen couldn't stay mad at her for longer than thirty seconds, it seemed.

"I can handle it," Gretchen said, though she hadn't even managed to get off the offending tire yet. And with the wedding looming in just six hours, things were starting to get tight on her timeline.

"She can't handle it," Dixie blurted. Gretchen's fingers gripped her daughter's shoulder. "Mom, you can't. You don't even know if we have a spare."

She'd been waiting to look, not wanting to disturb the flowers. "Of course we have a spare," she said anyway. She'd bought the van from a plumbing company, because the engine never seemed to stop running, had a lot of cargo space for her floral needs, and it had been cheap. And since Aaron's death, she'd needed to be more frugal.

The man came closer still, and something familiar triggered in her mind. He seemed to be staring at her with the same déjà vu expression on his face, and he asked, "Do I know you?"

She almost snorted. Was that a pick-up line? Practically everyone in Hawthorne Harbor knew one another—which made it strange that she didn't quite know his name either.

"I—I'm—" She cut off. He didn't get to sit at her personal table and know her private past. She'd spent every summer here, so if he had too, or he'd grown up here, he probably knew of her. "I'm Gretchen Samuels. I spent summers on my granddad's lavender farm back the way you were coming."

A smile lit up his face, which only made him more handsome. An injustice, really, because how was she supposed to defend against his straight, white teeth and those eyes that now shone like stars?

"Gretchen Samuels. You don't say." He stepped again, almost close enough now to reach out and touch her. She remained stiff and unyielding, still unsure of who he was. "And this must be the little girl I delivered right along here somewhere. What'd you name her again? Was it...Dixie?"

All at once, understanding slammed into Gretchen's chest. She gasped at the air, her mind racing, tumbling, aligning his face and his voice with the events of her past.

"Drew Herrin?" she whispered.

His laughter filled the sky, completely eradicating any remaining misgivings she had about accepting his help. After all, he'd guided her through her one and only labor, and they'd all survived that harrowing event.

"So," he said once he'd quieted. "Can I take a look at it?"

She stepped back, drawing Dixie with her. "Be my guest." She gestured to the stubborn lug nuts, sure they'd never come off, even for him. He seemed bigger than she remembered, but she'd been in a lot of pain and lying on the backseat of a car.

Drew crouched and touched the rim with one finger.

"Dix, that's the paramedic who delivered you."

"It is?" Dixie looked back and forth between Drew and Gretchen. "No way!" Dixie loved the story of her birth, and Gretchen had told it to her many, many times. Especially after Aaron's passing, Dixie wanted to know more and more about him. It wasn't uncommon for Dixie to climb into bed with Gretchen and say, "Tell me something about Dad I don't know."

She crouched down next to Drew. "What are you doing?"

He glanced at her, that same kindness in his face though he'd grown into his age now. Gretchen hugged herself and watched as he told her about the lug nuts. "This one's stripped," he said with a sigh. He didn't look at Gretchen when he said, "Someone probably used the wrong sized tool on it. I'll see what I have in my truck."

He left the X-shaped tool she'd found in the back of the van on the ground where she'd dropped it and headed back to his truck. Dixie skipped after him, already completely at ease with him. She'd gotten really good at spending time with adults since Gretchen had come to Hawthorne Harbor and started The Painted Daisy. Weddings required her to work afternoons and evenings, and that meant she needed to rely on others to help with Dixie. It had been difficult at first, but they'd both had three years of practice, and Gretchen wasn't surprised at all to see her sticking to Drew like his new shadow.

"Oh!" She pulled out her phone and dialed the elementary school they'd been heading to. Dixie was now late, and

Gretchen's anxiety increased with every passing moment Drew didn't return with the right tool.

She explained the situation to the school secretary and hung up just as Dixie bounded back and opened the back of the van.

"Whoa, whoa," Gretchen said. "What's—what are you doing?"

"Drew said we need to make sure we have a spare before we do anything else."

"He can't find the right tool, can he?" She glanced back to where he still rummaged around in the back of his truck. He was probably secretly hoping there was no spare.

Dixie reached into the van, and Gretchen leapt forward. "Let me, Dix. Let me." She lifted the very edge of the floor mat and tried to peer underneath, the way she had when she'd retrieved the lug nut tool. Gingerly, she shifted the roses she and Dixie had clipped that morning, pushing them further forward. She tried to ignore that the towels were nearly dry, that some of the flower heads drooped a bit.

She could still do the boutonnieres, the centerpieces, and the bride's bouquet. This wedding was all roses, from cream, to white, to pale purple and pink, to deep crimson red. They'd just need a bit of extra floral tape, maybe some well-concealed pins. She'd taken one flower arranging class at the community center in Seattle, the year Dixie started school and Gretchen didn't have much to fill the empty hours at home.

She'd been in the middle of a baking class at the time of Aaron's accident, and she pushed those thoughts away as she finally freed enough of the floor mat to peel it back. She stared into the empty space where the spare should've been.

Pure defeat slumped her shoulders and she spun when she heard Drew's deep voice ask, "Did you find the spare, Dixie?"

A slip of annoyance mixed with embarrassment and entered her bloodstream. She drew in a deep breath and steeled herself. "There's no spare."

"No spare?" Dixie stepped past her as if she didn't believe her.

Gretchen's mind raced. She had a broken down van full of flowers she needed for a wedding in six hours. Scratch that. Five hours and forty-five minutes. Dixie needed to go to school, as she was going home with Jess, a boy only a year older than her whose mother was Gretchen's best friend.

Her pulse thumped in her chest, and she pressed her palm over it, feeling the *ba-bump*, *ba-bump* against her skin. Could she cancel the wedding? She shook her head at herself. There was no way she could pull out of the wedding now. She'd already taken half of the money, and there was no one to replace her. She'd lose a ton of business if she didn't show up as promised, with the contracted bouquets and arrangements.

"How about we get all these flowers into the back of my truck?" Drew asked, already reaching past her, a wide smile stretching his mouth. "Then we better get Miss Dixie to school and your mom—" His eyes flicked toward her for only a fraction of a second. "To the florist. And then I have to check in with my boss."

So he was going to be late for work because of her. Great.

"That's not necessary," she said as he lifted an armful of red roses and turned toward his truck. Her anxiety kicked up a notch at the thought of what was in the back of his truck, and what might happen to the flowers back there.

"Mo-om," Dixie whined. "Help us move these flowers. I have music this morning and I don't want to miss it."

Gretchen got to work, relieved when she found a tarp lying in the bed of Drew's truck. They got the flowers moved in only a few minutes, and she spread the almost dry towels over them to preserve the petals as much as possible.

She climbed into the cab, the situation far from ideal. She needed that van to transport the arrangements this afternoon, and very little funds to get it fixed. *One problem at a time*, she told herself. She'd get Dixie to school and get her flowers into the refrigerator at the shop and go from there.

Drew waited out front while Gretchen ran Dixie into the front office at the elementary school and checked her in. Dixie hadn't missed music and that gave Gretchen a measure of relief.

When she climbed back into the cab with Drew, the atmosphere turned a bit charged. She hadn't realized how much of a barrier Dixie had provided, and she pointed to the right. "My shop is that way."

Granddad used to load her bike in the back of his truck and bring her downtown on the weekends. He worked the farmer's market with his lavender oils, soaps, honeys, and sachets. He infused lavender in everything, and his lemon lavender scones and dark chocolate lavender bark with salted almonds were bestsellers at the markets as well as the Lavender Festival. She'd ridden all over the town, laid on her back in the park, and gone swimming in the inlet on the west side of town.

Her chest pinched as she thought about her grandparents and their farm. They'd sold it five years ago, and at the time, she hadn't thought she'd miss it that much. She'd been completely engrossed in her life in the city, and though Hawthorne Harbor was only two hours away from Seattle, Gretchen didn't make it out to visit them as often as she should.

As the familiar shops passed—a bakery called The Honey Bun, a cluster of restaurants including a pizzeria, the 602 diner, and several fast-casual places Gretchen frequented each week—Drew glanced at her. "She's a great kid," he said.

"She always was," Gretchen agreed. "Remember how she didn't even cry when she was born?" She basked in the happy warmth of the memory and catalogued it so she could tell Dixie about it that night.

Drew chuckled and nodded. "That's right. I'd forgotten about that. You know, that scared me," he said. "We want babies to cry when they're born. Clear that liquid out of their lungs."

"Yeah, of course."

The barbershop went by, with the salon right next to it. The dog groomer, with its big white van that made house calls and had the cutest cartoon dog on the side, the library, and the movie theater.

"How long have you had the florist shop?" he asked.

"Three years." She nodded for a reason she couldn't name. Her stomach growled, reminding her that she'd skipped breakfast. Her head felt a little soft, like she needed more sleep to truly function properly. She had a few packaged snacks at the shop, and that would have to do, because she didn't have time for food today.

"So what brought you and Aaron back to town?" Drew pulled to a stop at the light, looking at her fully.

"Oh, uh." Gretchen hadn't had to explain about her late husband in a couple of years now. "Aaron passed away three years ago." She gave short little bursts of her head. "My grandparents had already sold the lavender farm, but I've always loved Hawthorne Harbor, so Dixie and I decided to come here. The Painted Daisy was up for sale, and I'd taken a class, so..." She told herself to stop talking. Most people didn't know what to say once they learned of Aaron's death, and Gretchen had learned to fill that silence.

Drew wore a look of sympathy. "Gretchen, I'm so sorry." Those dark, caring eyes pulled at her, and she cleared her throat and pointed at the light, which had turned green.

Drew watched her for another second and then eased forward, no awkwardness in his expression or body language at all. Gretchen supposed he probably dealt with emergencies and death more than the average person.

"Anyway." She exhaled, glad to almost be alone with her flowers again. "I was able to rent the land with my grandmother's flowers on it. Thankfully, the new owners hadn't demolished them yet. And now I do this." She tried to sound happy about it. Most days she was. She made enough to keep her and Dixie in a comfortable home, albeit with a vehicle that was almost as old as she was.

He nodded, something storming across his face. She should ask him about his family, as she knew a different neighbor must live next door to her granddad's farm now. Before she could ask, he pulled over in front of the shop.

"I'll call someone to go get that tire changed for you." He draped his hands lazily over the steering wheel. "Heck, my crew and I might be able to do it. Depends on how busy we are."

"You don't have to do that."

He started to unbuckle and she practically lunged for the door handle.

"I can get the flowers," she said.

"There's way more than you can carry." He didn't seem to take no for an answer, and Gretchen was already too tired to argue. Her head ached, and her stomach clenched, but together, she and Drew got the flowers into her shop.

"Thank you so much, Drew," she said. "Again. You're

always there when I need you." And he always had been. He'd been kind to her when she came to visit for the summers. Shown her how to harvest lavender, hang it in the cellar to dry, and steep it to draw the most fragrance from it. Not to mention delivering Dixie a decade ago and then helping with the flat tire this morning. Thank you didn't seem adequate, but she didn't have anything else to give him.

He saluted with a smile. "Happy to help." He ambled back toward his truck, and she marveled at how laid back and carefree he'd always been. Everything in her life felt so tense, and she envied his nonchalance.

Gretchen waved and went inside her shop. Pressing her back against the closed door, she shut her eyes and just breathed.

3

By the time Drew arrived at work, he was eighty minutes late. He checked in with Jean, the supervisor, and detailed what had happened out at mile marker seventeen. "Do you think we can send a couple of guys out there to take care of the van?"

"Seeing as how I've got Russ doing inventory for the third time this month, I think we can spare you two." Jean pulled out some paperwork that she'd probably looked at a dozen times. "This is really more of Adam's department, though." She peered at Drew over the top of her glasses, the question clear in her expression.

"Oh, don't call Adam." Drew waved his hand dismissively, his tone dry. "I'll let him know what happened." For some reason, Drew wanted to take care of the van for Gretchen. It wasn't his fault her tire had gone flat, or that she'd used the wrong tool and stripped the lug nuts. It wasn't his fault that her van had no spare tire, or that her husband had died, leaving her with a cute daughter to raise alone.

But he just wanted to do this for her. Maybe then, at least for today, his life would have meaning.

He left Jean's office before she could tell him he had to turn the flat tire case over to his brother. Adam would send out two of his officers, and everything would become so clinical. Besides, Drew had Gretchen's keys, and their weight in his pocket made him smile as he poked his head into the medical supply room.

Russ held a clipboard and surveyed a cupboard, a scowl on his face. Drew knocked twice on the door. "Russ, let's go. Flat tire."

He didn't even protest or ask why two paramedics were needed for a flat. He tossed the clipboard on the nearest shelf and followed Drew out to his truck. "We're not taking the bus?"

"I ran across a woman with a flat tire on my way in," he said. "It's not an emergency medical issue." He climbed into the cab. "Jean let us go, because there's nothing else going on." For the first time in the year he'd been back in Hawthorne Harbor, Drew was happy about the non-emergency nature of most of his days. Other days were slammed, and those times were hard too. He couldn't really decide what he hoped for on the job, honestly.

He pulled into Larkin Tire and Oil and headed inside to get a spare tire. "Hey, Bennett," he said to the man who was close to his step-father's age. "Got an old van that needs a tire for a spare."

"What year?" The older gentleman started tapping on a keyboard that used to be beige. The whole place smelled like rubber and grease, and Drew inhaled a noseful of it. He'd loved working with his father in the sheds behind the farmhouse, and he remembered days when he had dark stains along his fingers and under his nails.

"No idea on the year," Drew said. "It's one of those big Chevy ones. Three rows of seats. Ten-passengers, probably." Gretchen had taken all the seats out, but he'd seen vans like hers before. "You know, it looks like the plumbing vans."

"I got it," Bennett said, hitting the Enter key with more force than was reasonably necessary. "Ninety-nine dollars."

Drew hadn't thought through everything, clearly. He had the money, but he hesitated, wondering what Gretchen would think of him paying for the spare tire. She'd refuse him if she were here. Her independence and self-reliant spirit had been strong out on the Lavender Highway. Both times.

But she wasn't here, and she needed the spare. So he pulled out his wallet and slid his debit card across the counter. Russ watched him and then wandered over to the bulletin board, where flyers announcing *buy three tires and get the fourth free* hung.

"I'll have Jakey load it up for ya," Bennett said, and Drew turned toward the exit.

Russ gave him five seconds of peace before he said, "You bought the tire?"

"She'll pay me back."

"Who is this woman?"

Drew had a few extra moments to gather his thoughts together while Jake loaded the tire in the back of his truck and hit the tailgate a couple of times. He got in the vehicle and turned the key. "Remember how I delivered that baby ten years ago out on the Lavender Highway?"

"Before my time, but I've heard the story at least a dozen times."

"Oh, come on. I don't tell it that often."

"Yes, you do." Russ chuckled, his deep bass voice vibrating through the whole truck. "Every year at the Safety Fair." He started checking the times off on his fingers. "Every time we get together with the joint units for chicken wings. Every time—"

"Okay, okay." Drew laughed with his best friend. He glanced at the African-American man he'd worked beside before he left for Medina, and who'd still been here when he'd come back. They got along great, which was lucky as they spent a lot of time together.

"It's literally the most exciting thing that's ever happened on the job." Drew lifted one shoulder into a shrug.

"What about that hiker that got lost on Hurricane Hill?"

"That was a good day too." Drew sighed, trying to put his finger on exactly why that day he'd delivered Dixie in

February had been so significant to him. "It's just that, this wasn't an emergency because someone was bleeding, or because a glass broke in the kitchen sink. This—delivering that baby—it was like...magic. I helped a life come into the world."

"We help lives on every call we get," Russ said.

Drew agreed, because it was true. But delivering that little girl really had been different. He liked to think it was because it was Gretchen's baby, and he'd been friends with her for a number of years. Aaron too, as they'd lived next to his mom and dad while Aaron finished school. Drew had gotten busy with his own education, and moved out, and by the time Gretchen and Aaron left town with their five-month-old baby, they hadn't spoken since the day after Dixie's birth, when Drew had stopped by the hospital to check in on the two of them.

"So you like this woman?" Russ asked, his voice just on the edge of casual, suggesting his curiosity.

"I delivered her baby ten years ago," Drew said, forcing his voice into nonchalance too. "And then helped her into town. Nothing to like."

"And then begged Jean to let us go fix a flat tire. Which you paid for." Russ's eyebrows practically reached his hairline.

"Don't read anything into this," Drew said as they approached mile marker seventeen. "There's the van." With the two of them, they got the old tire off and the spare on in only a few minutes.

Drew was about to toss the ruined tire into the back when a police cruiser pulled to a stop alongside the van. The passenger side window went down, and Adam leaned across the seat. "Drew? What's goin' on here?"

Drew leaned his elbows on the car door and stuck his head in the car. "Hey, Adam." He smiled at his brother. "We've got this."

"Got a call about this abandoned van."

"I came across the owner on my way in from the farm." Drew rubbed his hand along his jawline where his beard itched. "I convinced Jean to let us come out. There's nothing going on today."

Adam's look of disapproval wasn't lost on Drew. "You should've called," he said. "This is a police matter."

"Sorry." Drew grinned and pulled out of the car. He tossed the ruined tire into the back, where a sliver of silver caught his eye. He traced his finger along the length of it. "That's a blade she drove over." Drew turned and scanned the road but couldn't see any other debris. Adam hadn't moved either.

"Dinner at my place tonight?" he called through the still-open window.

"What're you making?" Drew asked as Russ practically sprinted over.

"I'm in," he said, leaning into the window. "I haven't been grocery shopping in a week."

"I was thinkin' fish 'n chips." Adam draped one hand

over the steering wheel and gazed toward the water. "Maybe shrimp or something."

Sounded like he hadn't gone shopping either, but Drew didn't have anything else going on. "I just have to go out and get Blue and Chief from Mom and Joel after work."

"And take that van back," Adam said.

"Yeah." Drew turned away from the police car and took Gretchen's keys from his pocket. He tossed Russ his. "See you back at the station."

Russ groaned. "Can't we...I don't know. Maybe I'll drive in a ditch on the way back."

"Don't you dare," Drew said. "That's my truck, and Jean will never let us do non-emergency jobs again." He tapped on the doorframe. "I'll come for dinner, Adam."

"See ya." The police cruiser inched away, and Drew envied his brother. He could get in his car and drive around, looking for whatever it was cops looked for. He didn't have to stay in the office if he didn't want to.

He drove Gretchen's van back to The Painted Daisy and pulled around the back, where there were only two parking spots. Across the street sat the largest park in town, where the Lavender Festival took place every summer. Tall trees provided shade, and a couple of people had their dogs chasing Frisbees.

Drew inhaled the salty scent that permeated the seaside town, grateful for his life here. He faced the back of the building and saw a door labeled *floral deliveries*. He knocked on the door and then entered, calling out, "Hello?" The shop smelled like roses and pollen and something fresh, and the temperature was several degrees below that outside.

"I'm in the back," she called. A hall in front of him had a door on the left, leading to a bathroom, and on the right a big, metal door that looked like the walk-in fridge in the restaurant where he'd worked in high school. Beyond that, multi-height displays of vases and flowers sat on a single table, with an entire wall of refrigeration units that held various colors of flowers.

Gretchen came into the hall, wiping her hands on a green apron. "Coming."

"It's me," he said as she started to turn right.

She spun to her left, surprise flickering across her face as her hands flew to her throat. "Oh!" She recovered quickly, her shock melting away into recognition. "Drew. What are you doing here?"

He held out her keys and kept his position in the hall. "I got your tire fixed and drove your van over."

"You did not." She cocked her hip and her blonde-streaked auburn hair fell over her shoulder. With a slight wave, it caught the light from above. She gazed at him with a sparkle in her large, brown eyes. He couldn't see the smattering of freckles across the bridge of her nose now, the way he could in this morning's sunlight.

"I did. You needed it this afternoon, right?" He rocked back on his heels, satisfied that he'd helped her.

"Yeah, I use it to deliver." The corners of her mouth lifted slightly. "Thank you, Drew."

Drew shrugged like he'd done nothing. "Well, the tire's all fixed. We dropped the bad one off at Larkin's, and Bennett said he'd have it ready for you by five."

"Can I get it tomorrow?" She ran one hand along her forehead, as if reorganizing her thoughts from the outside of her skull.

"I'm sure you can." Drew watched her closely, unsure of why an alarm was going off in his head. "Why?"

"The wedding is at four, and I have to set up at three," Gretchen said. "I probably won't be done until nine tonight."

Drew's eyebrows shot up. "Really? You stay the whole time?"

"It takes an hour to set up, and then I stick around to make sure all the groomsmen and the bridal party have what they need. I might be able to sneak away before five, but I might not." She leaned against the wall, and she looked slightly pale to Drew. His medical training kicked in, but he didn't want to ask intrusive questions.

"My friend will bring Dixie home. I'll get her fed and in bed, and then I have to go back and clean up."

"They don't keep the flowers?"

"They'll keep some of them, sure. Some brides give them away. Whatever they don't want, I'll haul out." She glanced toward her workroom, and Drew fell back a step.

"All right, well, good luck." He didn't want to take her time. Surely, the tire incident had set her back already, and she didn't need him here talking to her. "See you around town." He turned to leave, but spun back to her as a thought struck him. "Oh, there's the Hawthorne Harbor Safety Fair next weekend. You should come as my special guest."

Her forehead wrinkled as her eyebrows shot up.

"I mean." Drew laughed as he realized how forward he'd sounded. "We have a special luncheon for people we've helped over the years. You and Dixie should come." Drew had never invited anyone as his special guest. He did his job, sure. He showed up every day, and he'd helped people over the years, yes.

He'd just never felt like he'd made a difference—except for Gretchen, Aaron, and Dixie Samuels. *He* had delivered that baby. *He* had felt responsible for that success. It was the only time he'd truly felt like he'd achieved what he'd hoped to achieve when he'd signed up for his first emergency technician class.

"When is it?"

"Next Saturday. Lunch at eleven-thirty. The Safety Fair starts at one for the general public. We'll have the fire engines out, bounce houses, great food catered. Dixie would love it."

"I'll see," she said, a completely non-committal answer. But Drew would have to take it. So he nodded and backed up another step.

"All right. Well, let me know if you need more details. It's at the firehouse three complex, right downtown. Couple of blocks from here."

"I'll look at my calendar. I have a lot of weddings in the spring."

Drew thought he heard something hiding in the tone of her voice, but he couldn't riddle out what. So he just lifted his hand in a wave and ducked out the way he'd come in. His heart did a little tap dance in his chest, and he couldn't name why.

4

Gretchen worked though her fingers went numb from the cold. She worked though her stomach roared at her to eat something. She worked though her head pounded and her feet ached.

She would not miss this deadline. She couldn't afford to. While hers was the only all-local, all homegrown flower shop in town, it wasn't the only one people had to choose from for their floral needs. If it were, perhaps she wouldn't have to worry so much. She certainly wouldn't have been able to keep the front of the shop closed while she frantically wrapped stems and secured baby's breath boutonnieres.

A chime like an obnoxious doorbell made her lift her head. Her phone, which she'd propped in front of her, showed a text from Janey. Her best friend and fellow single mother, Janey was picking Dixie up from school and caring for her until Gretchen could get over there that evening.

The two women helped each other a lot, as Janey worked in Olympic National Park as a park ranger. They coordinated her days off with Gretchen's busy times, and they'd made things work. Jess, Janey's son, was a year older than Dixie, and the two got along great. Thankfully.

Headed over to get the kids! the text read.

Gretchen's heart flew to the back of her throat. If Janey was already on her way to get the kids from school, Gretchen should be loaded and on her way to the reception center. Without answering the text, she put her head down and finished the last two wrist corsages and placed them delicately in the box for transport.

Taking a few precious seconds, she downed two painkillers and got her van loaded. The new tire in the front seemed to shine like black gold, and she realized Drew had not mentioned the cost of it.

This new worry ate at her, especially because she couldn't just call or text him to find out. She didn't have the man's number, or know where he lived, or anything.

But she absolutely would not allow him to pay for her new tire. She knew where his mother and step-father lived, and she went out to clip flowers every morning. She'd find out how to get in touch with him from Donna.

She spun to re-enter the shop and retrieve the vases. Her vision blurred, and agony tore through her head. Instinctively, she reached out and steadied herself against the trusty, brown van. The last thing she needed was to faint in this back alley, where no one would find her for hours.

Everything settled back into its normal place, and she moved through the doorway a little slower than she'd planned. Once everything was loaded into the back of the van, she got in the driver's seat.

Her stomach cramped, but she kept a tight grip on the steering wheel. She could eat as soon as the wedding was properly flowered.

Magleby Mansion sat on a bluff overlooking the water, on the northwest crown of Hawthorne Harbor. Anyone who was anyone got married there, and Gretchen had done more floral arrangements at the Mansion than anywhere else.

Securing the sponsored business label from them had been huge, something she'd accomplished in her first year in town. Honestly, the contract with the Maglebys had probably kept The Painted Daisy afloat all this time, and she navigated toward the back entrance of the event hall with ease.

She could do without having to deal with Mabel Magleby, who owned acres and acres of land in town and made sure everyone knew it. The Maglebys had loads of money, and were some of the original settlers in Hawthorne Harbor. Mabel's great-great grandfather had been the first mayor in town, something she liked to point out at City

Council meetings when discussions were had about things she didn't like.

Nearing seventy herself, Mabel still hovered around every aspect of the events at the Mansion, as she lived in a back cottage and had no children, grandchildren, or pets to speak of. Her event center was literally her entire focus, and Gretchen ignored the spicy look from the elderly woman as she backed her van toward the wide French doors that were already open.

The Mansion sported white and brown rock, cut into craggly shapes and fitted together. The grounds boasted of the finest Washington Hawthorne trees, after which the harbor and town were named.

Mabel made sure there were dozens of bushes, flowering plants, and spruces in all their varieties. She had a knack for picking out interesting foliage and making the gardens unique and beautiful. Someone in her family had extremely long vision, as the shade trees had all been placed strategically, and now produced exactly what the center needed to have outdoor and indoor events.

Gretchen leapt from the van as soon as she had it parked, welcomed by the scent of sugar browning into caramel. She'd done enough weddings at the Mansion to know the menus, and it seemed like today's lucky couple was getting the crepe buffet.

"You're late," Mabel said.

Gretchen gave the older woman a single nod. "I'll be ready in time."

Mabel had deep lines on her forehead and between her eyes. Decades of frowning could do that to a person. Her blue eyes were sharp, and she didn't miss much. "That tire looks new." She folded her bony arms and looked to Gretchen for an explanation.

"I got a flat," Gretchen said as she flung the back doors of the van open. "That's why I'm running a bit behind."

Mabel's expression softened, and she tucked an errant wisp of hair back up into her elegant bun. She wore a navy blue dress with pink rose buds on it—classic and chic all in one. As she lived alone, Gretchen wondered if she had someone online with whom she shared the town gossip. She'd certainly have a lot of it, dealing with events from birthday parties to weddings to anniversaries.

"I'll get Jaime to come help you." Mabel patted her arm as she passed.

Gretchen's first instinct was to refuse the caretaker's help. But something flinched inside her—could've been her hammering headache, or her twisting stomach, or her trembling hands—and told her to accept the help.

"I would appreciate that," she said, gathering the box of corsages and boutonnieres into her arms.

AN HOUR LATER, AND NOT A SINGLE MINUTE LATE, GRETCHEN adjusted the vase on the bride and groom's table a fraction of an inch and stepped back. It was perfect.

She retreated to the back of the room, which held a dozen tables in black iron. Her funky, colored vases brought life to the stone, the wood on the floor, and the dark metal furniture. Everywhere she looked, roses looked back. Tall and short, bunches and singles, pink and white. Satisfaction and a sense of pride pulled through Gretchen.

She'd woven roses into a massive wreath and placed it on the arch leading out to the garden, where the ceremony would take place. The dinner and reception would also be held here, and everything was set.

Erica, the bride's mother, entered the room already wearing her wrist corsage and her blue mother-of-the-bride dress. She gasped and her fingers fluttered around her mouth. "Gretchen, it's wonderful." Her eyes flitted around the room as she took in everything. "Absolutely perfect."

"Thank you." Gretchen hadn't meant for the words to come out a whisper, but she realized her exhaustion had extended to her vocal chords.

"Let me get your check, then I need to sit down. We're almost ready!" She bustled out of the reception room and returned a moment later.

Gretchen took the payment and said, "I'll be back at nine to take down anything Belinda doesn't want to keep or give away."

Back in her trusty van, she had time to go over to the tire shop and get her spare, but she couldn't make herself do it. She and Dixie lived in a little house between the Mansion and Larkin's, and all Gretchen wanted to do was go home.

She pulled into the driveway and leaned her head against the seat. *A few more hours*, she coached herself. Janey would bring Dixie home at six, so Gretchen had a few minutes to relax, unwind, and make something to eat before her daughter got home.

Dixie loved grilled cheese sandwiches and vegetable beef soup, so Gretchen turned on the radio in her kitchen and got to work. She loved being home alone for just a few minutes, something she thought she'd never like.

In Seattle, when she was home alone, she always played music. She'd taken classes just to get out of the house. And she'd planned to volunteer in Dixie's first grade class. But she'd never had that opportunity.

Her aches and pains and sadness melted away as bread browned and upbeat songs blasted through the house. She'd just pulled the last sandwich from the pan when the front door opened and Dixie called, "Mom?"

Gretchen rounded the corner and gave her daughter the biggest smile she could muster. "How was school?" She hated not being able to pick Dixie up at three o'clock, but life was life. Dixie didn't seem to mind, and she'd be okay for an hour tonight too while Gretchen went back to the Mansion to clean up.

Dixie turned back and waved at Janey, whose black SUV inched out of sight after that. "School was great. I got to play the xylophone in music the whole time."

Gretchen beamed at her daughter. "How was your piano lesson?"

She scowled at that one. "Janey wouldn't pass off my song. She said it needs another week."

"Well, then I'm sure it needs another week." Gretchen watched the displeasure roll across Dixie's face as she dumped her backpack next to the fridge.

"I guess."

"I'll sit with you in the morning," Gretchen offered. "We'll get it." She turned back to the island. "I made sandwiches and soup."

Dixie brightened after that, claimed to not have homework, and fell asleep in Gretchen's bed while she read a book about famous composers. Gretchen loved that Dixie enjoyed music, liked to sing and learn about the theory behind it, and read books she'd read before about Johann Sebastian Bach. Aaron had very much been into the symphony, the ballet, and had been an excellent violinist himself.

Though he hadn't played for years, his love for classical music had obviously infected Dixie. Gretchen carefully extracted the book from her daughter's fingers and crept from the bedroom. Her own tiredness had not been alleviated with painkillers or the few bites of sandwich she'd eaten.

Maybe she was coming down with something. Her stomach coiled like a snake about to strike, and she'd been able to eat very little though she felt hungry. She simply felt...off. But she had flowers to take down, so with every door locked at her comfy cottage, she returned to the Magleby Mansion.

A cheer erupted from the front doors at the same time she entered from the back. A smile touched her face as she remembered her own wedding day. She'd been the happiest bride, because she'd been marrying her one and only true love.

A pang of loneliness hit her right behind the heart. It seemed so unjust that she had to lose him so early. Would she ever find someone to love as much as she'd loved Aaron? She wasn't sure that was possible, and she'd barely dated since his death anyway. Dixie only deserved the best, and Gretchen was content with providing for the two of them.

Why then, was Drew's face floating through her mind?

Distracted, she stepped onto an uneven stone, and her ankle rolled. A hot bolt of pain shot up her leg and a cry burst from her mouth, only amplified when her knees hit the hard floor moments later. The walls spun and blurred into brown and white streaks while she tried to find a decent breath.

"Hey, you okay?" Someone touched her arms, but Gretchen couldn't seem to find the person. *Okay, okay, okay* echoed in her head.

She closed her eyes. If she could just have a minute, she'd be fine. Her vision would clear and she'd stand. Get her flowers taken down. Go home. Maybe stay home tomorrow.

"Gretchen?"

She thought the voice belonged to Jaime, who'd helped her carry in the flowers earlier. Of course he'd be here. He was probably making sure everything got cleaned up after the wedding. She'd seen him at plenty of other events while cleaning up.

"I'm fine," she managed to say, though her voice was breathy. Her hand touched stone beside her and the smell of caramel and chocolate assaulted her senses. At least things were working again.

With Jaime's help, she got back to her feet, blinking all the while. "Thank you, Jaime." She gave the man a smile she hoped would convey her gratitude. He was about her age, married with two daughters, and lived just down the hill for easy access to the property. His dark eyes held nothing but concern.

"Did you hit your head?" he asked.

"No, I just twisted my ankle." She tested her weight on it, and it hurt but not so much that she couldn't work out the kinks and walk. "I'm fine, honestly."

He dropped her hand and gestured toward the reception room. "They're finished, so we can go in."

Gretchen squared her shoulders and set a time limit for herself to beat. She found if she made clean up a game, it went by faster and got done with less moodiness. She'd started it when Dixie was a toddler and used to throw tantrums about the simplest of chores. Now she'd empty the dishwasher, practice the piano, and clean up her laundry without too much of a fuss. Gretchen could certainly get the leftover flowers in a box and in the back of the van before she ran out of energy.

She had the two remaining centerpieces and all the vases in the box, thinking she was done already, when she spied the wreath on the arch. She went outside to get the ladder, avoiding the uneven parts of the floor, and found it in its customary spot off to the right, leaning against the side of a storage shed. She stepped onto the grass and tried to lift it.

Not happening.

She tried again anyway, trying to remember how she'd used it to hang the wreath that afternoon. Her mind felt soft around the edges, because she couldn't recall. She did manage to lift the ladder a few inches off the ground—only to have gravity reclaim it.

The metal made a crunching sound against the bones in her foot, and the painful headache she'd been nursing all day exploded. Only agony existed, and she was aware of a howl tearing through the darkness before she toppled backward.

Her head whiplashed against the ground, and while it wasn't stone, a sound like gunfire rattled through her skull. Every muscle went limp, and she gazed up into the star-filled sky, wondering how long it would take for someone to find her.

Dixie loves stars. The thought rotated slowly in her sluggish mind.

A flash of silver blocked out the pinpoints of light. Somehow, she had the wherewithal to throw her hands over her face as the ladder descended toward her. Thankfully, she lost consciousness before impact.

5

Adam pulled open the silverware drawer and withdrew a fistful of forks. "Time to eat," he said as he tossed them on the counter next to the salmon he'd just extracted from the oven.

It wasn't fish and chips, but Drew didn't care. It was food he hadn't had to make, and his brother had always been exceptionally skilled at making the seafood easily obtained from the docks into something delicious.

Russ took the biggest piece of salmon and spooned the butter lemon sauce over the top. "I can't believe you can cook like this and you aren't married."

"He's seeing Anita Andrus," Drew said without thinking. Adam's growl reminded him that the relationship wasn't quite public yet. "I mean..." He flashed frantic glances between his brother and Russ, who scooped half the roasted potatoes onto his plate.

"Did you go see Mom and Joel this morning?" he asked, hoping Russ was so enamored with food that hadn't come from a box that he wouldn't remember the name Anita Andrus.

"Yeah," Adam said. "They looked good." He dished himself some food and headed for the couch a few feet away. His brother had been taking carpentry lessons from Joel, and together they'd remodeled Adam's house. The once separate living and dining and kitchen area was now one big room, delineated with a rug in the sitting area and a pot rack hanging above the kitchen island. Though it was more open, the house now radiated a kind of warm coziness it hadn't before.

Outside, the wind rattled something in the yard, and one of Drew's shepherds barked. He tried to find Blue and Chief, but Adam hadn't quite gotten to widening the windows and the dogs were nowhere in sight. They were fine. They loved to run and lie in the grass, and Adam's neighbors had a couple of cats they liked to torment through the fence slats.

Drew joined his brother on the couch. "Food's great."

"Did you invite Gretchen and her daughter to the Safety Fair?" Russ asked as he perched on the edge of the recliner to eat.

Drew tried to act like it was no big deal. That he went around inviting everyone he'd ever met to the special guests portion of the upcoming event. "Yeah."

"Did she say she'd come?"

Why did Russ care? He speared two potatoes and put them both in his mouth. Drew watched him for another half-second, trying to figure out the line of questioning.

"She has a lot of weddings in the spring," he finally said, echoing what she'd told him.

"I invited that woman from the crosswalk."

"The hit and run?" Adam asked, glancing up from his food.

"The guy barely bumped her," Drew said. "She didn't even lose consciousness."

"She's the closest to wounded that I've helped," Russ said.

"You held her elbow while she stepped up into the bus." Drew shook his head, a smile pulling at his mouth. He understood why Russ would invite her though.

"Yeah, well, she said she might come."

A thread of unease pulled through Drew. He couldn't be the only one there without a special guest. *Of course you can.* He'd done it every year before leaving for Medina, and last year after he'd returned to town too.

"Joel says they'll need help with the lavender harvest this weekend," Adam said after a beat. "And Mom wants us to come for dinner on Sunday."

"All right," Drew agreed without really thinking about what he was committing to. He finished dinner, thanked his brother, got his dogs loaded in the back of his truck, and headed out.

He stopped at Duality before going home, because he

was hoping for an hour or two on the couch, Blue and Chief on either side of him while a baseball game blared on the TV. And that required snacks. Maybe one of those baked-then-fried loaded potato skins. He'd collected the food from the eatery and had just picked up a bag of chocolate when his phone shrieked at him.

The candy hit the floor in his haste to answer the after-hours emergency operator. "Drew Herrin," he said, no wasted words, no wasted time.

"We have a woman with injuries, unconscious, as the Magleby Mansion. Location?"

"Duality," Drew said, already striding toward the exit. "I'm five minutes away." So a slight exaggeration, but he could speed on the way up the coast.

"We're routing a bus," Trudy said. "It's twenty minutes out."

"I have a bag in my truck. Anyone else?" He swung himself into the truck and had it on the road in only moments.

"Dispatch is in calls."

Which meant the call had gone out simultaneously. He'd see Russ and Adam up at the Mansion for sure. He just wanted to get there first. So he ended his call and focused on his destination.

When he arrived at the Mansion, it wasn't hard to tell where the victim was. People stood around in a semi-circle, with a woman kneeling on the ground, cradling someone's head in their lap. Frustration blipped through

Drew. They'd already moved the injured person. Never good.

"Paramedics," he called in a loud voice, soliciting the attention of the handful of people there.

"Drew," someone breathed. "Thank goodness. It's Drew Herrin."

The crowd parted, and Drew saw Mabel Magleby was the one kneeling on the grass. And Gretchen Samuels had her eyes closed, seemingly asleep.

His stride faltered as time stalled for a heartbeat. He had one brief moment to admire her beauty before reason and duty kicked in and he continued forward. Shaking the confusing thoughts of her fair features from his mind, he set his bag on the ground and said, "Tell me what happened."

"I found her." Jaime Allcott stepped forward. "She was here to take down her flowers. She sprained her ankle and fell in the hallway before we even started. She seemed fine, and I guess she came to get the ladder. When she didn't come back, I started to wonder where she'd gone, because she'd left her box and vases inside."

The ladder now leaned up against the building. Blood was smeared across Gretchen's face, but her chest rose and fell. Airway seemed normal. "Where was the ladder when you found her?"

She definitely wasn't alert. "Gretchen?" he said loudly, hoping she'd respond with a twitch, a jerk, or perhaps even wake up. "Gretchen, it's Drew Herrin. Can you hear me?"

Nothing. No eye flutter. No flinch.

"Jaime?" Drew glanced up. "Where was the ladder?"

Jaime's feet shuffled. "On top of her. She was on her back. She was already unconscious."

On top of her. Drew's chest seized a bit. "How long do you estimate she was missing before you found her?" He picked up her hand and pressed his fingernail against hers. This pain test could help him determine how unconscious she was. A slight pull in her hand as she tried to recoil from the pain.

Good. Better than nothing.

He pulled a stethoscope from his bag and looped it around his neck. "How long, Jaime?" Maybe the man needed to be treated for shock. It could be difficult to find someone passed out, with a ladder on top of them, with the amount of blood she had on her face.

Drew didn't wait for an answer before putting in the earpieces and listening to her heart. It seemed strong enough—there. He cocked his head and listened again, focusing on a blade of grass haloed in lamplight. A murmur. He wondered if she knew about it, had felt lightheaded at all lately.

If a ladder had fallen on her, she could've been knocked unconscious. She could've fainted first. She could have multiple fractures or broken bones in her ribs, torso, and legs. He couldn't assess any of that—a doctor and an x-ray machine was needed.

He only stabilized. Revived. Gave comfort and hope. Oh, and he could deliver a baby.

"Why'd you move her?" He looked at Mabel, who gazed at him with a flash of indignation, but it softened quickly.

"I didn't want her to be alone."

Drew understood how she felt, but he couldn't fathom why. It just didn't seem fair that someone like Gretchen should have to do anything alone—like lift a ladder. Or come back here at nine o'clock at night to clean up flowers and vases.

"The ambulance is coming," he said. "I need you to let her lie flat. She could have broken bones if a ladder fell on top of her."

Mabel seemed to grip Gretchen more tightly.

"It's okay," Drew said. "She responded to a pain stimulus. She's breathing okay and her heart's beating." Irregularly, but no one deserved to know that. Her nose was probably broken if the blood on her face was any indication. No matter what, she'd wake up with a hefty headache.

Like a flash of lightning, he thought of her daughter. She'd said earlier that she would put her to bed before coming to take down the flowers. She was probably home alone.

A siren, faint and in the distance, met his ears. He needed to do something about Dixie before he climbed in the bus and took her to the hospital. What had she said her friend's name was? The one picking Dixie up from school?

He couldn't remember, and he frowned at himself. "Does anyone know who I can call about Gretchen's daughter? I think she's home alone."

"I can go over there," Mabel said.

Drew sized up the elderly woman. "Would Dixie know who you are?"

"Janey Germaine," another woman said. "She and Gretchen are best friends."

Drew nodded his thanks and stayed at Gretchen's side. "Gretchen, I'm going to call Janey and have her go get Dixie, okay? Then we're going to take you to the hospital." He grinned down at her, something inside him softening at the peaceful expression on her face. Somehow he was able to look past all the blood and the swelling in her nose, and see a gentle soul in Gretchen Samuels he'd never looked for before.

Startled at the softness of his feelings, he leaned back and pulled out his phone. After Trudy answered, he said, "I need the number for Janey Germaine."

"I'll connect you. Hold, please."

DREW SAT IN THE EMERGENCY WAITING ROOM, HIS FINGERS steepled together and his eyes on the gray plastic door in front of him. He'd employed nearly every ounce of patience he possessed, and still the nurse hadn't come to tell him anything about Gretchen.

Legally, she couldn't give a diagnosis to him. But seeing as how she had no family over the age of ten, Drew simply couldn't leave her in the hospital by herself. Unconscious. Alone. Overnight.

No, he wouldn't do it. Though his eyelids grew heavy, and he'd thought about that loaded potato skin at Duality more than once, he maintained his seat and waited.

He'd probably only been there for a half an hour. Simply checking her vitals, assessing that nose, and ordering the x-rays would take that long. Which meant he should be hearing something very soon.

Someone sat down next to him, smelling like Old Spice and butter. "Janey got Dixie."

Drew startled at the sound of Adam's voice. "Oh, that's great." His voice raked through his dry throat, but he didn't dare leave to go get a drink.

"How is she?" Adam asked.

"Still waiting to hear."

Adam settled his head against the wall and closed his eyes, apparently ready to wait it out with Drew. His brother's presence comforted him, and Drew finally leaned back in the chair and let his hands fall into his lap.

Five minutes later, a nurse walked through the door. Drew stood, the amount of hope floating through his chest ridiculous. "How is she?" The rest of the waiting room was empty, so Drew knew Roxanne had come about Gretchen.

"She's awake, which is a great sign." Roxanne gestured for him to come back. "You two can come back if you'd like. She's frantic about her daughter, and I told her someone who knew what was going on was here. She wants to see you."

Drew looked at Adam, who waved for him to go. "I don't need to come back."

But Drew did. The craving to reassure Gretchen ate at him, almost an ache in the back of his throat. He couldn't quite classify it, didn't understand this pulsating desire to be the one to take care of her. He followed Roxanne through the door and down the halls wide enough to pass two patient beds side-by-side.

"She's in there." She gestured him into a room. "I'll give you a few minutes."

Drew said, "Thanks, Roxy," and walked through the doorway.

"Drew," Gretchen rasped as soon as she saw him. "Where's Dixie?"

He stepped tentatively into the room, his heart fluttering up near his voice box when he saw the neck brace, the temporary wrist cast, and the gauze across her nose and cheeks.

"I called Janey, and she went to get her." He edged closer to the bed, a strange inkling to reach for and hold Gretchen's hand. His fingers twitched in that direction, but he pulled them into a tight fist. "Do you remember what happened?"

Always the EMT, he watched her struggle to find the memories, sort through them, and put them in order. "It's okay if you can't," he said quickly. "You were unconscious for quite a while."

"I was at the Magleby Mansion."

"That's right," he said, hoping to encourage her, keep her talking.

"I needed to get the ladder to take down the rose wreath. It was really heavy. I dropped it on my foot." She shuddered as if she could still feel the pain. But her speech slurred along the edges, and he knew she'd been given some heavy painkillers.

"That's all I remember." Her eyes drifted closed, but she jerked them open again.

"A ladder fell on top of you," he said gently. "It looks like they've got your wrist in a splint, and they've taken care of your broken nose. They're concerned about your neck, thus the brace."

Her eyes filled with tears, and Drew shut his mouth. "You feeling okay?" He reached out and touched her arm, thinking maybe she just needed human contact. She turned her arm, and his fingers slid down to hers.

"You're going to be fine," he said in his best paramedic voice. Soothing and soft, but firm and authoritative. "Do you need me to call a nurse to get you something?"

She gave one shake of her head, closed her eyes so that a single tear tracked down her face, and squeezed his fingers.

And Drew thought maybe *he* was the one who needed the human contact. He certainly liked holding Gretchen's hand far more than he liked Chief nosing his fingers.

6

Gretchen heard voices beyond her veil of consciousness, and she struggled toward them. The anchor she'd been holding onto had disappeared at some point, and she felt like she was drowning.

Dixie. Where was Dixie?

She broke the surface of unconsciousness and opened her eyes. The room was dark save for a rectangle of light coming in from the hallway. Two figures stood there, facing one another. One spoke words she couldn't hear and glanced her way.

The other wore a long-sleeved doctor's coat and looked at her too. She approached, her face becoming more and more familiar with each passing second. Problem was, so was the throbbing pain coming from her foot.

"Gretchen," the doctor said in that kind, strong voice they must teach medical personnel in school. She sounded like Drew had, like whatever she said would come true simply because she said it. "I'm Susan Harris. Do you remember meeting last night?"

Gretchen recognized the voice and the face, but the name had eluded her. She nodded anyway.

"How are you feeling?" Dr. Harris asked.

Gretchen moaned, identifying pain now in multiple places from her nose to her toes. The doctor reached for the nurse's button and pushed it. "I'll get you something for the pain. Mister Herrin here has been sitting with you. Is that all right with you?"

The memory of his fingers in hers slammed into Gretchen's skull and rattled around. "It's fine," she said, meeting his gaze. He didn't seem embarrassed that he'd stayed, but he did look worse for the wear. "Don't you have to work tomorrow?"

"No," he said. "It's my day off."

Dr. Harris kept her eyes on him as she continued with, "He's not family, so I wasn't sure if you'd given him permission to stay or not."

"He can stay," Gretchen said, unsure as to why she didn't want him to leave. He possessed a charming handsomeness, sure. Maybe she simply didn't want to be alone. No matter what, if she had to pick someone to take care of Dixie, it would be Janey, and out of her options for who could stay with her, Drew was...perfect.

"I don't suppose I'll be out of here in time to open my shop in the morning?" She looked at Dr. Harris hopefully even as another blast of pain shot through her right leg and into her hip. She fought unsuccessfully not to wince.

"I'd like to keep you," Dr. Harris said. "Get a better look at that foot. Make sure the nose really isn't broken."

"My nose isn't broken?" Gretchen tasted blood on the back of her tongue, and Drew had said her nose was broken.

"Just bruised." Dr. Harris flipped a page on a clipboard when the nurse entered. "She needs another thousand of ibuprofen. We think you threw your hands up to protect your face from the ladder." She glanced at Gretchen and passed the notes to the nurse, who exited. "You've got bruising on the backs of your forearms, and that would explain how your wrist got sprained."

Gretchen sifted through the memories floating around in her mind. She remembered going to the Mansion. Collecting all the vases and leftover centerpieces. The defeat she'd felt at still seeing that rose wreath twined through the arch.

She'd gone out into the gardens to get the ladder, but it had been too heavy for her to lift. She'd dropped it on her foot, which screamed with pain as it reminded her to ask for help next time.

"I fell down," she said, the memory suddenly emerging. "When I dropped the ladder on my foot, I fell backward."

"Yes, your right foot is broken," Dr. Harris confirmed. "Luckily, that's the only broken bone you suffered."

"The ladder did fall on me," Gretchen said, a dose of

adrenaline spiking her heart rate and causing both Drew and the doctor to whip their attention to the monitor when it emitted a loud beep.

"You're okay," Drew murmured.

Dr. Harris said, "I want to do more x-rays on the foot and make sure it doesn't need surgery. We'll put a proper cast on it, and you should be able to go home by Friday."

Two days. What was she going to do in the hospital for two days? Who would take care of Dixie?

"My daughter...." she started but didn't know how to finish.

Dr. Harris exchanged a meaningful glance with Drew and backed up a step. "I'll leave Mister Herrin to iron out those details with you." She disappeared through the rectangle of light, leaving Gretchen alone with Drew.

He pulled up the only chair in the room and sat beside her. His fingers touched hers, and they were warm and wonderful. She sighed as the nurse re-entered the room and administered the next dose of medication.

"You should be feeling better in about a half an hour," she said. "Please call if you aren't." She looked at Drew pointedly. "She needs to rest."

"I promise I won't keep her up."

The nurse left, pulling the door closed behind her, drenching them in hospital darkness, which was more gray than black.

"Dixie is with Janey," he started, his hushed voice almost a whisper. "She's going to take the kids to school, but then she has to go into the park. I told her I'd pick Jess and Dixie up from school and bring them here." He ducked his head so she couldn't see his face.

"You don't have to do that."

"I knew you'd say that." He shook his head as a smile slipped across his mouth.

Gretchen hated this feeling of weakness, of pure help-lessness. She'd felt like this while lying in the car, waiting for the ambulance to arrive, ten years ago. She'd felt like this in the years leading up to her first pregnancy, almost desperate to have a baby. And in the years following Dixie's arrival, when she and Aaron had had to face the fact that they'd been very, very lucky to get a child at all. And she'd never felt as helpless and desperate as she had when Aaron had passed away.

She'd vowed then to never be so reliant on another person. The pact with herself had held true for three years. *She'd* made things happen for her and Dixie, and *she'd* gotten back up on her feet when life seemed to want to kick her down.

"Who's going to do it if I don't?" he asked.

Gretchen pulled herself from her past and looked right into Drew's gorgeous brown eyes. Deep and rich like the Belgian chocolate she used to splurge on in Seattle, she almost lost herself inside them.

"I'll figure something out."

"Right. And that something is that I'll pick them up and bring them here. Dixie will want to see you, and you're not leaving until Friday." Determination blazed in those eyes now, and Gretchen flailed for a different solution.

"Then, I thought I'd take them out to my family's lavender farm. I was going to go out there anyway, and it's a great place for a couple of kids." He took a deep breath. "I've already talked to my mother, and she's baking chocolate chips cookies for the kids." He chuckled. "My step-father is going to make sure the goats get a bath so the kids can touch them. We have chickens they can feed, and horses to ride, and of course, everyone loves hide and seek in a lavender field."

Gretchen couldn't help the smile that touched her lips. She and Drew had loved playing hide and seek in the lavender fields. She'd loved roaming her granddad's land, and her own yearning to wander through rows of lavender hit her powerfully behind her lungs. "I really couldn't..."

"You really can," he said. "It's the same farm where we used to roam, out near the tip of the harbor. They'll love it."

Her eyes widened and her breath lodged in her throat. Her brain couldn't seem to grasp any one thought, so she blurted, "I thought your last name was Herrin."

Lines appeared between his eyes as he frowned. "It is. Why?"

"I know the Loveland Farm really well. I rent my flower garden from them. I thought your family must have moved." Confusion raced through her. "Why is it called the Loveland Lavender Farm now?"

He sucked in a breath. "That's right. You rent the flower

garden." One, two, three heartbeats of silence followed his declaration, and then he filled the small hospital room with his laughter. It was one of the purest, most wonderful sounds Gretchen had ever heard, and she couldn't help adding a giggle to the chorus.

But that made her ribs hurt, so she cut off quickly.

"Yes," she said when he quieted. "I rent that land from Joel Loveland. Not a Herrin."

"He's my step-father," Drew said, his demeanor turning subdued in a single breath. "Different last name, because my father died nine years ago, and my mother got remarried."

She tightened her grip on his fingers. "I'm so sorry." He obviously still ached for his father, which Gretchen understood completely. A full minute passed while she lost herself inside memories she'd rather escape from. She wondered if he was doing the same.

"Did you know he bought my granddad's farm?" she asked. She wasn't sure why she'd asked. Of course Drew knew.

Sure enough, he nodded. "A few years ago, right?"

"Five years ago. My grandma died a while back. Granddad traded in lavender for coconuts," she said. "He lives in Hawaii now." A smile slipped across her face as she thought of her wrinkled granddad wearing a tropical shirt and swimming trunks while he harvested coconuts.

She exhaled, wishing she'd been more attentive to him before he'd left the mainland. "My husband died a couple of years later, and I came here anyway, though I had no family left and nowhere to live."

He squeezed her hand, and she took comfort from the strength and power in his. "Where are your parents?"

"California." She pressed against the memories of her family in San Francisco. "My brother lives there too."

"And you couldn't go there?"

"No," she said firmly. "I couldn't go there." Though they'd spent time together as she came to Hawthorne Harbor as a teen, she'd never told anyone about her family, or about why she came to visit her granddad alone.

Drew looked like he wanted to ask more questions, but thankfully he fell silent. The medication was starting to work, because a keen sense of drowsiness swept through her and she let her eyes drift closed.

"I'll be right here," he whispered, starting to pull his hand away as he inched toward standing.

She gripped it, unwilling to let him go quite yet. "Hold my hand until I fall asleep," she said. "Please?"

"Of course." He sank back into the recliner and Gretchen closed her eyes, wondering why it was so bad to ask for help when it came from someone as gentle and gracious as Drew Herrin.

GRETCHEN WOKE WITH DARKNESS AROUND HER AND A COLD, empty hand. She wiggled it under the blanket while she located the door. Soft, even breathing met her ears and instantly transported her back three years, when she used to sleep with another living, breathing human being next to her each night.

Oh, how she missed that. Dixie slept in the big king bed sometimes, but it wasn't the same as that deep draw in, and that slow exhale out.

She listened to the comforting sound, trying to decipher how she felt about the person making it. Drew Herrin.

Not her husband.

Not even close.

Where Drew was dark and chiseled and strong, Aaron had been light, and rounded and barely able to help with a jar of pickles. He spent most of his time behind a screen or on the piano bench, and it was clear that Drew used a different kind of bench to occupy his time.

After several minutes of thought, she decided it was okay to like him. Aaron had been gone for a while now, and those first inklings of attraction had certainly popped through Gretchen when Drew had held her hand.

She drifted back to sleep with a smile on her face and hope in her heart that the fireworks hadn't been one-sided.

The next time she woke, sunlight streamed into the room and two nurses stood at the end of the bed. They asked her questions about her pain, where it hurt most, what it was on a scale of one to ten. Drew was gone, and breakfast got wheeled in, followed immediately by Janey, her son Jess, and Dixie.

"Mama!" Dixie darted forward, the relief and happiness on her face evident.

"Careful, remember?" Janey cautioned, but Gretchen opened her arms wide to hug her daughter. She took a deep breath of Dixie's hair and got the clean scent of soap and strawberries.

"Hey, munchkin. How are you?"

"Good. Janey bought us doughnuts on the way over." She smacked her lips as if she'd just finished.

"Hey, that was a secret." Janey grinned at Dixie and leaned down to hug Gretchen too. "You sure you're okay?"

"I'm fine." But Gretchen held on for an extra moment, so glad to see such familiar faces. Janey wore her park ranger clothes, her high hiking boots, and her dark hair back in a ponytail. Her son, Jess, almost a spitting image of her except for her late husband's blue eyes instead of Janey's dark ones, lifted his hand in a wave. Gretchen caught sight of a spot of powdered sugar on the boy's sweatshirt, and smiled at him.

"So Drew ran home to shower," Janey said. "He said he'd be back by ten or so. He's planning to stay the day and then grab the kids at three." She put her arm around Jess's shoulders. "And then he's taking you guys out to the lavender farm, so be good."

"Are you sure he—?"

"Don't even ask," Janey said, her eyes turning sharp. "I've known Drew Herrin my whole life, and you can't find anyone better to entertain kids for an afternoon."

Gretchen wasn't sure if that was a compliment or not,

but she didn't protest again. Drew had been fun to hang out with in the summers she'd spent here. She didn't know him very well now, though. But she didn't really have any other options. Janey had to work. Gretchen herself couldn't get out of bed. Which made her life increasingly difficult when Dr. Harris walked in and said, "Oh, we've got a crowd in here. Good morning, everyone. I'm here to take Gretchen on her first walk."

7

Drew looked at himself in the mirror and could admit he appeared exhausted. Sleeping in a semi-sitting up position could do that. And that recliner was the most uncomfortable chair he'd ever sat—or tried to recline—in.

Janey was taking the kids over to see Gretchen this morning, and Drew cleaned up his beard so it was nice and neat. He wasn't sure what he'd do all day in the hospital room with Gretchen, but he wanted to look his best whatever he did.

Showered and shaved, he stepped into his kitchen. His brother liked to call it a science experiment gone wrong, and his mother had labeled it a laboratory more than a kitchen. Drew didn't mind their teasing. He could make sandwiches and pour himself a bowl of cereal despite the three electric ice cream makers and the two hand-operated ones taking up most of the counter space.

Next to the three notebooks where he'd kept detailed facts and figures of all of his recipes, his trials, his successes, his failures, he picked up a pen. He'd spent part of last night before he'd been able to drift into a shallow, uncomfortable sleep brainstorming flavor combinations.

Lavender had a sweet, floral, and soapy flavor, and he'd paired it with other sugary things like honey and white chocolate. But last night, as he'd done something he hadn't thought he'd do anytime soon—holding hands with a pretty woman—he'd thought about going sweet and sour. Maybe savory. Maybe all three.

Augustus had won with lavender and white chocolate once. Drew had taken that idea from the other man, actually. He'd won with lavender and blueberry, but Drew detested blueberries in anything but muffins, so he'd bypassed that particular flavor combination. And the last time Augustus had won, Drew had been in Medina. He couldn't bear to know anything about the man, as Augustus was a direct line to Yvonne, and Drew hadn't been able to deal with anything remotely related to her while he was in Medina.

Because she was the entire reason he'd left Hawthorne Harbor. Yvonne Hammond—Augustus's daughter—had refused to help Drew with his recipes, which suited him just fine. Her family owned one of the biggest lavender farms surrounding Hawthorne Harbor, and sometimes one of them sat on the judging panel. To protect them both, she'd kept herself out of that part of Drew's life.

"So..." He tapped the pen against the counter and reached for the top notebook. Flipping to a clean page, he wrote *lemon* and then below it *orange* before drawing two question marks. He'd made sherbets before, and his favorite was actually raspberry. He added that to the list and made plans to get over to the year-round farmer's market in Seattle so he could get the orchard and vine-fresh fruit he needed to make the citrus purees and extracts.

A plan started to come together, much more than his tired mind could grasp onto last night. But with the sweet lavender, the rich cream, and the zesty citrus, he'd need something to cut through it.

"Black pepper," he announced to his ice cream making kitchen. He wrote it down and closed the notebook. As he gazed out the window his mind filled with the image of Gretchen, and he had the sudden urge to take her one of his specialty ice creams.

Anxiety cut through his stomach, nearly eradicating his idea. He hadn't shared his creations with very many people —his mom and step-dad, Adam, and Russ. A safe lavender and honey with the paramedic crew for his birthday last year. He'd never entered the Lavender Festival's Creation Contest, but he was determined to do so this year. He still had four months to develop and perfect the recipe he'd use to win the title.

But he could take Gretchen a taste of his white choco-late ice cream with lavender and ricotta. He had all the ingredients, and he didn't even need to consult the notebook for the recipe. He'd made this treat so many times, he could do it from memory.

So he got out his heavy pot and measured whole milk into it. He added sugar and several drops of lavender-infused vanilla. He melted the white chocolate over a double boiler and separated five eggs while the ice cream base warmed.

He ladled the hot mixture into the egg yolks to temper them, and employed his patience while he stirred the custard until it thickened. With a scoop of ricotta in the ice cream base, he poured in the melted chocolate and added a couple of cups of cream.

While the mixture chilled, Drew went into the backyard with Blue and Chief, who wore identical expressions of joy that he'd finally come outside. "Hey, guys. Did you get breakfast, huh? Huh?" He scrubbed the dogs as he glanced toward their food bowls. Adam had come by as he'd promised and taken care of Drew's dogs.

Now, he picked up a tennis ball and held it for both dogs to see. "Wait," he coached. "Wait." Blue sat first, his tongue hanging out though they hadn't even started playing yet. "C'mon, Chief." Drew pointed to the ground, and the stubborn dog sat. "Okay go!" He threw the ball and both shepherds tore after it. Blue, the younger, more agile of the two German shepherds, got the ball first two-thirds of the time, and he always seemed pretty proud of himself as he trotted back to Drew.

His phone rang and he threw the ball again before answering it. "Hey, Mom."

"Drew, you sound good."

"Why wouldn't I sound good?" He silently cheered as Chief got the ball when Blue bobbled it.

"I thought you might be tired this morning."

"Well, yeah, but I'm okay. Am I still good to bring Dixie and Jess out to the farm this afternoon?"

"Of course. I've already started the first batch of cookies."

"First batch?" He picked up the ball and threw it again. "Mom, there's two of them."

"And you're coming. And Adam is bringing Anita for dinner."

Drew's stomach dropped toward his boots. "Mom," he said. "Really?"

"Really. We have people to cook dinner for." She sounded delighted, and Drew didn't have the heart to tell her that ten-year-olds probably didn't like meatloaf and asparagus.

"All right." Blue dropped the ball at Drew's feet and sat back on his haunches, waiting with that perpetual grin on his doggie face.

"Joel and I were talking this morning."

Oh, boy. Drew couldn't wait to hear what she had to say next. He bent, picked up the ball, and tossed it again. Chief didn't even go after it, but flopped to the ground several feet from Drew.

"We'd like to offer Gretchen to come out to the farm-house while she recovers."

Drew couldn't even make sense of her words. "What?" His throwing arm hung limply at his side.

"Well, she's not going to be able to live alone, not with her foot broken the way you said it was. Joel and I are here, and her flowers are right here, and we think she should come stay with us until she gets back on both feet."

Drew had started to shake his head about the time his mom had said *broken*. "Mom, she's not going to do that. She has a fiercely independent streak."

"Well, can't you at least ask her?"

No, Drew did not want to ask her. Gretchen would *not* like the idea, and he'd end up looking overeager. He wasn't sure if Gretchen's middle-of-the-night hand-holding was out of pure desperation not to be alone, or because the chemistry he felt with her was flowing both ways.

"I'll think about it."

His mother grunted, but Drew simply couldn't commit to asking Gretchen such a thing. "Her foot might not even be that bad," he said. "The doctor wanted to do more x-rays this morning." He turned back to the house. "Look, Ma, I gotta go. I'll see you this afternoon, all right?"

He hung up, refilled the dog's water bowls and threw the ball one last time before heading inside and switching on two of the electric ice cream makers. He poured the chilled base into the machines and let them work their magic.

By the time he showed up at the hospital, it was a bit

past ten. Gretchen sat in the recliner with her foot propped on the bed.

"Hey, look at you." He smiled at her and set the temperature-controlled bag containing the ice cream on her rolling table. She had great color in her face this morning, and she'd braided her hair. "Have you been up and walking?"

"Yes." She moaned and rubbed a spot on her knee. "It's horrible."

He chuckled. "Well, it keeps the blood moving to the injured areas. Have you gone in for the extra tests?"

"They're going to come get me in a few minutes." She yawned and ran one palm over her eyes.

"I brought you something that might tide you over." He reached into the bag and removed the plastic container of ice cream. His heart bobbed against the back of his throat. He was really going to share it with her. Ask her for her opinion on the recipe. Reveal that he dabbled in ice cream and dreamed of winning the town's Lavender Festival Creation Contest.

What would she think? For some reason, her opinion was extremely important to him. Yvonne had always expressed that he could win, but she'd never initiated any conversations on the topic. She'd never asked him how his recipes were coming.

"It's white chocolate lavender ice cream with ricotta." He popped the lid and handed the container to her.

She took it without looking at it. A flirtatious glint entered her eye. "And where did you get this?"

"I, uh, made it."

"You made it?" She accepted the plastic spoon he passed to her.

"Yeah, I made it," he said with more confidence. "This morning."

She finally tore her eyes from his and looked at the ice cream. "I didn't know someone like you knew what ricotta was."

"Someone like me?"

She waved her spoon in the air like a wand. "You know, with all those muscles and whatnot."

Drew had no idea why he couldn't have muscles and make ice cream, but he put a smile on his face and said, "Give it a try. I want to know what you think."

She took a bite without hesitating. Only a moment later, her eyes widened. "Wow, Drew. This is fantastic." She scooped herself another taste.

"Are you just saying that?"

"No." She ate more of the ice cream. "You should sell this stuff."

He basked in her compliment. But pretty much everyone in town had bottled, bunched, or baked lavender into something, packaged it, and was trying to sell it. He didn't want to throw his hat into that ring. He just wanted to give some validity to his mad scientist hobby he'd been nurturing for the past six years.

"Time for the x-rays." Roxy stepped into the room

pushing a wheelchair in front of her. "Oh, hey, Drew." If she thought it strange to see him there, she didn't say so.

"I can take her over," he said.

"Yeah?" Hope entered Roxy's face. "We were slammed in emergency this morning, and I'm so behind. If you could take her to radiology, that would be amazing."

Drew's curiosity jumped. "Slammed in emergency?" He took the chair from Roxy.

"Three people got burned when the hot oil splashed at the bakery this morning. A mother who sliced all the way to the bone when a glass broke while she was washing it."

"I didn't hear any calls." Drew pulled out his phone like they'd be there now.

"Everyone drove themselves in." Roxy turned to leave. "She needs to be there in fifteen minutes."

"We won't be late."

Roxy left, and Drew turned to face Gretchen. She'd polished off all the ice cream and was licking her lips. Drew's face flamed with enormous heat, and he glanced away. "So, can you get from that chair to this one on your own?"

"Better not risk it." She scooted to the edge of the chair, and he put his hand under her arm. Supporting her, he helped her transition from one chair to the other by pivoting on her good foot. She groaned as she sank into the seat.

"When's the last time you had pain meds?" He checked the end of her bed for her chart, but it wasn't there.

"This morning." She sounded tired, and Drew was glad she didn't have to walk over to radiology. He pushed her onto the elevator and pressed the button for the bottom floor.

"I don't like hospitals," she said so quietly, he could barely hear her.

"No?" Drew eyed the huge elevator, which could hold two rolling beds and the people needed to push them. "I spend a lot of time here, so I don't mind it."

"When Aaron was in the accident that took his life..." Her voice drifted into nothing, and the atmosphere in the elevator turned charged and awkward.

"Car accident?" Drew cleared his throat, torn between whether he should've asked or not. But the simple truth was he wanted to know. He wanted to support Gretchen in everything, and the strength of his fledgling feelings surprised him.

Gretchen studied her hands and nodded. "He'd stayed late to finish some work, which honestly, wasn't that abnormal."

The elevator opened and Drew eased her into the hall, moving slowly so she had time to talk before they arrived for the x-rays.

"I often went to bed alone, but I never woke up alone. When I did, I knew there was something wrong."

"I'm so sorry, Gretchen."

"The police didn't find his wallet in the glove compartment because it was smashed completely in. Aaron was in surgery for hours and hours." She glanced left and right, and Drew suddenly wanted her to stop talking. The tight pain in her voice caused his chest to squeeze uncomfortably.

"The other driver had fallen asleep," she continued. "Crossed the center line, and hit Aaron head-on."

Drew pressed his eyes closed. He wouldn't have wanted to be summoned to that emergency scene, despite what he'd thought about having a more exciting day at work. He had nothing he could say to her, and thankfully the door to radiology loomed.

He put his hand on her shoulder with only a few steps to the department, and she reached back and patted his fingers. Electricity roared through him, and he had to believe she could feel the current too.

"Gretchen Samuels," he said upon entering radiology.

"I can take her." A woman stood from behind the desk.

"Wait." Gretchen looked up at him with a face full of fear. "You'll be here when I get back, right?"

He smiled at her, hoping to convey as much comfort as possible. "Right here."

She nodded, and Drew passed her over to the radiology nurse. He tucked his hands in his pockets and watched Gretchen disappear down the hall. His phone vibrated, and he pulled it out of his pocket, using it as the distraction he needed from his confusing feelings about the girl he used to spend summertime with in rows of lavender.

His heart lurched for a whole new reason. Because the text was from Yvonne Hammond.

Hey you! I'm going to be back in town for a few days next month and wondered if you wanted to get together.

Get together?

Drew looked up, shocked to know he still had Yvonne's number in his phone and utterly baffled as to why she'd want to get together with him. They hadn't spoken in three years. Not a text. Not a written note. Nothing.

So why was Yvonne texting now?

Gretchen slept after her appointment in radiology, and Drew left her snoozing to go get the kids. Jess pulled open the door and climbed into the cab of Drew's truck first, saying, "Hey, Drew," like they were old friends.

"Hey, there." He grinned at the easy-going nature of the boy. Janey had done a great job of raising him on her own after her husband's death in a ferry fire. Drew had been one of the first on-scene, but the scuba cops had done the bulk of the work in getting survivors back to land, where Drew and his crew could then work on them. If Drew remembered right, Jess had been a baby when his father had died.

Dixie climbed up after Jess and pulled the door closed. She didn't say anything, and Drew wondered what was bothering her. He wasn't sure how to ask, so he put the truck in gear and headed toward the farm.

"Your mom's asleep, so we'll go see her after dinner," he said, glancing over at the girl. Dixie barely nodded.

The elementary school sat south of Main Street, so he took the central vein out to the Lavender Highway that led north. "You guys want to stop and get a snack?" Duality came into view, and Drew's mouth watered.

"Sure," Jess said. Dixie said nothing.

Drew's heart kicked out an extra beat as he turned into the parking lot. Everyone piled out, and Drew positioned himself next to Gretchen's daughter. "What'd you do in music today?" he asked.

"We didn't have music today."

"Oh. Well, what did you have instead?"

"PE."

"Do you like PE?" He opened the door and held it for the kids while she said, "Yeah, I guess."

"One thing, okay guys?" he called after them. "Whatever you want."

Once he had his pancake wrapped sausage link, and the kids had their candy, they got back in the truck. He said, "So, have you guys been out to a lavender farm before?"

"Yeah," Jess said in a bored tone, and Dixie said, "My great-grandparents owned a farm. My mom says I came to visit when I was little, but I don't remember."

"We have horses and goats and chickens." He glanced at the kids, glad Dixie was talking again. "What do you want to do first?"

"Horses," Jess said.

Dixie said, "Goats."

He chuckled. "We'll have time to do it all." They arrived at the farm in fifteen minutes and Drew called, "Ma?" when he got out of the truck. His mother appeared on the front porch of the farmhouse, wearing an apron and a wide smile.

"That's my mom," he told the kids. "She's made cookies, and she can't wait to feed you guys dinner."

She received the children with a hug for each of them and a quick, "Hello," before taking them into the kitchen to get a cookie. Drew supposed he probably shouldn't have bought them candy on the way out, but as they petted goats and fed chickens and finally saddled horses, neither of them seemed pale or ill.

"Up you go, Jess." Drew held out his hand to help the boy up, but Jess didn't need it. He landed in the saddle like he'd ridden a horse every day.

He grinned, and Drew pulled out his phone. "Let's take a picture for your mom." He still hadn't answered Yvonne's text. He wasn't sure if he should, or if he should simply delete it. He'd been devastated when she'd left him, and it had taken a year before he'd stopped blaming himself for the break-up.

He pushed Yvonne from his mind and tapped to take the picture.

"Don't send it to her," Jess said, his smile slipping.

"Why not?" Drew admired the photo and turned to help Dixie onto her pony.

"She gets nervous about me doing stuff like this." Jess wore a disgruntled expression when Drew faced him again.

"You don't think she'll find out? You aren't going to tell her?" He tapped the stirrup. "Right there, Dix. Left foot." The girl stumbled a bit, but Drew righted her.

"Probably not," Jess said. "I'll just tell her about the goats and chickens."

Dixie pushed off the ground and Drew helped her land in the saddle. "Oof," she said, surprise racing across her face before it split into a smile.

He gathered the reins of both horses and led them out, thinking about what Jess had said. He'd never known Janey to be afraid of anything. In high school, she formed the rock climbing club and led the group into Olympic National Park on weekends.

Of course, that was before her husband had been killed when the ferry he piloted from the northern point of town over the United States border and into Victoria, Canada had caught fire and sunk with him on board.

"Maybe we shouldn't ride the horses if she's going to be mad about it." Drew glanced over his shoulder, and the identical looks of wonder and joy on Jess's and Dixie's faces squashed that idea real quick. So Drew put his worries to rest—he could deal with Janey Germaine's wrath if he had to.

He walked them through the neat lavender rows, pointing out the different varieties of the plant while Blue and Chief kept the overeager chickens away.

"What's that?" Jess asked, pointing to something on his right. Drew followed his finger and spotted the old wishing well his father had installed a few years before his death.

He chuckled and changed course. "I don't suppose either of you have any coins with you?" He certainly didn't carry cash and when both children said they didn't either, Drew said, "Well, just another reason to come out here again."

They arrived at the old stone well, and Drew helped Jess and then Dixie down. "My dad built this," he said, peering over the edge. "My brother—you guys know Chief Herrin, right? He's my older brother."

The kids nodded and joined him with their hands splayed against the rough rock of the well.

"Anyway, Chief Herrin really wanted to make the high school football team. So my dad would come out into the fields every night and practice with me and Adam." Memories flooded Drew's mind, all of them happy, with footballs being thrown while the sun set and laughter filled the sky as they headed back to the house for their favorite treat: ice cream sandwiches.

His mom made them from scratch, using a thin, crispy gingerbread cookie and lavender honey ice cream. Drew had gotten his love of eating ice cream from his father and his obsession with crafting ice cream from his mother.

"Anyway," he said, realizing he'd fallen silent and that Jess was now staring at him. "The summer before Adam's tryouts, Dad came out here and started building this wishing well. He said he needed the water this far out anyway, and if Adam tossed in a quarter every day for a month and made the same wish, he'd get what he wanted."

Dixie stepped closer to his side. "Did he do it?"

"He sure did." Drew reached up and ran his finger along the top of the roof, which went to a sharp point. The well had seemed so magical when his father had first built it. "Adam came out every day for a month with a quarter he'd earned by raking grass, or hauling lavender, or working around the house for my mom. He'd toss it in, close his eyes tight, and make his wish. Silently." Drew made eye contact with both kids, smiling at them. "That's the trick. You can't say your wish out loud."

Dixie closed her eyes for a few seconds. "I don't have a quarter."

"Like I said, we'll have to come back." The sun was starting to edge toward the ocean on the west, so Drew turned his back to the well and leaned his weight into the wall. "I'm sure I can rustle up some quarters for us."

"I already know what I want to wish for," Jess said, copying Drew and leaning into the well too.

"I don't know that we'll be able to come every day," Drew said.

"Maybe you could come and make our wishes for us," Dixie suggested.

"But then you'd have to tell me your wish out loud." He tapped her on the forehead. "I think once is probably

enough. Come on, we better get back before dinner starts."
He helped the kids back onto the horses and led them back
to the barn.

He showed them how to brush down the animals and
put them in their stalls. When they approached the house, a
forest green SUV sat in the driveway, which meant Janey
had arrived. Adam's truck sat beside it.

"Looks like we're last." Drew increased his speed.
"When we get inside, let's get washed up quick, all right?"

"Drew?" Dixie's sweet voice lifted into the sky.

"Yeah, sweetheart?" He paused and let Jess go into the
farmhouse first.

"Mom said you were there when I was born."

He crouched in front of her. "I sure was." A sense of
pride filled him, and a smile tugged at the corners of his
mouth.

"So you knew my dad."

Drew straightened as he exhaled. "I knew your dad a
little bit," he said. "He and your mom lived out here. Right
over there." He pointed southwest, where the frame of
another house could barely be seen through the trees. "I
wasn't living here, so I wasn't real close with them. But I
knew your mom a little bit from when she came to visit in
the summertime. And yeah, I knew your dad, sure."

Dixie's hand fitted into Drew's. "I miss my dad. Do you
miss your dad?"

The question took Drew by surprise, and that grief that

normally allowed him to go about his day undisturbed hit
him hard behind his heart.

He managed to nod, and his voice was only a little rough
around the edges when he said, "Yeah, I miss my dad."

"But you have Joel now."

Drew didn't want to go into how he'd been a lot older
than Dixie when his dad died, that he hadn't lived at home
when his mother got remarried. But all he did was nod.
"Yeah, I have Joel now." He pushed the door open and
tugged on Dixie's hand to get her to enter first. She went
inside, and he looked up into the sky, hoping for one last
breath of peace before the craziness of dinner began.

Then he faced the bright, loud atmosphere of the farmhouse and joined his family and friends. As he greeted his
brother and put the forks out where his mother dictated, he
realized there was one person missing.

Gretchen.

Somehow they all fit around the dining room table, and
Joel said a blessing on the food. Conversations broke out,
about school, about the farm, about the National Park,
about the happenings of the police department. Drew
enjoyed the vibrant, boisterous meal more than he'd
thought he would, and as Anita stood to join his mother in
making coffee, Drew leaned back in his chair.

"Can I go play with Chief and Blue?" Jess asked
his mom.

"If it's okay with Drew."

"Sure, go on. There are balls in the box in the utility room next to the washing machine."

Jess started to get up, and Dixie did too. They rummaged around in the box to find a toy for the dogs, who waited with their tongues hanging out of their mouths. Blue whined, as if he thought he could find the ball faster.

"So did you ask Gretchen about coming out and staying here at the farm?" His mom placed a steaming mug of coffee in front of him.

Drew's whole body seized, but he managed to lock his gaze onto Dixie's. "Mom," he said quietly.

"I just don't think it would be good for her to try to manage on her own. It's not necessary."

Drew looked to Janey for help. He wanted her to jump in with, "Oh, I'll be there to help her," but she sat silently, watching him.

"We have all those bedrooms upstairs," his mom continued as if an awkward hush hadn't fallen over the table. "She's going to need help."

"She has a broken foot," Drew said. *And we're not together*, he added silently. "She can't go up and down stairs."

"I can help her," Dixie blurted out as she rushed toward the table. "And Drew, you could come help too, right?" She looked from person to person at the table. "My mom would love to stay out here. She talks about her granddad's lavender farm all the time."

Janey finally leaned forward and touched Dixie's arm. "We should talk to her about it first, honey."

"Can we go now?" she asked. "Mom said we could come visit her tonight. We can ask her right now."

Dread filled Drew, and he pressed his eyes closed in a long blink. "I can take you to see your mom." He pushed back from the table and headed into the utility room to get his jacket.

He found Janey with Dixie in the front living room, zipping Dixie's sweatshirt before the little girl practically skipped out the front door.

"This is a bad idea, right?" he asked Gretchen's best friend.

"Oh, I don't know." She tucked her hands in her back pockets. "Depends on how it's presented. Gretchen doesn't like to accept help or be viewed as a charity case." She put her hand on Drew's shoulder as she passed. "Good luck."

Drew chewed on her words all the way to the hospital, but he still couldn't figure out a way to ask Gretchen to come live at the farm with his parents—who she probably barely knew—and make it seem like it wasn't for her bene-fit. How could he make it into something they needed from her?

In the end, he didn't even get a chance to say anything. Dixie beat him to the room and had barely burst through the door when she said, "Drew's mom said we can come stay at the farmhouse while your foot gets better, and I really want to."

Gretchen looked up from the magazine she was reading. "What?"

"Please?" Dixie ran to her mother's bedside. "Please, please, please? They have horses and chickens and this wishing well I need to throw a quarter in every day and make a wish or it won't come true."

Gretchen scoffed in helplessness and looked over Dixie's head to Drew, who still had no idea what to say.

Gretchen listened while Dixie and Drew managed to piece together a story about a wishing well—which apparently Drew's father had built before he'd died—and "the best horses on the planet, Mom," and the fact that Drew's step-father needed help with harvesting the lavender.

"I have a job," Gretchen said. She'd checked her schedule that afternoon after the x-rays, and she had an anniversary party on Saturday night she was providing centerpieces for. And she didn't have a wedding on the day of the Safety Fair, but the evening before.

She'd closed her calendar app at that point, because her foot ached and her brain couldn't handle more than the minimal things she'd done that day. She wasn't sure how in the world she was going to put in a ten-hour day in only a week.

"You could still run The Painted Daisy," Drew said. "But you'd be closer to your flowers out at the farm, and my mother would *love* to help with that. She's always saying how much she admires those gardens you maintain." He didn't seem to be lying, though Gretchen couldn't tell just by looking. She was a mom though, and her fibbing radar wasn't going off.

"You don't have to decide right now," he said.

But Dixie pouted and said, "I don't want to be home alone, Mom. If we stay out there for a week or two, Joel and Donna will be around, so if you need to rest, you can. And I can feed the chickens, and play with Drew's dogs—"

"My dogs live with me," he said quickly, his gaze even on Dixie.

"But you come out to the farm a lot, don't you?" She looked up at him, almost a pout on her face.

"Not a lot," he hedged and that dishonesty alarm sounded in Gretchen's head. She both liked and disliked the idea of having help with Dixie. Needed but didn't need the compassion of Drew and his family. Wanted and didn't want to spend more time with him.

Her feelings felt like she'd stuffed them into a small roller coaster car and set them down a twisty track with multiple loops. She couldn't make decisions with so much wind in her face, without knowing which way the coaster was about to throw her. So she said nothing.

"You won't be able to drive," Drew said, almost securing her decision right then.

"My foot is only broken in one spot," she said. "It doesn't need surgery."

"It's in a full cast," he said, his eyes sliding down to where her foot lay. She wanted to move it but she couldn't hide it. "You can't drive with your right foot in a cast. How are you going to get to the shop and back?"

"Or out to the flowerbeds?" Dixie challenged.

Gretchen had never felt so ganged up on before, even when Aaron and Dixie wanted to go to skip school and work and hop on a ferry to Whidbey Island. In the end, she'd relented, called and excused Dixie, and they'd spent a great day on the beach together. She'd wished Aaron was more spontaneous more often, but he operated like clockwork. In the shower at six-thirty, out the door by seven-thirty. He'd worked long hours, and Gretchen hadn't minded until that last year before his death.

"I'll think about it," she said, her standard mom-answer that bought her time to think about what she should do. Time to get off this roller coaster of confusing emotions she hadn't felt in fifteen long years.

"Can I tell you in the morning?" She stroked Dixie's hair, her insides softening at the pleading look on her daughter's face. She didn't dare look at Drew, because her attraction to him flowed through her the same way her blood did. Surely he'd see it, and she didn't want him to see it yet.

"C'mon, Dix," he said, extending his arm toward her. "I'll take you back to Janey's."

"I don't want to go to Janey's," she complained, but she

moved to Drew's side. He put his arm around her and it looked so natural. Gretchen's heart banged against her ribs as she watched the two of them interact. He seemed to have already forged a relationship with her after just one day, and Gretchen experienced a rush of jealousy that tightened her throat. Since Aaron's death—and even before it—the two of them had been inseparable. But Gretchen had sensed some distance between them the past few months. She'd eased up on the asthma nagging, letting Dixie manage her inhaler on days she had PE and not asking her about how things had gone during gym class.

"Say good-bye to your mother."

Dixie turned back and ran over to the bed. "Love you, Mom."

Gretchen ignored the way the bandage on her wrist pulled, and the zing of pain radiating through her bruised ribs as she hugged her daughter. "Love you, too, Dix." She held her tight, never wanting to let go. "Be good for Drew and Janey, okay?"

"I will." Dixie gave her a fast smile before rejoining Drew in the doorway. He waved and ducked out into the hall, leaving Gretchen to dream about tracing her fingertips along his bearded jaw moments before she kissed him.

THE NEXT MORNING, DR. HARRIS ARRIVED AT THE SAME TIME

the sun burst through the window. "You can go home today," she said, scribbling something on Gretchen's chart. "Who's coming to pick you up?"

"Drew Herrin."

Dr. Harris nodded without missing a beat, finished her notes, and hung the clipboard on the end of the bed. "So they'll bring in breakfast, and I'll get the nurses going on your discharge papers." She smiled at Gretchen. "I'm glad you've got Drew helping you."

Gretchen wanted to ask her what she meant by that, but Dr. Harris exited before she could. She wondered what the doctor would think if she knew Drew was just going to drop her off at home to fend for herself and Dixie.

The fear she'd entertained last night—that she couldn't take care of herself and Dixie on her own—slammed into her with the force of a tsunami. She scooted to the edge of the bed and swung her legs toward the floor. She couldn't put weight on her foot for six weeks, and she couldn't reach her crutches either.

So she couldn't even get out of bed. How was she supposed to get herself from town to her flowers and back? Desperation nearly choked her, and the scent of eggs and orange juice turned her stomach.

Just when she was about to press the button to call the nurse, Drew walked in.

"Morning," he said easily, his smile filling his face and crinkling his eyes. Gretchen's tension fled, because Drew could help her. Drew could fix anything. Drew was talented, and strong, and capable—everything she was not.

"I need my crutches," she said. "Dr. Harris said I could go home this morning."

"You don't want to eat?"

She pressed her mouth into a tight line and shook her head. "I wanted to take a quick walk while I wait for the paperwork. Then I just want to go." Her hatred of hospitals felt suffocating, and she wanted to escape this room she'd been trapped in for two days.

He crossed the room and set a bag on her bed. "Janey put together some clothes for you to wear home." He picked up her crutches and helped her position them. "How far do you want to go?"

"I'm not sure." She hated the effort it took to simply move herself a few feet. Hated that she had to do it in front of this man she'd been crushing on and hoping he'd hold her hand again. They moved into the hall, Gretchen's breath coming quick with the exertion it required to walk.

Her arms hurt, her good leg started to tire quickly, and she only made it around the nurse's station once before returning to her room, completely spent. Drew slipped out into the hall while Gretchen changed, and it took her several long minutes to maneuver the cast on her foot and inflict the least amount of pain on her ribs, wrist, and head.

She wiped the sweat from her hairline just as someone knocked. "Yeah," she said.

Dr. Harris walked in. "I sent a prescription for a

painkiller over to Swanson's. You should pick it up on the way home and take it religiously for the first few days." She paused and fixed Gretchen with a stern, doctorly look. "Drew's just told me that you're going back home. With Dixie."

"I—"

"I can't release you if that's your plan," Dr. Harris said. "You can't be alone on these painkillers, and it's not a ten-year-old's job to watch over you. You can't drive. You shouldn't be doing anything but getting up to use the bath-room for about a week."

Gretchen kept her mouth shut about the anniversary flowers she needed to do. She could sit on a barstool if she could get someone to harvest the flowers and drive her to her shop.

Making a snap decision, she said, "I'm not going home," as Drew pushed the door open and leaned against the frame. He was so handsome her breath caught in her throat.

"Where are you going?" Dr. Harris challenged.

"Drew's family farm." Gretchen switched her gaze to his. "If that's still okay."

"Of course it's okay."

"His step-father needs help with the lavender, and I know every inch of my granddad's farm."

Dr. Harris stabbed a pen in her direction. "No lavender harvesting." She turned back to Drew. "She shouldn't be doing anything but resting."

He raised both hands in acquiescence. "No lavender

harvesting. Got it." His winning smile could charm anyone, even doctors apparently, as Dr. Harris turned back to Gretchen with a satisfied smile.

"Then I can let you go."

Embarrassment warmed Gretchen's face. She positioned her crutches under her arms and hobbled out of the room, Drew carrying her purse and personal belongings behind her. It seemed like a mile to his truck, but she made it. He put her crutches in the back and set her bags on the floor between them.

"So." He exhaled. "I didn't eat breakfast either, and Duality has these amazing burritos with potatoes and eggs and sausage..."

Gretchen produced a small, shy smile. "I like the ones with jalapenos in them."

"Really?" Drew started the truck and laughed. "I would not have guessed that about you."

"No?" She hadn't flirted with a man in many long years, but it almost felt like riding a bike. "What else wouldn't you guess about me?"

He pulled out of the hospital parking lot before giving her a sideways look. "I wouldn't have put you and Janey together as best friends."

"Oh, well, we're more alike than you think."

"Why's that?" He looked both ways at a stop sign before proceeding. "Because you both have kids? The single mom thing?"

"Yeah." Gretchen giggled. "The single mom thing. It's a

pretty strong binder." Anyone who'd raised a child—or attempted to raise a child—on their own would understand. Anyone who hadn't...well, in Gretchen's experience, they didn't understand the challenges as easily.

"I suppose it is."

"So let me play," she said, wanting to tuck her left leg under her body and turn toward him. She couldn't, because she couldn't lift her right leg without help, and she didn't want to make a fool of herself any more than necessary.

"Let's see...you've lived in Hawthorne Harbor your whole life..."

"False," he said.

Surprise shot through her. "Really? You left?"

"For a couple of years."

"Where'd you go?"

"Medina Fire Department."

"Wow, so you're—you're a firefighter too?"

"Not in Hawthorne Harbor. But yes, I did the training, and I could be a firefighter if I wanted to."

"But you don't want to." She wasn't really asking. Her curiosity seemed never-ending.

"Do you like being a paramedic more?"

"Yes," he said simply. "There's too much...devastation in firefighting. All you see is ash and destruction. With emergency medicine, I see the problems and I can fix them. Or at least stabilize them long enough for someone else to fix them."

Gretchen wanted to touch him, reach over and squeeze

his fingers so he'd know his words were safe with her. But he was too far away, and he pulled into Duality in the next moment anyway.

He didn't get out right away, though. "Thank you for accepting my mom's offer to stay at the farm."

"Dr. Harris wasn't really giving me a choice." Why couldn't she just tell him she'd have chosen the farm?

"I didn't mention anything to her, I swear," Drew said. "She overheard me talking to Roxy. That's all."

"Mm-hm." Gretchen gave him what she hoped was a flirty smile. "Maybe you'll have to convince me by buying my breakfast burrito."

He returned her grin, and his dark eyes sparkled with fun and desire when he said, "Done."

She thrilled when he touched her arm to help her from the truck, and she knew in that moment with his skin on hers that this attraction between them was definitely dual-sided. "So I checked my schedule," she said as he held the door open for her so she could maneuver with her crutches. "And I'm free next weekend for the Safety Fair."

Drew brushed her hair back off her face, gazed into her eyes, and said, "That's great, Gretchen."

And it was great. Going out to the lavender farms sounded great. Not having to shoulder every responsibility for a few weeks was going to be absolutely great. And when she bit into the spicy breakfast burrito Drew had purchased for her, that was pretty great too.

But not as wonderful and calming as the man sitting next to her, eating his milder version of the best breakfast burrito in the state of Washington.

10

Drew thought it would be easier to lift Gretchen into his arms and carry her into the house than it was watching her struggle up the five steps to her front door. When she finally made it, she was sweating and her face was an odd shade of gray.

"You okay?" he asked.

"Fine."

Unable to do more, he entered first and held the door open so she could hop-step inside. "There're a couple of bags in the hall closet there." She nodded to a closed door on his left. A living room sat on the right, and she moved in there and collapsed on the couch. "I just need a minute to catch my breath."

Drew appreciated the scent of lemons and the lived-in but clean appearance of her house.

"Dixie's room is down the hall on the left. Mine is on the right, but I can pack my own things."

Nerves wiggled in his chest, and he wondered if Janey wouldn't have been a better choice for this particular task. He had no idea what a ten-year-old needed in the way of clothing, what shoes to bring, or if she'd like anything to occupy her time outside of the farm. He threw in jeans, shirts, socks, and the three pairs of shoes he saw sitting in the closet.

As far as he could tell from the stack of music books on the girl's nightstand, she liked to play the piano. He didn't seen crayons or coloring books, novels or journals. So he grabbed the top few music books and put them in the bag.

He found Gretchen in her bedroom leaning on one crutch while digging through a drawer with her other hand. Watching her for a moment, a rush of affection for her roared through him. She had beautiful eyes and he liked the way she held her mouth in a determined line as she continued to search for what she wanted.

With a jolt, he realized he was staring. "I, uh, got Dixie's stuff. I'll go put it in the truck and be right back."

She startled and almost fell down without the help of both of her crutches.

"Whoa." He darted forward and latched onto her arm. "I've got you." Electric pulses shot up his arm in time to his heartbeat and his eyes locked onto hers.

She was completely steady now, with heat riding in her expression, but he said, "I've got you," again anyway. He really wanted to have her in his arms, in his life. He wanted to know everything about her, and tell her everything about him.

He couldn't make his voice say a single thing.

"Did you get Dixie's inhaler?" Gretchen finally broke the silence. "I think she usually keeps it in the bathroom."

Inhaler? "Does she have asthma?"

Gretchen nodded, her throat moving as she swallowed. Drew tracked the movement against her creamy skin, wondering what it would feel like against his fingertips, his lips. He cleared the fantasy from his mind and turned, releasing his hold on Gretchen's arm. "I'll go grab it."

He hadn't gotten her toothbrush or anything for her hair either, and Drew added the personal hygiene items to Dixie's bag and took it out to his truck. He leaned against the tailgate, and drew in lungful after lungful of the crisp spring air.

He couldn't be alone with Gretchen like that again, not if he wanted to keep her out at the farm until she could take care of herself. His face cooled, but his heart still hammered against his ribs as if he'd just lifted the heaviest weights of his life.

Dr. Harris hadn't said anything about the heart murmur either, and maybe her body had simply been compensating for her injuries.

Something banged inside the house and he practically sprinted back through the front door. "Gretchen?"

"I'm fine," she called. He followed the sound of her voice

down the hall, bypassing the one that went left and continuing into the great room, dining area, and kitchen, where Gretchen stood with ice cubes strewn around her feet.

"I just dropped the ice cube tray," she said.

"I can get you a drink." Drew hurried forward and took the glass from her hand. He didn't need to clean up broken shards as well as water.

"I want to get my own drink," she said in a surly tone.

"Yeah, well, I want a million dollars." He tossed a smile in her direction and picked up the ice cube tray, shaking the four cubes that were still in the plastic into the glass. He filled it with water and set it on the counter in front of Gretchen. "You're going to have to get used to someone helping you for a while."

"I will never get used to it."

Drew gathered up all the melting cubes and tossed them into the sink. He settled his weight against the countertop and faced her. "Why not?"

"Because, in the end, only you can take care of yourself." She drained the last of the water and met his eye with a challenge in hers.

"Do you really believe that?" he asked.

"Yes, I do."

"I think that's really sad."

"Well, you weren't left without a job, without a way to pay bills, with a seven-year-old daughter to somehow provide for." She hopped on her good foot so she faced him. "When you go through that, see who'll be there to help."

Sadness pinched behind his heart. "My parents would be there."

"Lucky you."

"Why didn't you go back to California so your parents could help?"

"I already told you I couldn't go back there."

"But you never said why." She didn't have to do everything alone. She *chose* to.

Gretchen lifted her chin. "I left my bag on my bed. It's ready."

Drew wasn't ultra experienced with women, but he knew when a conversation was over.

I can't do this.

That was one kind of final.

But so was *I left my bag on my bed.*

Yvonne's text haunted him as he collected Gretchen's bag, put it in the back of the truck, and returned to the porch to help her down the steps and into the vehicle.

When he arrived at the farm, his mom and Joel greeted them in the driveway. Joel grabbed the two bags, and his mom took over assisting Gretchen into the house. Drew trailed behind, his emotions swirling around and around themselves.

The ride out to the farm had been filled with tension and he hadn't known how to break it. He stepped next to his mom, who was filling coffee mugs with the hot liquid and whispered, "She can't sleep upstairs. She can barely walk."

His mom gave him a look and turned back to where

Gretchen sat at the kitchen table. "Here you go, dear." She pushed the sugar bowl closer. "So we only have one extra bedroom here on the main level. Do you think Dixie would mind sleeping upstairs alone? Or she could stay in the bedroom with you. It has a queen-sized bed."

Gretchen sipped her coffee and took a few extra moments to answer. She wouldn't look at Drew, and he stayed over by the coffeemaker. He didn't want to appear too friendly out here, otherwise his eagle-eyed mother would know about his crush on the pretty florist.

"I'll ask her after school," Gretchen said. "Honestly, sometimes she sleeps with me, and sometimes she doesn't."

His mother patted Gretchen's hand. "Well, you just leave everything to me. I'm so glad you're here. It's been so long since I've had someone to take care of in this house."

"Hey," Joel protested as he entered the kitchen, having taken the bags up to the second-floor bedrooms. "You take care of me."

She laughed and handed Joel a mug of coffee. "I suppose that's true."

Drew watched their exchange, glad his mother had found someone to love again. He wished he could find someone to share his life with, and his gaze wandered to Gretchen's. Would she ever allow someone into her life? Into Dixie's? Would she be able to rely on someone again, accept their help?

He hoped so, and he turned away from her at the table and reached for another mug. After filling it with coffee, he nodded at Gretchen and escaped through the back door. Knowing his mother, she'd have a schedule set up for who would take Dixie to school, who would pick her up, and how Gretchen could get back and forth to her shop before he got back from feeding the chickens.

Sure enough, when he returned to the farmhouse after taking an extra-long hour out with the animals, his mother greeted him with, "Gretchen has an anniversary dinner tomorrow night. She needs help getting the flowers in the morning, and then you'll drive her over to the florist on your way to work." She glanced at Drew as if expecting his perfect compliance. "Is that all right?"

"I guess. Can I bring the dogs out here for the weekend? Maybe Dixie could have Jess over and they could play with them."

"Sure, bring the dogs. What time do you need to be to work?"

"Nine."

His mother turned from the stove, where she was browning sausage for what Drew hoped was her chicken and bell pepper Alfredo pizza. "Gretchen, dear, how long will it take you in the flower gardens?"

Gretchen looked at Drew. "Depends. Do you know the difference between a daisy and a tulip?"

Drew blinked, unsure of how to answer.

"Oh, he's helpless with flowers," his mom said. "He knows lavender, that's for sure. He knows roses. He's good with honey." With every word his mother said, Gretchen's head tipped a little more, like one of his dogs trying to figure out a new command.

"Really?" she said. "Honey?"

"Oh, Drew here is a budding ice cream chef." His mother seeded a green pepper, and Drew knew he'd be asking her to save him some pizza.

"Mom," he said. "Stop talking, please."

"Oh, you." She mimed throwing the green pepper at him and laughed.

He focused on Gretchen. "I can get your flowers. You'll just have to boss me around a little."

"I think I can do that." She grinned and ducked her head but not before he saw the hint of a blush in her cheeks. "So maybe seven-thirty," she said.

He groaned. "That's early." He usually worked out before going over to the hospital, but a seven-thirty call time for picking flowers would push his wake-up time to six.

"I can have Dixie help."

"I can do it." Drew spoke maybe a little too quickly, or a little too sharp. No matter what, he'd drawn the attention of his mother, who managed to chop the peppers into rings without even looking at them. How she didn't cut off her fingers, he didn't know.

"Well, I have to get to work," he said, glad for a reason to get out of the kitchen. "I'm on until ten tonight," he told his mother with a quick kiss to her temple. "You'll save me some of that pizza, right?"

She laughed and promised she would. Drew headed out

to his truck without looking back. He really wanted to, but he couldn't give his mother any more fuel for her suspicions.

THE NEXT MORNING, DREW LIFTED WEIGHTS AND RAN ON THE treadmill, showered, and loaded up the dogs. Out on the farm, he let them loose into the lavender fields and walked around the fence and into the expansive flower gardens Gretchen maintained. He found her there already, her auburn hair tied back into a ponytail. She wore a pair of baggy jeans with an overly large pair of field boots—well just the one—and her sweatshirt zipped all the way to her throat.

He didn't blame her. The wind coming off the ocean today held a certain iciness he hoped would be gone in a few weeks.

"You doing my job?" he asked as he came up behind her.

"Just looking," she said. "I knew you were here. Your dogs are loud."

"Only Blue," he said. "He seems to think everyone wants to know what he has to say." Drew chuckled as he noticed the clumps of lavender getting jostled in the distance from where Blue and Chief romped through the fields. The distinct sound of Blue's bark met his ears, and he couldn't help feeling the same joy as his dog running through the field.

He drew in a deep breath, getting the salty brine mixed with a heady floral scent and Gretchen's powdery skin. His hand hovered over hers though it rested on her crutch. She released it and tucked her fingers into his, a sigh slipping through her lips.

"I'm a little nervous," he admitted, not quite sure when he'd decided to have this conversation with her.

"About what?"

"Starting something with you."

Before she could respond, Dixie called, "Mom! Mom?"

Gretchen dropped his hand, and he automatically moved farther down the row. "Out in the garden, Dix."

The little girl came skipping over from the farmhouse, and when she saw Drew her whole face lit up. "Drew!"

"Hey, Dixie. Should we help your mom get the flowers she needs?"

"I have a list," Gretchen said, and Dixie plucked it from her fingers and read it.

"This is easy. C'mon, Drew. Follow me." The little girl traipsed past him and over a couple rows. Drew grinned after her and looked back at Gretchen. She watched her daughter with the same fondness, and when her eyes met his, something passed between them.

"We'll talk later," he said.

"Looking forward to it." Gretchen started back down the row, and Drew went to work with Dixie to get the flowers her mom needed, a thread of happiness pulling through him at these two females that had come back into his life.

11

G retchen got her anniversary centerpieces finished in plenty of time. She sold a few bouquets for dates that evening. Janey, still dressed in her forest green park ranger garb, came to pick her up in time to get the vases over to the Lions Lodge, a premier restaurant with a beautiful banquet room in the back.

"The blue one on the far table," Gretchen told her friend. Janey picked up the appointed piece with white, pink, and orange daisies arranged artfully. Gretchen absolutely loved daisies, and she'd been working for the past year to cross-pollinate her favorite colors to breed a new one. She hadn't had Dixie and Drew pick any of those, as they held a special place in her heart, and she wanted them to be used for something special.

If she were being honest, she wanted the indigo daisies with white centers in her own wedding bouquet.

She continued directing Janey as to where to put each centerpiece, and Florence Francis came in to inspect the work. "Lovely, as always, Gretchen." She bent down and gave Gretchen a hug. "I can't believe you didn't cancel. When I heard about your foot, I felt so guilty."

"I'm fine, honestly." Gretchen waved her hand like her injury was no big deal. "Happy anniversary, Flo. Thirty years. Wow."

The older woman laughed and straightened. "So, are you seeing anyone?"

"No," Gretchen said just as Janey said, "She sure is."

"Janey," Gretchen warned.

"Ooh," Flo said, volleying her gaze between Gretchen and Janey. "Who is it? One of our local boys, I bet."

Gretchen tilted her head, trying to hear the meaning between those words. "What does that mean?"

"It means you've always loved this place. Too bad your grandparents sold before you had a chance to buy that farm you've always loved."

Gretchen *had* loved her granddad's lavender farm, and from what she'd seen, Joel hadn't done much to keep it thriving over the past five years. She'd wondered why he'd bought it and done nothing with it, but she hadn't had time to ask him or Donna about it.

She'd thought about asking Drew—he'd been on her mind all day long—but she still didn't have his phone number.

"It's Drew Herrin," Janey said despite Gretchen's warning.

"Oh, my. Drew Herrin." Flo patted her hair as if Drew was in the room and she wanted to impress him. "He's quite handsome."

Janey grinned wickedly. "That he is."

"I'm not seeing Drew Herrin." Gretchen nodded toward the empty box. "Grab that, Janey, and let's get out of Flo's way. Her family will be arriving soon."

Thankfully, Janey complied and they headed out to her SUV. "I'm not *seeing* Drew Herrin," she repeated as Janey opened the door for her.

"But you want to."

"No, I don't." She sank into the bucket seat and let Janey close the door behind her.

She got behind the wheel and started the Jeep. "Why won't you let yourself like him?"

"I...don't know."

"Dixie likes him. He's great with the kids. You should've heard Jess going on and on about this wishing well Drew showed him. My son usually doesn't put more than three words together, and he talked about the horses at that farm for twenty minutes."

Gretchen remembered how easily Dixie had taken to Drew too. And how much she'd talked about the farm last night while they lay in bed together. She hadn't read the way she usually did. No, everything had been "Drew this," and "Drew that."

"He is really handsome," Gretchen said, admitting the tiniest detail that everyone could see anyway. There was something about a neatly trimmed beard that made her heart pitter incessantly.

Janey laughed as she turned down Main Street and drove past all the familiar shops. "He sure is. And what about him dropping everything to take care of you? Come to your rescue, putting you up at his parents' place? He's like your knight in shining armor. Or a paramedic uniform."

Gretchen's defenses went right back up again. "I don't need a knight in shining armor."

"Of course you don't. But aren't you tired?"

"Tired?"

Janey glanced at her. Turning north, she set the Jeep on course for the farm. "Yes, Gretchen. Tired of shouldering everything yourself? Tired of making all the decisions? Don't you want someone to take Dixie so you can sleep in for just one day? Someone to pick up dinner on the way home when you don't feel well. Someone to share each day with." Janey's voice grew quieter and quieter with each sentence she spoke.

"I do," she said. "I think I'm ready to find someone to share my life with again."

"Janey." Gretchen reached across the console and gripped her best friend's fingers. "I've never heard you talk like this."

"I miss Matt with my whole heart," she said. "But our marriage was young, and our baby younger. I haven't dated because I honestly wasn't sure I should, for Jess's sake, because I didn't think I could ever love someone as much as I loved Matt." She shrugged, her coat slipping off her shoulder a bit. "But seeing the way Drew looks at you, I've realized that I wouldn't have to love someone as much as Matt. I'd just have to love him."

Gretchen absorbed her friend's words, wondering if she'd been focusing on the wrong things these past three years. "How does Drew look at me?"

Janey laughed again, the sound bouncing around the interior of the Jeep. "You really can't see him at all, can you?"

"I see him." Gretchen clenched her arms around her stomach. She'd seen his strength as he helped her in the flower fields, seen his handsome face while she dreamt last night, seen his kind spirit every time she thought about what he did for a living, seen his determination whenever he asked her if she'd taken her meds and how she was feeling.

"Then admit you like him." Janey pulled up to the farmhouse and twisted toward Gretchen, a teasing smile on her face.

"I'll admit I'm interested in him."

"Ah-ha!" Janey pumped her fist in the air with another laugh. "That's at least a start. Now, let's go make sure our kids haven't worn Donna and Joel right into the ground."

EACH NIGHT, GRETCHEN SAT DOWN WITH DONNA AND DIXIE to make sure everyone knew who was driving to school and who was picking up from school the next day. Sometimes it was Janey, sometimes Donna, and sometimes Drew. Even though he didn't live out at the farmhouse, he came every morning and did a few chores. As the days passed, he became her flower errand boy without having to be asked, and Gretchen enjoyed her time with him in the mornings before the sun truly rose.

He never complained about the early hour, or making multiple trips to her van and back with armloads of flowers. He never seemed frustrated with her bossy voice telling him to be careful, to wrap the stems in damp towels, and to drive slower. He didn't seem to mind helping her or with taking Dixie out to the wishing well. He had a quick smile, and warm hands, and a way with kids and dogs Gretchen could only marvel at.

"So," he said, clapping his hands together on Thursday evening as he joined her on the porch. "I'm helping in the flower shop tomorrow for the wedding. I hope that means I'll get to run out and get you lunch." He gestured to the other half of the porch swing. "Can I join you?"

"Sure." She had a blanket across her legs and her hoodie zipped up tight. Drew had seemed cautious with his conversations and the way he touched her while out here at the farm, and Gretchen understood why. He held her hand in the morning and if they were alone in his truck. Nothing more. He never brought up "starting something" with her either, and since she was having a hard time untangling her feelings for him, she'd remained silent on the subject as well.

He sank into the swing, setting it into motion as he laughed. "I haven't sat out here for a while." He cut her a glance out of the corner of his eye. "I don't do a lot of sitting when I'm at the farm. Lots of work to do."

"You work hard around here," she said, adding another positive trait to the list she was keeping in her mind.

"Well, my day job isn't very taxing," he said. "Not a lot of emergencies in Hawthorne Harbor."

"Thankfully," she said.

"Yes, thankfully." He pushed off with his toe, keeping them rocking back and forth, back and forth. "Where's Dixie?"

"My mother has her peeling potatoes."

With that, Drew's hand found hers and Gretchen thrilled at the touch of his skin, the warmth in his hand. She sighed and leaned her head against his shoulder. "So the wedding tomorrow," he said, his voice taking on a husky quality. "And you're still planning on the Safety Fair on Saturday?"

"Yes." She snuggled closer, though her internal defenses were lifting into place. "I really appreciate all your help this week."

"I'm really glad you decided to take it."

"I don't have much choice, do I?"

"You always have a choice, Gretchen." His lips pressed

hotly against her temple, and fireworks popped through her system, sparking all the way down to her toes. Her smile was instant and she couldn't seem to straighten her lips even when she tried.

"I wanted to ask you something," he said, gently pushing them every time they swung forward.

Gretchen swallowed, telling herself that sharing things was a normal thing for people to do as they got to know each other. "All right."

"Have you dated anyone since Aaron died?"

"No."

"Why not?" He didn't sound judgmental, only curious.

"It took me a while to figure out what to do," she said. "He had some life insurance, but not enough to keep me and Dixie in our condo in Seattle. I sold that, and made the move back here."

His fingers tightened on hers, but he didn't say anything.

"I needed something to support myself and Dixie, and I met with your step-dad about the land with the flowers—which was why I didn't know your family still owned this land. I thought they'd moved." She paused, her memories flowing back to when she'd first driven the Lavender Highway after being away for so long. Joel had met her in the garden, and she'd had no idea Drew's family was still connected to the lavender farm she'd loved so much.

"It was a lot of work to get the flower gardens back in shape. They haven't done much with my granddad's farm."

"No, Joel and Mom bought it to preserve their own farm,

as well as the farm of the neighbors they'd had for decades. They didn't want someone coming in and bulldozing the lavender, or hosting a big festival, or anything like that."

"Do they do anything with the lavender?" There used to be several rows of Pacific Blue lavender, her favorite variety of the flower.

"Joel used to, but he's getting older. His hip bothers him most days, especially when the weather is colder. I take care of the animals and maintain all the equipment. We both tend to the lavender, but I don't have enough time to take on another farm full of it."

"My granddad's farm was eighty acres, with twelve different varieties of lavender." She felt warm and woozy, full of great memories of her summers out at the farm. "I loved summer on the lavender farm. Granddad would tell me stories about his father, and he showed me how to ride horses..." Her voice trailed off into happiness. "It smelled so good out here, and everything seemed more magical than my dumpy two-room apartment in Carlsbad."

The swing went back and forth several times in companionable silence. Gretchen wondered if she'd revealed too much, but then she decided she didn't care. She wanted Drew to have some insight into her life, and it didn't make her weaker if he did.

"So are you interested in dating?" he asked.

Gretchen's face heated and she giggled. She shifted on the swing until she could look up into Drew's face. "Depends on who's asking."

He gazed at her evenly, his dark eyes dancing simultaneously with hope and anxiety. "*I'm* asking, Gretchen. Me. I'm asking if you'd like to go out with me."

A slow smile arced across her face at the same rate her heart went from beating normally to racing. "Then yes. I'm interested in dating again." She swallowed, finding her throat so dry and her fantasies filled with anticipation.

"Great." Drew swept his lips across her temple again, jerking away when Dixie yelled, "Drew?"

"On the porch." He launched himself from the swing on its next move forward, almost like he didn't dare let Dixie see them cuddling on the porch. Probably smart. He put his hand on the screen door. "So maybe I could get your number," he said.

Gretchen grinned at him. "Sure."

Dixie arrived, practically knocking the screen door down as she spilled onto the front porch with Jess in hot pursuit. "Drew, Jess has to go in a minute and we haven't gone out to the wishing well yet."

"Well, he might have to miss a day."

"I can't miss a day," Jess whined. "I washed all the dishes for your mom, and I have my quarter."

"We don't have time to saddle the horses," Drew said. "It's almost dark already."

The kids stood there and stared at him, and Gretchen wondered how he'd won them over in only a few days. They'd do anything he said, and Dixie did chores around the farm every day to earn her quarter for the wishing well.

"You have an ATV in the shed," Gretchen said.

Drew whipped his attention to her. "Have you been snooping around?"

Giddiness pranced through her. "Joel goes out with me. I'm being safe."

"You have an ATV?" Jess asked. "Can we take it out to the wishing well? Please?" He glanced over his shoulder. "And don't tell my mom. She'll say we have to go now if she even hears the word ATV."

Drew cocked one eyebrow and stepped past the children. He called into the house, "Janey, can you come out here for a sec?"

"What are you doing?" Jess hissed. "She's—hey, Mom."

Janey gave him a suspicious look and took in the scene on the porch before saying, "What's up, Drew?"

"Jess would like to take a quick trip out to the wishing well. On an ATV."

Jess's shoulders sank and he sighed. "C'mon Dixie. Let's go have Donna save our quarters for tomorrow."

"Can he go?" Drew asked. "I'll be driving, and it's a quick trip out on the ATV. Maybe ten minutes there, and ten minutes back."

"Do you have a helmet for the kids?"

"We used to have helmets in the shed," he said.

"I saw some," Gretchen offered. "Dixie has my permission to go."

Dixie cheered and joined Drew, slipping her hand into his. "Please, Janey? Jess *can't* miss a day of his wish."

"What are you wishing for?" she asked her son.

"Oh, no," Drew said. "He can't tell you out loud."

"Why not?"

"Then it won't come true."

Jess joined Drew and Dixie, creating a united front against Janey. "Please, Mom. It's only twenty minutes."

Janey looked at them and then Gretchen, who lifted both shoulders, knowing her friend would say yes. "Oh, all right."

Everyone whooped, and Jess gave Drew a high five before hugging his mom. "Thanks, Mom." They went down the steps and headed toward the sheds on the west side of the farmhouse.

Janey dropped into the spot Drew had just been in on the swing. "He's great with them."

"They seem to love him." Gretchen watched until she couldn't see the kids and Drew anymore. She honestly had no idea how to classify the feelings dancing through her veins. "He asked me out."

"It's about time." Janey laughed and lifted her arm over Gretchen's shoulders. "I hope you said yes."

"You know what?" She grinned at her friend. "I did."

12

Drew marveled at the way Gretchen could take flowers and make them into works of art. With floral tape, pins, and the eye of a professional, she put together delicate corsages, traditional centerpieces, and huge show-pieces for the bride and groom.

He got her whatever flower she requested, retrieved more tape when she ran out, and brought her a chicken Ceasar salad from the Souper Salad down the street. He made several simple sales of rose bouquets to anyone who came in.

When they only had twenty minutes left until they needed to leave to get over to the reception center, a woman pushed into the florist.

"Jenna Blackman." Drew smiled at the raven-haired woman he'd grown up with. "What can I help you with?"

"Is Gretchen here?" Jenna tipped up onto her toes and

tried to see past Drew. Gretchen's workroom had a large window that faced the shop, but it was tinted so she could see into the shop, but they couldn't see her.

"She's putting the finishing touches on a wedding. We're closing in five minutes to head out." He flinched when he realized he'd used the word "we're" like he and Gretchen owned and operated The Painted Daisy together. He hoped Jenna hadn't noticed.

"I need to talk to her about a wedding." Jenna's face filled with happiness as her smile widened. "I got engaged!" She held out her left hand like Drew should examine the engagement ring and gush over it.

"Let me see if she has time to talk right now." Drew edged away from Jenna and hurried into the back room. "Jenna Blackman is here, and—"

"I got engaged!"

Drew jumped and his heartbeat accelerated when he realized Jenna had followed him into the refrigerated workroom. She pushed past him and approached Gretchen, who sat at her workbench, blinking.

"I *have* to have you do the flowers for the wedding, Gretchen. I just have to." Jenna positioned herself on the barstool Drew had been occupying for most of the day. "You're the best in town. You don't ship anything in." Her eyes shone with anxiety and hope. "Can you do it?"

Gretchen looked at Drew over Jenna's head. "Drew, I have a calendar under the front desk. Could you grab it for me?" She wiped her hand on the green apron she wore over her clothes, the faintest line of disapproval appearing between her eyes.

He didn't want to leave her here alone, but he nodded and hurried back to the front of the store. He found the calendar and returned to the workroom to find Gretchen holding Jenna's left hand and assuring her that the ring was lovely.

Relief washed across her face when Drew stepped between them and placed the calendar on the table. "When is the wedding?" Gretchen asked.

"Should I start to load up?" Drew asked. "We have to leave soon."

"Yes, please." Gretchen flashed him a brief smile. "I'll finish this wreath and we'll go."

Drew picked up a box of corsages at the same time Jenna said, "So our date is August fourth." He hated leaving Gretchen in there alone, but he reasoned that she usually ran the florist shop by herself. She didn't need him hovering over her, even if she looked uncomfortable around the bride-to-be.

They left several minutes late because of Jenna, and Gretchen exhaled heavily after he'd helped her into the van.

"Maybe we can grab some ice cream after we get set up," he said, glancing at her.

She smiled and gave him a sexy smirk. "Always with the ice cream."

"It'll be store-bought, but I suppose it'll have to do." He

turned onto Main Street and started toward the gardens where the reception was being held.

Both eyebrows lifted under her bangs. "You eat store-bought ice cream?"

"If the occasion calls for it." He chuckled as he drove.

"Seems almost criminal." She giggled and the sound of it drove his temperature higher. "So, what's the last flavor you made?"

"Lavender and orange with a dash of black pepper."

"Oh. Wow. That's…" Gretchen's mouth worked but no sound came out.

"I haven't tried it frozen yet. I'm still working on the recipe."

"How do you know if it's good?"

"I make the base first," he said, feeling like he was exposing part of his soul by talking about his ice cream experiments. And taking Gretchen to his house? Yeah, he wasn't going to do that anytime soon.

"And I taste it," he said. "The only difference between the base and the ice cream is the texture and the temperature. So I mix it up and put it in the fridge to get nice and cold. Then I taste it. Although, sometimes the way the ice cream is churned makes a difference. When I use liquid nitrogen, for example, I—" He made himself stop talking. One quick glance at her showed that he had said too much, too fast. He chuckled. "Sorry. I get a little carried away when it comes to ice cream making."

She turned and settled some of her weight into the door

instead of the back of the seat. Straightening the green sweater she wore, she asked, "Why is that, Drew?"

"Why is what?"

"Why do you like ice cream making so much?"

He shrugged, though he knew why. "It's just a hobby."

"Yeah, I don't think so." She watched him, and he almost squirmed under the weight of her gaze. "No one makes the bases, tastes them, and then washes them down the drain."

"I didn't say I washed them down the drain."

"Oh yeah?" She folded her arms, her smile beautiful and flirty. "What do you do with the base after you taste it? If it doesn't meet your cut to actually get made into an ice cream? Then what?"

"I...wash it down the drain." He laughed with her, and it felt so good. So right. And he was so happy he'd decided to ignore Yvonne's text. As soon as he could, he was going to delete it completely.

"So what are your goals with the ice cream recipes? Cookbook? Oh, wait! Do you have a blog online?" Her eyes practically shot sparkles they were glittering so much. "Can I find your creations on the Internet?"

"What? No." Drew scoffed, his fingers gripping the wheel a bit tighter. "I—look, I don't want you to laugh."

"I'm not going to laugh."

He hadn't even told his mom or Joel about why he'd been so focused on ice cream lately.

"You don't have to tell me," she said.

He wanted to. "Just promise you won't laugh."

"I'm not going to laugh. I promise."

It took a few moments for him to work up his courage. "So you know how they award a Lavender King or a Lavender Queen every year at the Lavender Festival?"

"Yeah." She drew the word out, obviously not getting where he was going yet.

"I want to win that," he said. "I've never entered, but I've been perfecting my ice cream recipes and skills for a few years now. I'm not sure I'm ready for the Creation Contest, but—"

"I'm sure you are," she said. "Do you need a taste-tester? I really like ice cream."

Drew looked at her, hope firing through him and filling him completely. "Really? You'd taste and tell me the truth?" The idea of having her over to his home to taste his creations made him as nervous as much as it excited him.

Her little laugh made a shiver cascade over his skin. "Of course. I'm not afraid to try anything either," she said.

"All right, then," he said. "Let's get these flowers where they go, and then you can try my honey lavender scone ice cream."

She blinked, her cute little smile still in place. "That sounds fascinating."

"It won't win." He pulled into the reception center. The Hawthorne Harbor Gardens weren't the Magleby Mansion, but not everyone could afford such a luxury location for their wedding.

"Why not?"

"Honey with lavender is too ordinary." He got out of the van, the scent of roses already in the air. He'd loved these gardens when he was a kid. His father had first taught him about botanicals by wandering through these gardens.

The memories flowed as he got to work, following Gretchen's directions and exchanging flirtatious smiles with her. An hour later, all the flowers were in place, and Drew drove back to his place, his nerves pulsing through his whole body. His hands felt slick on the steering wheel and when he parked in the driveway, he couldn't make himself get out.

Blue barked from the backyard, the sound faint through the closed windows.

"Are we going to go in?" Gretchen asked.

"Yeah." Drew ran his hand down his face and over his beard. "Yes, let's go in. It's kind of a mess, so..."

"I'll be kind." She opened her door, and that launched Drew into motion. He went around to her side and helped her get the crutches in position. Once inside, the scent of cream and sugar met his nose, and Gretchen said, "Smells great in here. When's the last time you made ice cream?"

"Like actual ice cream? A couple of nights ago. I made a lavender blueberry base last night." He made a face that got a laugh from Gretchen. "Augustus Hammond won with something similar a while back, but I don't like blueberries much."

"Augustus Hammond...he owns the Purple Haze Lavender Farm, doesn't he?"

"Sure does." And the Hammonds were very influential around town. Drew worried that even if his recipe was better than Augustus's, he wouldn't win. He pushed the cares away. He didn't even know if Augustus was going to enter the contest this year. Perhaps he'd been invited to sit on the judge's panel.

Drew led her into the kitchen, which looked like a mad scientist lived there. Normal people had toasters on their counters. He had a row of ice cream makers. Other single men probably had frozen pizzas in the freezer. He opened his and pulled out one of a half dozen plastic containers of ice cream.

"Wow," Gretchen said, taking in the kitchen. He tried to see it through new eyes, and he supposed the glass containers of sugar and malted milk powder lining the counter were odd. The big stock pot he used to heat milk and sugar. The stack of egg containers he hadn't taken out to the recycling bin yet.

"So, I, uh, eat out a lot," he said. "The kitchen mostly gets used for ice cream making." He tacked on a light laugh and got out two spoons. He cracked the lid on the container and handed her a utensil, reminding himself that it wasn't the first time she'd tried his ice cream.

"So give it a try." He stepped back and watched as she fixed him with the flirtiest look a woman had ever given him. She finally dipped her spoon into the ice cream and lifted out a bite.

Heat shot into his face as he watched the spoon go all

the way to her lips. He focused on her mouth, and then all he could think about was kissing her. The air between them became charged, and he didn't even know why.

He couldn't tell if she liked the ice cream, because her expression remained blank even as a beautiful blush crept into her cheeks.

She finally swallowed and a small cough broke from her throat. A giggle followed, and Drew exhaled in a loud burst. "Well?"

"Drew, that is delicious." She took another bite. "I like this one better than the white chocolate one you brought to the hospital last week."

"Yeah?"

She leaned her weight into the counter and took an awkward step closer. "Really great."

He received her into his arms, the weight and feel of her there absolutely perfect. "Could you taste the cinnamon?" he whispered.

"Yes, it sort of sat on the back of my tongue."

"And the lavender?"

"Just at the end, that great floral note. And the saltiness that indicated the scone was the best part."

"You think so?"

She leaned into him, tipping her head back to keep eye contact with him. "I think you could win Lavender King with that ice cream."

Drew chuckled. Every cell in his body urged him to kiss

Gretchen, but still he didn't. "I don't think I'd win with that," he said. "Like I said, it's a little too ordinary."

"There was nothing ordinary about that ice cream." She reached up and traced her fingers along his jaw line. "There's nothing ordinary about *you*."

Drew wasn't sure how to respond, and it didn't matter, because he was going to kiss Gretchen.

At least until his phone sang from where he'd tossed it on the kitchen counter. A part-nervous, part-frustrated laugh spilled from his lips as he glanced at it. Then alarm filled him. "It's Dixie." He released Gretchen and swiped the device from the counter and held it toward her.

"Dixie?" She peered at the phone and then took it from him. "Dixie?" she said into the phone. "Yes, it's Mom. I'm with Drew. He's..." Her eyes met his. "Busy."

She turned away from him but couldn't move far. So he heard her when she said, "Dix, I need you to take a deep breath...yes, Drew brought your inhaler out to the farm-house. It's probably in the bathroom."

Several tense seconds passed, where Drew put the lid on the ice cream and replaced it in the freezer. He went to the back door and whistled for the dogs. They came tearing into the house as Gretchen said, "Go ask Donna, baby. I'll be home in a few minutes."

He gestured toward the front door, and she set his phone on the counter before grabbing her crutches. He picked up his phone and followed her. "Is she okay?"

"She's having an asthma attack. She said something

about an animal in the lavender fields and she ran... I couldn't really tell what had happened. She couldn't find her inhaler."

"I'll call my mom." Drew held open Gretchen's door while the dogs loaded into the truck bed and his mom's phone rang and rang. "She didn't answer." He jumped behind the wheel and put the truck in gear. "Don't worry, Gretchen. I'm sure she's fine."

But Gretchen didn't relax, didn't even respond. She stared out the passenger window, her jaw working and her hands sitting very, vey still in her lap.

13

G retchen hated that she couldn't always be there for Dixie. Hated relying on Donna and Joel, Janey and Drew, to take care of her and her daughter. She supposed everyone needed help from time to time, but she felt like such a burden.

The worry wormed through her stomach, making it sour. If Aaron were here, she wouldn't be in this position. Anger flowed through her. Anger that he'd always worked so late. Anger that he hadn't been more careful that night. Anger that she now had to deal with everything alone.

She glanced over to Drew, his words echoing in her head.

I'll be right here.

And he had been right there, directly beside her, offering constant support and encouragement. So she didn't have to do this alone. Not tonight.

By the time they pulled up to the farmhouse, enough time had passed for Dixie to quiet. Donna rocked in the porch swing with Dixie's head in her lap, stroking the girl's fair hair.

"How is she?" Gretchen asked, exhaustion filling her whole soul. She still wasn't back to one-hundred percent, and her head ached.

"We found her inhaler, and she's doing fine." Donna smiled down at the girl with such love, Gretchen wondered how she could take her daughter and move back into her cottage. This farm, Donna and Joel—Drew —they felt like where she should be and who she should be with.

Gretchen took a deep breath and pushed it out. "Thank you so much, Donna." Her voice quivered a bit, and she let herself lean against Drew. His mother saw, but Gretchen wasn't sure she cared anymore. She'd almost kissed the man only twenty minutes ago.

Her whole body felt cold, and not only because the evening wind had kicked up.

"Come on, Gretchen." Drew took her in the house. "You should go to bed."

She sank onto the couch and wiped her hand down her face. "I can't. I have to go back and get the flowers."

"I'll do it."

"You have to be to work by eight tomorrow." She gave him a look she hoped made his insides quake with fear.

He didn't seem fazed at all as he sat next to her. "Please

let me do this for you." He lifted her fingers to his lips and kissed each one before looking into her eyes.

She couldn't argue with him. She didn't even want to. "Okay."

Satisfied, he leaned back into the couch and tucked her into his side. "Okay."

GRETCHEN WOKE WITH A START AND SAT UP STRAIGHT, HER eyes taking precious seconds to adjust to the dark. "Hello?" One thing about living out in the country was there was no light pollution. Everything was absolutely silent at night. Which made the sound she'd heard terrifying.

"It's me," Drew whispered from across the room. "My mother said you didn't take any painkillers before bed. Are you feeling okay?"

Her head pulsed with pain, and surprisingly, her forearms did too. She'd warded off a fifteen-foot ladder with them, so she supposed they had the right to hurt.

"I could use something," she said, finally able to drink in the form of his silhouette as the dim light filtered down the hall and framed him. "I can get up."

"No, just stay there," he whispered. "I'll grab you something to drink and get your pills." He left the door open, returning a few minutes later with a glass of water and a couple of capsules. She swallowed them, relief at the cool water already touching her scorched throat.

"Thank you."

"Everything went well at the reception center. I collected the rest of your money." He set something on the nightstand before retreating to the wall near the open door and sliding down it. She couldn't fully see him, but the way he took care of her was so endearing she couldn't help how much she liked him.

"What's on the menu for tomorrow's lunch?" she asked, settling back into her pillows.

"Salad and sub sandwiches from the Spring Fling. The firemen make their famous cranberry almond punch."

"Mm." Gretchen loved Carmen's catering company, and she couldn't wait to try the food. She felt drowsy, but surely the pills couldn't have kicked in already. "Why'd you choose to be a paramedic?"

"I like helping people." A short, almost bitter laugh filled the night. "Not that I do much of that. Hawthorne Harbor is really a quiet town for its size."

"Is that why you left three years ago?" She couldn't believe the question had burst out of her mouth like that. She really shouldn't have such personal conversations while so tired—or medicated.

"Partly," he said. "Medina was definitely busier, even on the EMT side of things. I was a firefighter there, and it just wasn't a good fit."

"What was the other part of why you left?" She liked talking to him in the dark. It was easier to ask questions, easier to give answers. She couldn't see him, and he couldn't see her and she almost felt anonymous.

"Yvonne," he said after a few seconds of silence.

"Ex-girlfriend?"

"Yes."

"Must've been bad to force you to leave the town you grew up in."

"It wasn't pleasant."

"I'm sorry." Gretchen wanted to know more, but her eyes felt so heavy, her brain so thick.

"She broke up with me, and I made the move to Medina." His voice had a soothing quality that lulled her further toward unconsciousness. "She left town after I did, and it took me a while to rebuild my heart, and to admit I didn't like Medina as much as I'd hoped I would."

"So you came back."

"Yes, I came back."

"I'm glad you came back," she said, her brain non-operational now and the effect of the drugs in her system taking root. "I really like you, Drew."

She woke with the sun pouring through the window, her bedroom door closed, and Drew nowhere in sight. She wasn't sure if his response had been real or part of her dreams.

I really like you too, Gretchen.

∾

Donna drove them all to the Safety Fair in a big, old SUV, and there were so many cars already there, she could only find a parking spot two blocks away. So she backtracked to firehouse three and pulled up to the curb. "You get out here, Gretchen. We'll go park and come find you."

Joel got out to help Gretchen to the sidewalk while Dixie said something to Donna. An Asian man who looked somewhat familiar approached them, a smile on his face. "Gretchen Samuels." He pulled her into a hug, and she giggled nervously as her ride and support system drove off to find a parking spot.

"It's so good to see you again." The man pulled back and held her at arm's length, a fond expression on his face.

"I'm so sorry," she said. "I can't remember your name."

"Peter Chee," he said without missing a beat. "I'm the EMT supervisor now. But I was on the bus when Drew delivered your baby."

"Oh, right. Of course." Gretchen gave him a warm smile and glanced around to find Drew.

"He's working the lunch line," Peter said. "He said to keep an eye out for you. I'll radio him."

Before Gretchen could stop him, Peter whipped a radio from his hip and spoke into it. Thirty seconds later, Drew appeared, wearing his paramedic uniform with an apron tied around his waist. She felt underdressed in cutoff shorts and a coral tank top, but she couldn't go home and change now.

"Hey, beautiful." He grinned at her and slipped his arms around her in a quick embrace. "Where's everyone else?"

"They went to park the car," she said. Peter seemed to have disappeared, and Gretchen started moving slowly toward the three big tents that had been set up alongside the firehouse. A truck sat under one, with kids climbing in and out. The food was inside the firehouse, and a line of people waited for a four-inch section of a sandwich and salad from one of three bowls. She'd wait too, because Carmen made some seriously great food.

Gretchen looked around for the woman who had first welcomed her back to Hawthorne Harbor, who'd helped her find the first apartment she and Dixie had lived in, and who had told her about The Painted Daisy being up for sale.

She found the raven-haired woman wearing black from head to toe, with a white apron cinched around her waist. She lifted her hand in a wave, and Carmen's face bloomed with a smile. She glanced at the table where she had her food set up, said something to her assistant, and came toward Gretchen.

Laughing, she grabbed onto Gretchen and held her in a hug. "How are you?" She stepped back and swept her gaze from her cast foot to the bruises on her arms and face. "I've been meaning to call you, but we've been insanely busy this week." She tossed a glance at Drew. "And you seem to be in good hands."

"Hey, Carmen," Drew said, keeping the distance

between him and Gretchen. He wore a warm smile and added, "I'm okay to step out with Gretchen for a bit, right?"

"Oh, definitely. I got what I wanted from you." She quirked a smile at him, and Gretchen watched the exchange with a bit of jealousy pulling through her.

"Always using me for my muscles," he teased, and Carmen laughed. She glanced behind her to the tent. "I have to go. Good to see you two." She left, and Gretchen wanted to hook her arm through Drew's so everyone there would know they were together. But with the crutches, she couldn't.

Drew nudged her toward the firehouse, and she went, her jealousy completely unfounded and ridiculous.

Behind the station, in the community park, several bounce houses had been set up, along with a fishpond and a face painting booth. Music filled the air and kids danced with three police officers in a roped-off area. People milled about, chatting and laughing, some of them with balloons on their wrists. Dixie would want one of those. And maybe the Hawthorne Harbor Police Department badge painted on her face.

"How are you feeling this morning?" Drew asked.

"So much better," she said. "Weddings just take it right out of me, you know?"

"Why is that? You don't work longer than you do on a normal day." He strolled right next to her as she hobbled along, and more than a few people threw curious glances their way. Gretchen didn't care. She didn't want to be alone anymore. Drew had awakened her to how lonely she'd become. How isolated from everyone—except maybe Janey.

"More emotional, I guess," she said, though she knew that was only part of it. The other part was that she really wanted to use those indigo daisies in *her* wedding bouquet. When she and Aaron had gotten married, there'd been no money for flowers. The bridesmaids bought their own corsages, and they hadn't matched.

Her parents hadn't helped at all, hadn't even come to the wedding. Granddad had given her a little money and set up a huge trellis on the farm. And then they'd lived with him for a few years, scraping by while Aaron finished school.

Truth be told, there hadn't been a lot of money until he'd landed the job at Pacific-Payne Enterprises in Seattle. And then they had money, but no time to spend together in order to enjoy it.

"Have I told you about a special breed of flower I'm trying to produce?" she asked.

"No." He paused at the edge of the shaded tent and looked down into the park. She joined him, glad when he put his arms around her and held her close to his heart.

"It's a daisy," she said. "They're my favorite flower. I love the bright orange ones, and the bright pink ones. And I want a really bright, really vibrant purple one. You can get sort of a fuschia-colored one. And a darker, more eggplanty one. But I want indigo."

For some reason, she'd always loved the color. She felt like it was overlooked in so many things. No one ever described a flower, a pair of pants, or the sky as indigo. Though it sat right in the rainbow, it was smashed between two more dominant colors.

"So I've been cross-breeding my pink daisies with red to make a more rosy color. Then I take that one and pair it with a blue daisy. I mix in some white from time to time, because they have such a unique center, and I'm trying to create it in my wedding flower."

As soon as she'd spoken the last two words, she wondered if she'd said too much.

Drew couldn't seem to do more than breathe and blink. "Wedding flower?" he finally managed to rasp out.

"Yeah." Gretchen lifted her shoulders in a fast shrug. She felt free and strong, and she suddenly didn't care if she'd revealed too much to Drew. "If I get married again, I want nothing but my indigo daisies on display."

A hearty smile replaced the shock on his face. "And I'm sure you'll have them." He swiped a quick kiss across her check and stepped out of the embrace. He backed up as he said, "There's everyone."

So he didn't want to display their budding relationship in front of his family, though she'd made it pretty clear to his mother last night. Or maybe Donna had just assumed Gretchen was really tired. Or perhaps Drew was worried about Dixie's reaction to him holding Gretchen, not his parents.

He waved at his parents and Dixie as they approached. "Hey. Do you guys want something to eat?"

Dixie skipped forward and put her hand in Drew's. "After we eat, can we go over to the face painting?"

"I don't see why not," he said. "I mean, if it's okay with your mom."

"Totally okay." As she moved toward the food tables with Drew, Dixie, Donna, and Joel, Gretchen hadn't felt this complete in years—probably since she and Aaron and Dixie had experienced their last Christmas together. Only the three of them, as Aaron's parents had traveled to his sister's for the holiday. Her parents and brother never came, and they never visited them, and Gretchen had made a ham, hot chocolate, and caramel popcorn. No pressure. No big mess to clean up afterward. They'd played board games and watched movies and fallen asleep in the same big bed.

She sighed as more happiness than she'd had in a long time settled into her bones. Sure, some of them might be broken, but she was still here, with a handsome man at her side and her adorable daughter scooping too much potato salad onto her plate.

After they finished eating, Harvey Carroll, the fire chief gestured them over to a spot under one of the tents with banners attached to the wall.

"Drew." Harvey shook his hand. "Who are your special guests?"

Drew half-turned back to them. "This is Gretchen Samuels and her daughter, Dixie. I delivered Dixie on the Lavender Highway ten years ago."

"Oh, that's right." The chief beamed down at Dixie. "I've heard that story many times. A miracle baby."

Dixie watched him with wide, round eyes.

The chief tapped the camera he manned. "Can we get your picture? The three of you?"

"Sure." Dixie bounded over to a spot in front of the banners, which read *Hawthorne Harbor Fire Department* across them in red letters.

"We might put it on our Facebook page," the chief said. "Is that okay?"

Gretchen didn't see why not. "That's fine." She tucked herself behind Dixie and handed her crutches off to Joel. Drew crowded in on the other side, slipping his hand along her back and holding onto her waist, providing an extra way for her to balance without her crutches. It was as if he knew exactly what she needed, and when, and he was there to provide it.

"Smile." The chief stepped behind the expensive camera and took a picture. "Want me to take one with your phones?"

Gretchen handed hers to Drew, who passed over his and hers before repositioning himself in the group. More pictures were taken, more smiles exchanged, and Gretchen wasn't sure a more perfect day could exist.

"Face painting!" Dixie announced, and Donna and Joel followed her as she ran down the steps and into the park.

"We'll catch up," Drew called after them. His mom waved to indicate she'd heard, and Gretchen was glad to be alone with Drew again. Though dozens of people were at the event, with more arriving every moment, she felt like there was just him and her.

"You should sit down," he said. "There're benches in the park. Do you think you can make it down the steps?"

"I'm great at steps now." It took several minutes, but she navigated the steps successfully. The grass, however, was much harder. She finally balanced on her good foot and put her crutches together. "I'll just hop." She'd only taken two hops when Drew touched her arm.

"Let me." He swept her off her feet in one fluid, strong moment. A cry of surprise—and delight, if Gretchen were being honest—flew from her mouth. She laughed as Drew carried her across the distance to an empty bench in the shade.

"There you go." He set her down gently. She exhaled, breathless and giddy for reasons she could only imagine at this point in her life. After all, she wasn't sixteen anymore. Or even twenty-six.

A man wearing a police uniform approached, and Gretchen vaguely recognized him as someone who'd come into the flower shop from time to time.

"Hey, Drew."

"Trent, how are things going?" Drew pointed at the policeman. "This is Trent Baker. He joined the Hawthorne Harbor police force, what? Three years ago?"

"Just two." Trent extended his hand and Gretchen shook it.

"Nice to meet you." She smiled at him, her memories of him returning. "You have a little boy, don't you?"

"Porter, yeah." Trent glanced over his shoulder. "He's here with my sister...somewhere."

"This is Gretchen Samuels," Drew said. "She's my—" His voice turned silent, and Gretchen swung her head toward him. His jaw worked, and his eyes held nothing but panic.

She giggled and swatted at his arm playfully. "We just started dating."

Trent nodded, a smile touching his lips but not his eyes. Gretchen could see the pain in his expression, and she wondered what had happened to his wife. Empathy pulled at her heartstrings, especially when a cute, towheaded boy sprinted toward them, calling, "Dad!"

Trent scooped the child into his arms and laughed. "This is Porter. You remember my friend, Drew? He's a paramedic."

Porter squirmed and Trent set him down. He gave Drew high five and said, "Aunt Liza said we can play baseball later."

"That's great." Drew beamed at the boy.

The boy tore off again, and Trent hooked his thumb after him. "I guess I better go. Nice to meet you, Gretchen. See you later, Drew."

After he'd moved out of earshot, Gretchen snuggled a little closer to Drew. "What's his story?"

"His wife was in a car accident too. Drunk driver."

"He's come into the shop before. He must date a little."

"I think he's had a bad experience here." Drew's mouth touched her temple. "Sorry about the awkward introduction. I didn't know what to say."

Gretchen watched as two paramedics spotted them. Peter Chee, who she'd met earlier, said something to the other man, and they changed course toward Drew. "Here comes some more of your friends. Better get it right this time." She looked up at him and giggled. He tightened his grip on her shoulder and squeezed her closer.

"Hey, guys," he said. "How's the Safety Fair going?"

"Great," Peter said. "Chief Carroll never overlooks a detail." He looked at Gretchen and back at Drew pointedly.

"Hey, so this is Gretchen Samuels, my girlfriend." He gazed down at her, and warmth filled Gretchen from head to toe. "I think you met Peter earlier."

"I did, yes." She glanced at the other man standing there, his eyebrows stretched so high she almost laughed.

"And that's Russ," Drew said. "He's my bus partner. He drives. I ride shotgun. We go out on calls together."

The African-American man extended his hand for her to shake, which she did. "So you have to deal with him at work."

"It's a rough job," Russ said.

"Hey," Drew protested. "I'm not difficult at all."

"As long as we stop by Duality for some of those twice-fried potato skins." Russ grinned good-naturedly at Drew, and Peter said, "Oh, I love those."

"Duality is the best," Drew said. His phone sounded and he leaned into Gretchen as he withdrew it from his back pocket. He frowned at the screen, his eyes growing dark with whatever the message was.

"Everything okay?" she asked.

"What?" He flicked his eyes to her without really looking at her. "Oh, yeah. Fine." He pushed the button on the side of his phone and shoved it back in his pocket. He spoke to his friends again, but Gretchen noticed his normal joviality was gone, and she wondered who had texted to steal that from him.

14

Drew had to do something about Yvonne. She'd texted him again, with Gretchen within eyeshot of his phone.

Just saw your picture on the Hawthorne Harbor Fire Department page. I can't believe you delivered that baby ten years ago! Has it really been that long?

He didn't know how to respond to that. Surely that picture had barely gone up in the last hour. Why was she taking an interest in the town—in him—now?

She was a Hammond, so she'd always been entrenched in the lavender traditions surrounding Hawthorne Harbor. But she'd chosen to leave town instead of having a grown-up conversation with him.

While Gretchen gushed over the unicorn Dixie had gotten painted on her face, Drew sent off a message to Yvonne. *Why are you contacting me?*

He wasn't sure he wanted to know, but he needed her to stop communicating with him.

Wanted to talk to you if possible.

He sighed, checking to make sure Gretchen was still occupied with her daughter. She was, and he loved watching the two of them together. They'd been through a lot with only each other to rely on and it showed.

When? he texted.

I'm not sure of my schedule yet. I'll let you know.

Frustration rose within him. He had no idea where Yvonne had gone, or what she was doing now. He didn't care.

As if every Hammond was drawn to him, Augustus caught his eye. Their gazes locked, and the older man started toward the bench, where Gretchen still talked with Dixie. Drew's parents had gone to find frozen lemonade— with lavender, of course—leaving him to face the lavender legend alone.

"Be right back," he said to Gretchen before standing and meeting Augustus out on the lawn.

"Are you entering the Lavender Festival Creation Contest this year?" Augustus asked, not wasting time with even a simple hello.

Drew still didn't have a perfect recipe. His flavors had eluded him. But the festival was months away still, and his confidence was high. "I think I am this year, yes."

"You said that last year." Augustus practically scoffed, but managed to turn the sound into a cough. "I'm doing another ice cream, so you'll have your work cut out for you if that's what you're planning to enter with."

"What flavors?" Because he better come with more than blueberries and honey.

Augustus actually laughed. "Nice try." He scanned Drew and definitely found him lacking before turning and walking away.

Drew sighed and turned around to find Dixie and Gretchen watching him. He returned to them and sat further from Gretchen than he had been previously.

"What was that about?" she asked.

"Oh, you know Augustus."

"Not that well, actually."

"He just told me he's entering an ice cream into the Creation Contest too."

"You'll beat him," Gretchen said, her voice every bit as calm and powerful as the one he used on patients. He wasn't sure he believed her, but he appreciated the vote of confidence.

So he nodded, determined not to let Augustus or Yvonne ruin this day. After all, he'd dreamt about the day he'd have special guests at the Safety Fair. He groaned as he stood. "So, should we go play some of the games they have set up?"

Dixie leapt to her feet and slipped her hand into Drew's. "I want to do the ring toss. You can win a goldfish!"

"Oh, boy." Drew exchanged a glance with Gretchen where she made hand motions that clearly said *No. No ring toss. No goldfish!* He chuckled and waited for her to find her balance on her crutches. He managed to enjoy the next couple of hours, but Yvonne was never far from his mind, and he decidedly disliked that.

OVER THE NEXT FEW WEEKS, DREW TRIED FOUR NEW ICE cream recipes. He brought Gretchen to his house in the evenings when he wasn't working and let her try them. She claimed to like them all, but Drew knew none of them were right for the Lavender Festival Creation Contest.

Impatience dug at him, but he crossed off lemon, orange, and raspberry as possible citrus flavors to go with the lavender.

He needed something else. But what, he didn't quite know yet.

His routine of helping her with the flowers in the morning, driving her and Dixie to work and school, and heading out to the farm after work brought him so much joy. If he worked the day shift, he and Dixie and Jess rode horses out to the wishing well in the evening. The kids hadn't missed a day in a month, and on the thirtieth day, Jess's whole face beamed.

"I did it, Drew."

Drew sure hoped his wish would come true, and he tousled the boy's hair. "What did you wish for?"

"I can't tell you." Jess gave him a *duh, Drew* look but

wiped it away quickly. "But my birthday is coming up, and I just know I'm going to get what I want."

Panic paraded through Drew, and he made a mental note to speak with Janey about the boy's birthday. She'd been spending most evenings out at the farmhouse too, even if it was just to sit on the couch while she caught up with her email on her phone. He'd caught her napping once or twice too, and he'd let her snooze on the couch while he took her son out with the horses he loved so much.

His mother had been glowing since Gretchen had moved in, and Drew had even detected a change in Joel, too.

On his days off, he spent time training his dogs. He wanted to sit in the flower shop with Gretchen all day, but he didn't want to appear desperate. So he taught Blue how to crawl and threw a ball for the shepherds until his arm ached. Then he'd take her lunch and spend an hour with her before heading back to the farm to work in the lavender fields.

As May dragged on, the plants that dominated the summer in Hawthorne Harbor required more and more attention. Each variety peaked at a different time, and each had to be harvested, bundled, and hung in the cellar.

Some got steeped in simple syrup to make lavender vanilla. Some got made into essential oils, that his mother then infused into soaps, lotions, and shampoos. Some was combined with culinary sugar, and salt, and spices. Joel used the lavender culinary products to make everything from lavender ranch mix and onion and chive with lavender dip mix.

No matter what, Drew felt like lavender had taken over his entire existence.

Gretchen had graduated into a walking boot, and more often than not, when Drew showed up at the farm, he found her on her granddad's land, cultivating, fertilizing, or cutting back row after row of lavender that had been abandoned years ago.

One warm evening, he found her wearing a cream sundress with vibrant flowers splashed across it, working along a tall row of yellow lavender. "Ah, Lavender Viridis," he said, smiling when she turned. She seemed stable enough in her walking boot and single running shoe.

"There you are." She leaned into him and let him kiss her forehead. Her auburn hair smelled like strawberries and felt like silk between his fingers. He wanted to migrate south and touch his lips to hers, but the timing had never been right. "I heard Blue barking twenty minutes ago."

"Yeah, he's around here somewhere." He glanced at the vibrant yellow flowers. "What are you doing with this?"

"I was thinking it would make a great cologne." She pinched off a flower and brought it to her nose. "It smells very masculine, don't you think?" She lifted it for him to smell.

"It smells like lavender," he said. "Maybe a little softer, not quite as sweet."

"But with the right base notes—maybe cypress or moss —it would be a great aftershave."

He chuckled and pulled her close to his side, glad her bulky crutches were gone. "So are you going to turn your bathroom into a perfumery? Enter the Lavender Festival Creation Contest and try to get the crown?"

"Maybe." She lifted one shoulder and dropped the yellow flower. "But not this year." She twisted and wrapped her arms around his waist. "This year, *you're* going to be Lavender King."

He gazed out over the rows and rows of lavender, the sun still high in the sky as spring had turned into summer. "I still haven't found the right flavor for my ice cream."

"It's only May."

"The festival is in eight weeks." Just saying it out loud made his chest tight. "Maybe I won't be able to enter this year." Disappointment cut sharply through him. He'd felt so sure that this year would be *his* year. He didn't want to face Augustus and explain why he hadn't entered.

"So let's brainstorm," Gretchen said, stepping out of his embrace and putting her hand in his instead. She moved down the row of lavender, sliding her palm across the tops of the flowers.

"I've done blueberry, raspberry, lemon, and orange. I don't think lime will work, because it's too close to lemon. Those sharp, acidic citrus flavors overpower the lavender, and they're almost bitter."

He wasn't quite sure how to describe what was going

wrong, only that it was. Lavender had to be the dominant flavor, even if there were others. The combination had to be unique. He thought he'd found the perfect amount of black pepper, but he wouldn't really know until he got the sour note right.

"Pineapple?" Gretchen suggested.

Drew thought about the fruit, which could be pureed easily. "I can give it a try." But he didn't feel great about it. "I need something that wouldn't be better as a sorbet or a sherbet."

"Well, citrus fruits are best in those." Gretchen always kept her eyes on the ground when she walked, as it was uneven and she still had that bulky boot.

"I'm sure there's something we haven't thought of," he said. "Using sour cream instead of so much heavy cream helped a lot, actually. But the citrus flavor is still wrong."

"Grapefruit? Tangerine? Mandarin orange? That might be milder than the sweet orange you've tried."

"Maybe." He wanted something without a rind. Something he couldn't zest and put in the base. He'd tried that, and while he liked candied lemon rind, it didn't feel that great on the tongue, frozen in an otherwise smooth ice cream. "What about another type of berry? Cherries, maybe?"

Washington State grew a lot of cherries. And they were sour.

"Cranberries?" she suggested.

Feeling more hopeful, Drew smiled at her. "Both of those sound like something to at least try."

A bell started ringing in the distance, and Drew's adrenaline spiked. "There's the dinner bell." He started to increase his pace, but Gretchen hung back. "What is it?"

She rubbed her arms as if cold. Sighing, she glanced toward the ocean and let her gaze linger there when she said, "I don't think I should stay with your parents much longer."

Disbelief tore through Drew. "What? Why not?"

"I'm walking okay on my own now. Dr. Harris says I can start driving as soon as this boot comes off."

"And that's not for three more weeks."

She looked right at him, trepidation in her expression. "Are you sure I'm not a burden to them?"

"Gretchen." He gathered her into his arms, glad when she came, thrilled when she pressed her cheek against his heartbeat. "You're anything but a burden to them. Have you seen my mother? She *loves* having you and Dixie at the farm. In fact, you're going to face a fight when it's time to go."

"I'm afraid Dixie will never leave."

"Maybe you should think about moving out here permanently."

"I can't live with your parents permanently." She shook her head and put some distance between them. "I need my own space."

Drew understood that, so he nodded and glanced

around at the rows of lavender they'd been walking between. "What about this farm?"

"Joel owns this farm."

"But he's not doing anything with it. Maybe you could ask him if he'll sell it to you."

Gretchen looked at him like he'd sprouted an extra head. "I don't have the money to buy an eighty-acre lavender farm. And the house hasn't been lived in for years. It'll need a lot of work to be habitable."

But Drew noticed how she gazed at it longingly, and he determined to talk to his step-dad about the lavender farm he'd bought but had never bothered to maintain. Maybe he could volunteer his time if Joel would teach him how to put shiplap on walls, or add exposed wood beams to the ceiling for decoration.

DREW ARRIVED AT JANEY'S HOUSE, WITH THE WINDOWS FILLED with yellow, cheery light, just as the chorus to *Happy Birthday* swelled through the screen door. He let himself in, and finished the song with everyone gathered in the kitchen.

Jess's face glowed with happiness and excitement in the candlelight as his mother set a cake with twelve flames in front of him. The song finished, and he took a big, big breath before blowing out all the candles.

Everyone cheered, cake got sliced and served, and Jess

started opening his presents. Drew had told Janey that Jess had made a wish for his birthday present every day at the well. She'd assured him she'd take care of it, but as each gift was opened, Drew could tell it wasn't the one Jess had wished for.

Drew stood behind Gretchen at the table, his anxiety for the boy growing, even though he grinned at the new helmet Drew had bought for him. He jumped up from the table and gave Drew a hug. "Thanks, Drew. Can I come ride the ATV tomorrow?"

"Of course, bud." Drew smiled at Jess as he returned to the table and reached for a paper plate holding some of his birthday cake. He obviously hadn't gotten what he wanted.

"I have one for you," Janey said, smiling. "But it's outside. It didn't fit in here."

Everyone began filing outside, and Drew secured Gretchen's hand in his. "I hope he gets what he wants. He made a wish at the well for a solid month."

The alarm on her face wasn't hard to find. "What did Dixie wish for?"

"I have no idea. Neither of them would tell me. But I know Jess's was related to his birthday. He said that much."

Janey had everyone stand in the driveway, with Jess in the front. The anticipation was killing Drew. He really wanted this twelve-year-old boy to get what he wanted. He'd have done almost anything to keep the magic of the wishing well alive and ensure Jess's happiness.

Janey punched in the garage code and the door started

to lift. Inch by inch, it revealed a brand new bicycle, with a big blue bow tied on the handlebars.

Jess yelped and ran forward. He reverently touched the seat and the back tire before running to his mom and hugging her tight. "It's exactly what I wanted, Mom! Thanks!" He sprinted in the house and came out wearing Drew's new helmet. He struggled with the clasp, and Drew moved through the crowd to help him.

"My wish came true," Jess said as Drew tightened the straps and fastened the buckle. "I can't believe it, Drew, but my wish came true!"

Drew's heart felt like it might burst with joy. "That's great, bud. Be careful, all right? I don't want to have to work tonight." He grinned at the boy.

Jess got on the bike and sailed out of the driveway and on down the street, whooping as he went. Janey laughed and Drew caught her wiping a tear from her eye.

"Thanks for the tip, Drew."

"Hey, I didn't know what he wanted." He gave Janey a smile and watched Jess for another moment. "How did you find out?"

"We moms can ask questions without really seeming like we're asking questions." She grinned at her son. "I figured it out just in time."

"Well, good job. Any idea what Dixie was wishing for?"

Janey swung her attention to him. "No, but I can start to work that into my conversations."

He nodded. "I think Gretchen would appreciate that."

He looked at her, radiant and beautiful simply wearing jeans and a bright blue blouse.

"You like her a lot." Janey wasn't really asking, and when he looked at her, she was watching Gretchen too.

Drew forced himself to chuckle so he wouldn't give too much away. He honestly didn't know how much he liked Gretchen. He simply knew he did. He wanted to share his hard days with her. His easy ones. His lazy ones. His busy ones. And he loved Dixie, and just like Jess, would do anything to make her happy.

Since he and Janey had been friends their whole lives, Drew nodded and said, "We're getting to know each other."

"Slow and steady," Janey said before patting his forearm. "Thanks for coming, Drew." She moved to stand beside her parents while Jess continued to ride up and down the street.

Dixie stood with her mom, and Drew returned to them. "He looks happy, doesn't he?"

"I hope my wish comes true," Dixie said in a wistful voice.

"I'm sure it will," Drew said quickly.

"What was it?" Gretchen asked.

"Mom." Dixie rolled her eyes. "I can't just tell you." She turned and walked away, and Drew sorted through possibilities for what she could want.

"We could ask my mom," he said. "She spends a lot of time with her in the kitchen and around the farm. Maybe Dixie mentioned something to her."

"Maybe." Gretchen seemed distracted, and Drew

needed to get home and feed his dogs. Plus, he'd boiled down a pot of cherries last night, strained them, pressed them, and sugared them into a syrup, and he was dying to try a lavender cherry with black pepper ice cream that night.

"I should go. The ice cream is calling me." He swept a kiss across Gretchen's cheek, enjoying the way she leaned into his touch, and headed for his truck. He'd barely buckled himself inside when the emergency ring on his phone sounded.

"Drew Herrin," he answered.

"Multiple-car accident in Bell Hill," the operator said. "We're calling in everyone. Buses leave as soon as you can arrive."

"I'll be there in five." He lamented his loss of ice cream making time, but the possibility of saving someone's life gave him the same high.

RUSS NAVIGATED THE AMBULANCE TOWARD THE SCENE, WHERE at least half a dozen police cars had already arrived, their blue and red lights flashing, flashing, flashing.

Another ambulance had arrived ten seconds ahead of them, and the two paramedics from that bus had their gear out and were approaching the first cop car. He pointed toward a red car that looked like it had been crunched to half its normal size.

Drew swallowed, preparing himself for blood, burns, and broken bones. He didn't see any smoke, but even an airbag produced enough heat to singe, and he jumped from the ambulance as soon as Russ put it in park. He had the heavy equipment bag from the back and Russ collected the stretcher in only breaths, and they approached the same cop.

"Where's the most dire need?" Russ asked, surveying the scene. Several people stood on the side of the road with minor injuries, talking to police officers. They could probably get themselves to the hospital to get checked out, or simply go home if they thought they were okay.

"Black truck down on the end," he said. "Hit from both sides after he tried to avoid the pileup. Both passengers are still inside; the doors won't open. The people inside are pretty panicked, but they're awake and alert."

"We'll get them out," Russ said, striding toward the truck, which sat perpendicular to all the other vehicles on the road. A woman and a man were inside, and the woman was clearly crying. Drew could see blood on the side of her face, but it was impossible to tell where it was coming from.

"I'll take the man," Russ said, and the two split to flank the truck.

"Ma'am," Drew said through the glass, which was cracked. "Are you hurt?" The window wouldn't go down because of the fractures, and Drew saw the blood was coming from her right ear. The situation suddenly more serious, he called over to Russ, "Ear bleed on this side. I'm stabilizing the truck with wheel chocks, and then I'm going to use the hydraulic spreader to get this door off."

He looked into the woman's eyes, a freaky sense of calm descending over him. "Ma'am, I need you to remain still and calm. I'm going to get you out of there."

Her face was paler than Drew would like, but she nodded. He wasn't sure how he remained so calm amidst so much chaos, but he got the wheel stabilizers in place and stopped next to Russ.

"How is he?"

"The airbag went off," Russ said, who was administering to the man through an eight-inch gap where the window had come down. "I think it probably burned his forearms. And his leg is stuck in the door. I'll check him once you get the woman out."

"What's her name?" Drew asked the man.

"Felicia," he said, his voice strained.

Drew hurried around the front and removed the hydraulic spreader from his bag. "All right, Felicia. I'm going to pop this door off the hinges. I need you to stay as far back as you can, all right?"

She scooted over on the seat and Drew positioned a pair of safety goggles on his head and then plugged in the hydraulic tool to his mobile power supply. He inserted the tip of the spreader into the seam between the door and the panel over the front tire and spread his feet to brace himself.

The metal of the truck moved as if it were hot, and he

cleared back the center bit so he could see where to insert the tool over the hinges. He closed the spreader, positioned it right above the top hinge and pressed the button. The door popped off only moments later. He repeated the action for the bottom hinge, and set the tool on the ground. With gloved hands, he grabbed onto the top of the door and pulled it back toward the handle. It came free, and he tossed it to the side, the way to the woman inside the truck now unobstructed.

"Clear," he called to Russ, and he stepped over to the bench seat. "Felicia, stay there."

He ditched the work gloves for rubber ones, and left the hydraulic tool behind in favor of a neck brace and his stethoscope. Her eyes were dilated, and her heartbeat quick.

"What hurts the most?" he asked, reaching for an otoscope, which would allow him to see if her ear drum was perforated or not. He hoped it was. That would explain the bleeding, though he would make sure she went to the hospital and got an exam from a doctor.

"My ear," she said. She shook her head. "No, my head." She seemed confused.

"Can you tell me what happened?" Drew looked in her ear, but he couldn't see any evidence of a burst ear drum. Not good.

"We came up over the hill, and there were just cars everywhere. We were going to a concert."

"No, we weren't," the man said. "My brother invited us for dinner."

Drew exchanged a glance with him. "How's your leg? As soon as I'm done here, Russ there is going to get you out."

"I'm hanging in," he said. "Felicia, don't you remember we went to the concert last weekend?"

She started to cry again, and Drew said, "Don't worry about it. All right, your ear drum looks fine. We need to get you to the hospital so they can assess your head injury. Did you hit your head in the crash?" She had a spent airbag on her side too, but it didn't appear that any injuries had resulted from it.

"I...don't know. Maybe?"

From the bruise purpling on her cheekbone, Drew guessed she had hit her head against the window, and that the bleeding could be from anything. Her symptoms showed she definitely had a concussion too, but he wasn't a doctor and he couldn't diagnose.

"Do you think you can slide over here?" Drew asked.

"Pauly?"

"I can't get out until you do, baby." He spoke in a gentle tone and squeezed her fingers. Drew watched their exchange as a pang of love made his heart sing.

She started to slide over, but she winced. "My knee hurts," she complained.

"Russ, the stretcher."

Russ appeared a moment later, and together, they helped Felicia out of the truck and onto it. Drew covered her with a blanket though the night was still plenty warm while Russ crawled into the truck to check out Pauly's leg.

"Do we need the jaws on the other door?" Drew asked when Russ crawled out.

"Yep." He picked them up in one hand and the power supply in the other and went around the truck.

"Felicia, don't go to sleep," he commanded when he noticed her eyes fluttering open and closed. "Stay with me. Tell me about Pauly. Is he your boyfriend? Husband?"

Tears leaked out of her eyes. "Boyfriend. I love him." Her voice could barely be heard above the hydraulic pump as Russ worked the spreader. The loud popping and groaning of metal drowned out everything.

"I haven't told him," she said, her eyes popping open. "Why haven't I told him?" She started to sit up, and Drew used one strong palm against her shoulder to keep her down.

"You'll have time to tell him. Neither of you are going anywhere." Drew gave her his calmest smile, infused all the confidence he had into his tone. She settled back against the stretcher, and Drew pushed her around to the other side so he could assist Russ if necessary. He had the door off and was crouched, examining Pauly's leg. The man wore an expression of agony, and he only seemed to have eyes for Felicia.

"I love you, baby," he said though gritted teeth.

"Love you too," she said before she let her eyes fall closed and she passed out.

"Felicia." Drew shook her shoulder, but she didn't even flinch. At least she'd got to tell Pauly she loved him, and all

Drew could think about for the rest of the night was Gretchen.

As he and Russ transported the patients to the hospital and filled out the paperwork, Drew's mind churned around questions. If it were his last night on earth, what would he want her to know? Did he love her? How could he make sure he didn't make the same mistakes with her as he had with Yvonne? Did he even know what real love felt like?

He finally got home close to midnight, and he bypassed his kitchen in favor of his bed. Sleep came quickly, and his dreams featured a certain auburn-haired beauty and various ways Drew could tell her how he felt about her. You know, as soon as he figured out exactly *how* he felt.

15

Drew didn't show up at seven-thirty like he had every other morning for the past several weeks. Gretchen didn't have any special events that day, and she could stand to open the shop a bit later than normal.

But it was so unlike Drew to be late that she worried. When he still hadn't arrived by eight o'clock, she called him.

"Hey, are you okay?" she asked when he answered in a groggy voice.

"What time is it?"

"Eight."

"Oh my—I completely forgot to set my alarm." He sounded awake now. "I'm on my way out."

"It's fine," she said quickly. "You don't need to rush. Dixie doesn't even have school today. Is everything okay?"

"I got called out on a job last night," he said. "I'll tell you about it when I get there."

She hung up, and let her feet take her over to the farmhouse where she'd spent her summers. At first, she'd come to Hawthorne Harbor with her whole family. They usually came for three weeks, beginning at the end of June and going through the Lavender Festival.

Then her father didn't come one year when she was eleven years old. She didn't know why. Her mom had brought Gretchen and her brother for another year, maybe two, and then she stopped coming too. The next year, Grandma had died, and Gretchen had cried and cried and cried. She still missed her grandmother with a fierceness she didn't quite understand.

When it came time to go to Hawthorne Harbor the following summer, no one made plans. Gretchen, thirteen, demanded to go, and Granddad had driven down to California to get her. He'd done that every year since, and Gretchen started staying all summer, not just for three weeks.

She'd wanted to ask her parents why they stopped coming, why they didn't even speak of her mother's parents anymore, but she never did. She felt like a stranger in her own house, and when she left after high school, she'd never gone back.

This farm had been the only place where she'd ever felt like she belonged. Though Aaron hadn't liked it as much as she had, Gretchen had adored everything about the farm.

Granddad had labored in the lavender fields, and he'd won the Creation Contest that last summer she'd lived on the farm, before Aaron got his job in Seattle and they moved.

Granddad had developed a new variety of lavender and spent hours arranging it into gorgeous wreaths, earning him the coveted title of Lavender King. Her ideas of cross-pollinating daisies had come from him, as had the belief that she could purchase The Painted Daisy and weave roses into wedding wreaths after taking only one class at a community center on floral arranging. He was the one who'd told her why her parents had stopped coming to Washington too.

She climbed the steps of the old farmhouse where she used to live and tried the doorknob. It wasn't locked, and she entered the house. The air was hot and stale, scented with dust and old wood. There was no furniture in the living room, dining room, or kitchen as she scanned from the front of the house to the back.

Morning light poured in through the wall of windows in the back, and shadows stretched long on the dirty floors. She stepped, leaving evidence of her presence, her fingers trailing along the chair rail she'd installed with Granddad the first summer she'd come alone. She'd almost nailed her fingers to the wall, and a sad chuckle came from her throat.

With two fingers, she pushed in the door to the bathroom and found it exactly as she remembered it. Sink, toilet, bathtub. Granddad used to have purple bath mats and a shower curtain with lavender plants on it. Now everything was just white upon white.

The door next to it led down a hall to three bedrooms, but she didn't go that way. She wasn't sure she was ready to see where she'd stayed when she came, nor the master bedroom where Granddad and Grandma had lived for so long.

Instead, she trekked to the back door and turned to go upstairs. With two bedrooms and a bathroom up here, she and Aaron had enjoyed relative privacy in the first few years of their marriage. Gretchen had cooked dinner for her husband and her granddad every evening, and the memories flowed over her, around her, and through her until she couldn't contain them anymore.

Drew found her in the bedroom where she'd nursed Dixie for those first few months of her life, tears streaming down her face.

"Hey, hey, hey," he said, his voice soft yet urgent at the same time. "What's wrong? What are you doing in here?" He knelt beside her and gathered her close, the scent of him masculine and comforting. She clung to his strong bicep, sure as the sun would rise the following day that she needed to be out here on this farm. Permanently.

He wiped her tears and looked into her face. "Talk to me, love. What's wrong?"

She shook her head. "Nothing's wrong. I...just miss my granddad. And there are powerful memories here." She pointed to the corner where her rocking chair had sat. "There used to be a chair there, where I'd sit and rock Dixie to sleep."

Drew stroked her hair, his jaw tightening. "You're not hurt?"

She quieted her emotions and swiped at her face. "No, I'm not hurt." She'd never felt so safe as she did within the circle of his arms. "I don't feel like going into the shop today."

"Really? It's Saturday. One your busiest days."

Her reality set in, and she knew he was right. "Yeah, I should go."

"I'll come with you until this afternoon. I don't have to be to work until two."

"That would be nice."

He helped her stand, and she took him over to the window where she'd stood so many times, overlooking the farm and wondering how she could follow Aaron to Seattle. She told Drew about it, and he kept her close to his side, his arm strong and secure on her shoulder.

"But I did," Gretchen said. "We left Hawthorne Harbor, and though I only lived a couple of hours away, I only came back to visit a few times." She looked at him, fresh tears pricking her eyes. "Granddad must've been so lonely."

"I'm sure he was okay," Drew said.

But there was no way for him to know that. Gretchen sniffled and watched the lavender wave in the perpetual breeze on the cape of Washington. "My parents stopped coming up here because Granddad and my father got in a fight. It was too hard for my mother to come alone, so she stopped coming too. My brother stayed away. Only I kept coming, year after year. And then I stopped too." She shook her head, the regret she'd harbored for so long finally surfacing.

"What was the fight about?"

"Money. Granddad had a lot of money, and my parents didn't. They never did, and it became a real source of contention between them." An inkling of an idea started in her head. Maybe her granddad would loan her the money to buy back the farm. Maybe she could get him to come live with her this time.

"I'm so sorry," he murmured close to her ear.

She drew in a deep breath to infuse strength into her soul. "Tell me about the job last night."

"Big pileup on the highway leading out of Bell Hill. I had to use the hydraulic spreader to get the door off to get this woman out of her truck."

Gretchen peered up at him. "You're kidding."

"I wish I was." Drew gave her half a smile and resumed gazing out the window. "You know, I've always felt a little unsettled here in Hawthorne Harbor. Don't get me wrong, I love this town, and I've learned I don't belong anywhere but here. But I've often wished there were a few more emergencies." He chuckled, but the sound was dark. "Ridiculous, right? I'm wishing for bad luck for the people of this town."

Gretchen wasn't quite sure what to say to soothe him. It simply seemed like a morning of reflection. "Was everyone okay in the end?" she asked.

"Yes, no casualties."

"Well, that's something. And you saved another woman." She nudged him with her hip. "You seem to be good at that."

That elicited a chuckle from him, and he kneaded her closer. "I learned something last night too."

"Oh yeah?"

"Yeah."

But he didn't continue. She twisted to look at him, the handsome lines of his face, his eyes a bit brighter for some reason. "Are you going to tell me what you learned?"

He finally tore his eyes from the lavender fields and looked at her. "The woman, she was with her boyfriend in the truck. She told me she wished she would've expressed her feelings for him earlier. And right there, while she was strapped to the stretcher and his leg was bleeding, she told him she loved him."

Gretchen's heart skipped a beat, and then another, then rushed forward at triple speed. "Oh," she managed. "Wow."

Drew leaned down, his lips touching her cheek. "And it made me realize I haven't been very forthcoming with how I feel about you."

Gretchen's eyes drifted closed, and she couldn't form any coherent words. She gripped his upper arm and was extremely glad she did when his lips finally touched hers. A sigh waved through her whole body, and the next touch of his mouth to hers became a real kiss. Gretchen had forgotten what it felt like to be kissed so completely, by someone who could convey how much he cherished her with such a simple gesture.

When the kiss ended, she pressed her cheek to his chest and listened to the strong, steady beat of his heart, hoping with every cell in her body that they could be together for a long, long time.

THEY SPENT AN HOUR IN THE FLOWER GARDEN, WHERE HE kissed her one more time before driving her into town so she could open the shop.

"How will you get home from work?" she asked.

"I'll call my brother or something." He didn't seem too concerned about it as he took the extra barstool at her workbench.

"So." She set several yellow roses on the bench. "Should we talk about Dixie?"

"What about Dixie?"

She busied her hands with clipping stems and stretching floral tape. "She's the main reason I haven't dated since Aaron's death."

"Ah, I see. And now you're worried about how she'll take...us."

"Aren't you?"

"Not really."

She glanced up at him, surprised. "No?"

"She's a great kid, and I think she already likes me, so

no. I'm not too worried about her." He abandoned the box of floral pins he'd been spinning. "Are you?"

"Yeah, a little." Her voice squeaked a bit too much to be casual. "I've never dated anyone, and I don't want her to think I'm replacing her dad."

"Do you want to talk to her together?"

Relief washed through her. "Yes, I think we should."

"When?"

"Are you working tomorrow?"

"Sunday is usually super slow or complete chaos, depending on who decides to roast or fry something they haven't before. I'm on the morning shift."

Gretchen giggled at his assessment of how people came to need emergency help. "How about tomorrow night then, before your mom's Sunday dinner with everyone from town?"

Drew laughed, the sound so wonderful it bathed Gretchen in happiness. "She does invite a lot of people to Sunday dinner, doesn't she?"

"I kinda like it," Gretchen admitted. "As long as I can escape to the porch swing when I get overwhelmed."

The bell on the front door sounded, and Gretchen left her yellow rose bouquet to go see who it was. Linnie Robbins, sporting a brand new—huge—diamond. Another wedding she needed to pay the bills, so she hitched her smile in place and gave Linnie the information paper she needed to make sure she got what she wanted and knew what payments were due when.

But all she could think was *Another wedding that isn't mine.*

She returned to the workroom and found Drew concentrating on his phone, his eyebrows drawn into a frown. It seemed they both needed a day to get through some personal things, so she settled back to work silently, her thoughts rotating around Drew's kiss and what it might mean for her in the future.

"Hey, I need to run out for a few minutes." Drew stood and headed for the door without looking at her.

"Oh, okay. Where are you going?" Gretchen focused on pinning the bouquet together, but she still saw Drew turn back and flash her a fast smile.

"I'll bring back lunch." With that, he headed into the alley, and she realized that his statement wasn't really an explanation at all.

16

Drew just wanted to get Yvonne off his text stream. Out of his life. Where he thought she already was. But she'd been texting him all morning, and now she wanted to meet for coffee.

No, he'd told her. Meeting for food or drink was what people did who were dating, and he wasn't interested in getting back together with Yvonne. Not now, not ever.

The image of Gretchen crying in that empty farmhouse ran through his mind as he crossed the street to the park. When he'd seen her there, his whole heart had collapsed, and he didn't want her to go another minute without knowing how he felt about her.

"Yvonne." Drew approached the statue in the center of the park, where the woman stood gazing up to the umbrella there. He'd suggested they meet here—a public place where they couldn't be mistaken for a couple.

She turned, and Drew looked into her familiar face. He felt nothing, and that was a huge blessing. He wasn't sure how he'd feel when he came face-to-face with her again, and he was relieved not to have any sudden doubts, any lingering attraction.

He stuffed his hands in his pockets. "I'm here. What do you want to talk about?" He'd tried to get her to talk to him on the phone, through a text, something. She hadn't wanted to, insisting she needed to see him in person.

Her porcelain face transformed into a smile. She scanned him from head to toe and ran her fingers through her dark hair. "Hey, Drew." She moved as if she'd step into him and kiss him, the way she had so many times before.

He jerked backward. "I'm busy," he said. "What do you need?"

Her smile slipped, and she reshouldered her purse. "I just wanted to..." She sighed and looked past him, over his shoulder. "I needed some closure."

"Closure?" Drew's impatience climbed, and he wasn't sure how much longer he could stand here. He wasn't sure why he'd come at all. "You're the one who left town while I was at work, and broke up with me through a text. A *text*, Yvonne."

So maybe Drew needed some closure too.

"I know." She nodded and focused on the ground. "I need to say I'm sorry about that." She lifted her gaze to his, and he found panic and hope in her eyes. "I'm sorry, Drew."

Something in his chest pinched, and he put another

step of distance between them. He liked Gretchen. He liked Gretchen a lot, and he wasn't going to get involved with Yvonne again.

"Apology accepted." His voice sounded like he'd gargled with glass.

"I'm moving back to Hawthorne Harbor." Her words landed like bombs in his ears.

"That's...great." He cleared his throat. "When?"

"This week." She tried to smile at him, but when he didn't return it, the gesture faded. "I'm going to be living and working out on my family's farm."

Drew felt like someone had punched him in the throat. She'd never been interested in his family's farm. She wouldn't even come out to see it. She proclaimed to dislike everything about lavender, and while Drew didn't live and work on the farm, she'd made it clear she wasn't interested in that life.

"What changed your mind?" he asked.

"My mother isn't doing well." She hugged her arms around herself. "My dad is working non-stop on his ice cream recipes, determined to win one more title for her."

Drew's mouth turned dry. Augustus had more time, more resources, and more experience than Drew did. And now he had extra drive to win. "Your mom is that bad?"

"We're not sure, and Dad just wants to give her another crown." Yvonne took a breath and shrugged. "And I just wanted you to know, so it's not awkward when we see each other around town." She edged forward and put her hand on his arm. Her touch felt like ice against his skin, and he let her keep her fingers there for two heartbeats before he gently backed up.

Her hand fell back to her side, and Drew started walking down the sidewalk. "All right. I'm going to go grab lunch." He eased away from her, surprised when she joined him.

"I'll come with you. Where are you going?"

His mind raced as he tried to think of something she didn't like. But Gretchen wanted the Hawthorne harvest club from Andy's Anchor, the sandwich shop across the street from firehouse three.

"The Anchor," he said, unable to lie.

"Oh, I love their hot meatball sub."

So did Drew, but he kept that to himself. It was early still, but there was a short line at the Anchor. Drew waited with Yvonne, feeling weird and awkward with the wrong woman at his side.

"So what are you up to these days?" she asked.

"Same old stuff," he said. She didn't get to know what his life had been like for the past three years. She'd left, and he wasn't going to tell her anything about his trials in Medina.

"Drew?"

He turned to find Janey behind him, her face colored with shock.

"Hey, Janey."

Her eyes skipped over to Yvonne, and since they'd all

grown up in town, of course she recognized her. "Yvonne. What are you doing back in town?" She looked at Drew again, and he heard her unspoken words.

What are you doing back in town and out to lunch with Drew?

"I'm moving back to town," Yvonne said, and she and Janey kept talking. Drew couldn't find a way to tell Janey that this wasn't at all what it looked like. He moved forward and ordered his and Gretchen's sandwiches, leaving Yvonne to order for herself.

"What is going on?" Janey hissed as he stepped to the side to wait for his food.

"Nothing," he whispered back. "She just showed up and said she needed closure."

"Have you told Gretchen?"

"Drew?" His order got called, and he stepped forward to claim the two sandwiches.

On his way past Janey, he said, "There's nothing to tell. Yvonne and I are over." And with that, he marched out of the sandwich shop, leaving Yvonne where she should be —behind him.

ANOTHER COUPLE OF WEEKS PASSED BEFORE DREW FOUND himself out at the farm without Gretchen and Dixie around. Her walking boot had finally come off, and she'd taken her daughter to the beach. They hadn't spoken to Dixie the way they'd planned, because that day had been weird for both of them.

Janey obviously hadn't said anything to Gretchen about seeing Drew and Yvonne at the sandwich shop, and he was glad. He'd spoken true—there was nothing to tell.

He and Gretchen continued to hold hands on the porch swing after Dixie went to bed and steal kisses out on the farm when the girl was busy riding her favorite horse.

School had gotten out for the summer on Friday, and Gretchen wanted to have a "much-earned vacation" with just the two of them. Drew couldn't argue, though he wanted to tag along if only so he wouldn't have to be alone.

Gretchen had filled the void in his life that he'd thought firefighting would. Caring for her and learning about her these past few months had been nothing short of wonderful. He still counted down the hours at work, but not because he was bored, but because he couldn't wait to get back to her and Dixie.

He walked into the farmhouse and found his mom asleep on the couch in the living room. Concern spiked his heart rate but he calmed when he saw her peaceful expression and the soft rise and fall of her chest.

She wasn't known for napping, but Drew supposed she'd had quite a lot of excitement at the farm these past several weeks, and he tiptoed past her and entered the kitchen. Joel wasn't there, so Drew grabbed a sports drink from the fridge and headed out to the barn.

He found Joel there, brushing down Lucky Star, his

favorite horse. "Hey, Joel." Drew picked up a rope someone had dropped and began coiling it. "Mom's asleep. Is she feeling all right?"

"Oh, she had a touch of the stomach flu in the night and didn't sleep well." Joel gave him a reassuring smile. "She's all right."

Drew nodded, the questions he wanted to ask his stepfather building behind his tongue. "Joel, can I ask you something?"

Joel glanced up, his smile gone now. "Sure, I suppose. About what?"

"The farm next door."

Joel started nodding as if he'd been expecting Drew to come asking questions about it.

"You don't work it," Drew said. "The lavender's gone wild. Did you really buy it so no one else would?"

"About, yeah. I didn't want someone to buy it and come in and build a hundred-home subdivision." He finished with Lucky Star and wiped his hands down the front of his jeans. "I don't have the time or manpower to maintain the farm, but well, your mother thought you might want the place one day."

Pure surprise snaked through Drew. "Really?" He wondered what he'd done over the years to show her he wanted to be a lavender farmer and not an EMT. "I love my job."

"You've been restless for years," Joel said. "You come out here almost every day, even before Gretchen and Dixie started living here. You take care of the horses, feed our chickens, and visit with our nanny goats."

"Well, I—I—" Drew didn't know what to say. He did love the farm; he always had. But did he want to own and run one himself? The idea didn't take long to root itself into his brain and settle there.

"You maintain all of my equipment, for which I'm grateful. I just keep telling your mother to be patient with you. That you'll figure things out on your own." He came forward and while Drew had always liked Joel, he'd never really made room in his heart to love the man the same way he'd loved his dad.

"You come out in the summer to harvest. You're practically running the farm as it is."

Drew shook his head, knowing there was a lot more than the physical things he did necessary to run a farm. "I don't do the money side of things. I don't plan the watering schedule and make sure the plants are thriving. I get to do all the fun stuff."

"Then hire someone else to do the stuff you don't like," Joel said, grinning. "That's why I asked you to do the tractors and the goats."

"There's outbuildings to maintain," he said. "You do all of that."

"Because I like it. I'd do it for you too, if you wanted."

Drew's gaze wandered southwest, to the farm that sat there. He couldn't see it from inside the barn, and he walked down the aisle and looked beyond the white fence that delineated the two properties. "I've never honestly thought about being a lavender farmer."

Joel clapped his hand on Drew's shoulder. "Well, maybe you should. It's a good living." He walked past him and headed back into the house. Drew stayed outside a bit longer, his mind sifting through things. Gretchen things. Farm things. Lavender things. EMT things.

He didn't feel equipped to make decisions by himself, and he wished Gretchen were here so he could talk to her. It almost felt like they needed to discuss this and then make a decision together, because he wanted her in his life for always, and he didn't want to condemn her to a life of farming if she didn't want it.

She loves this farm, he thought. *And the one next door.* Though he'd found her crying in that upstairs bedroom a couple of weeks ago, he'd quickly learned the tears weren't because of sorrow. She had good memories at that farm, even if the circumstances that brought her to it each summer weren't ideal.

He wandered over to the fence and leaned against it, the way he had several times over the years as he conversed with her granddad. He'd been a nice guy, a hard worker, and really smart about his lavender plants. The fact that they were still thriving all these years later without anyone caring for them proved that.

"Drew!"

He turned at the sound of his mother calling his name. He hurried down the fence line until she could see him. He waved until he caught her attention and she pointed to her wrist. Dinner time.

He walked toward her, and she went back inside. Once he'd entered the kitchen, he washed his hands and gave his mom a quick hug. "Feeling better?"

"It's amazing what an afternoon nap can cure," she said. "Joel said he mentioned the farm next door to you."

"Donna," Joel said from his place at the kitchen table. "Let the man think for a day or two."

"Or a week," Drew said. "I don't know, Mom. Honestly, it's a lot to think about."

"And you'll probably want to talk to Gretchen."

Drew knew he hadn't done a great job of keeping his relationship with Gretchen a secret from his mom or Joel. "Yes," he said slowly. "I want to talk to Gretchen about it."

"She mentioned moving back to her house a few days ago," his mom said, sending his heart crashing against his ribs. "Dixie dang near dissolved into tears." His mom bustled around the kitchen, putting steaming white rice in a bowl and pouring chicken stir fry over it.

"I'll admit, I don't know what I'll do out here without them." His mother sniffed and turned to set the bowl on the table. "Let's eat." Her eyes looked glassy, and Drew realized his mom loved Gretchen and Dixie.

"Mom," he said, but he didn't know what else to add.

"Sit down, sit down," she said, her tone impatient and yet emotional at the same time. "I'm fine."

"What else has Dixie told you?" he asked after serving himself some food. "Anything about her wish?"

"She's mentioned it a time or two, but she won't tell me what she wished for."

"Any hints? Gretchen's pretty worried it won't come true, and Dixie'll be devastated." Drew caught his mom and Joel exchanging a look, but neither of them said anything.

"What am I missing?" he asked.

"The wish is about you," his mother said carefully. "I don't know the whole thing, obviously, but Joel overheard Dixie talking to Harriett, the horse she likes, and she said your name."

Drew's gaze flew to Joel's. "What did she say?"

"I didn't really catch all of it, and I didn't know it mattered until a few days later when your mother was helping Dix wash the dishes."

Drew's heart constricted when his step-dad used Dixie's nickname. They really did love the little girl, and Gretchen moving back to town would be devastating for everyone.

"She said she wasn't sure her wish would come true, because her mom can be really stubborn," his mom said. "And that's when Joel realized he'd heard her talking about her wish too."

"Yeah, but what did she say?" Drew had completely abandoned his food, his curiosity over this conversation too much to absorb.

"Again, I didn't catch it all, but it sounded like she was worried about you leaving them. Her and her mother. That you were only here because her mom's foot was hurt, and when it got better, you'd leave."

His throat narrowed. "I don't see how the two conversations fit together."

His mom put her fork down. "I had to explain it to Joel too. You men." She shook her head. "It's obvious her wish is that you and her mom will get married. And she's worried that won't happen because her mom is really stubborn and you're only in their lives until her mom's foot heals."

Drew just stared at his mother. Thankfully, blinking and breathing were involuntary, because his brain had gone completely blank.

"That's how I felt." Joel chuckled. "But now that I've had time to think about it, I think your mother is right."

"Excuse me," Drew managed to whisper before pushing away from the table and leaving the farmhouse. He drove back into town without really seeing the road. He wasn't sure what time Gretchen would return from her trip to the beach, but it didn't matter. He needed time to sort through everything. He needed the silence of his kitchen, and the concentration required to put together complex flavors into an award-winning ice cream.

NINETY MINUTES LATER, HE SPOONED THE VIBRANT, BABY PINK ice cream from the electric freezer and into a bowl. The cherries had been a close fit, but they'd been a bit too sweet and had taken over the lavender.

He'd been wanting to try cranberries for a few days, but he hadn't had time. Something else was always occupying his mind, but now, he didn't want to think. Didn't want to question his life choices. Didn't want to think that maybe he'd been doing the wrong thing for the past eighteen years.

So he mixed the milk, the sugar, and the lavender leaves and steeped them gently. He gave them all the time they needed to extract the greatest flavor. He let the milk cool and then reheated it, adding the egg yolks to thicken the base and give it body. Then he added a cranberry puree and the cranberry syrup he'd made several days ago, the dark red liquid turning the base the beautiful bright baby pink color it would maintain through freezing.

He'd added the black pepper—only three-fourths of a teaspoon—to the mixture just before freezing, and now the moment had come for him to taste it. He'd sampled the base without the pepper and it had been a perfect combination of sweet and sour, and he hoped the savory would come through with the additional seasoning.

He took a deep breath and dipped his spoon into the lavender cranberry ice cream. He put it in his mouth and let the flavors flow over his tongue. The lavender was definitely prevalent, there right on the front of his taste buds. The cranberry hit him next, and it was the perfect blend of sugary, candied berry with that sour punch. The black pepper lingered in the back of his throat, but the lavender was the dominant aftertaste.

He let the spoon fall to the counter, not a single critique coming to mind about his ice cream. "This is it," he said to himself. He took another bite just to make sure he hadn't hallucinated the flavors. Still delicious. Still perfectly balanced.

His first thought was to call Gretchen and tell her. He wasn't sure where she was, but he picked up his phone and dialed her.

"Hey," she said, fuzz ringing in the background.

"Where are you?" he asked.

"Driving back from the beach. We're probably thirty minutes away."

"I think I just made the ice cream worthy of a Lavender King. You wanna stop by and taste it?"

"Are you kidding? Yeah, we'll stop by your place."

"Great." He couldn't erase his smile as he scooped the ice cream into a plastic container and put it in the freezer. He loved ice cream soft and fresh from the maker, but he also liked it hard, sculpted into a perfect sphere with a sprinkle of nuts on top.

"Nuts." He stood still in his kitchen, wondering what he had in his cupboards that he could garnish his ice cream with. For the competition, he couldn't simply scoop the ice cream and call it good. He hadn't even thought past the recipe yet, and he would definitely need to.

He worried that nuts would add another flavor he didn't

need, but having crunch would definitely be welcome with the smooth texture of the ice cream. Exhausted both mentally and physically, he left his ice cream lab and went out to his porch to wait for Gretchen.

Blue and Chief scratched against the gate, and he let them out with the words, "Stay by me." They obeyed, and the three of them sat on the top step and waited. Drew absently scratched Chief's head, his relationship with Gretchen different now for some reason. Different, and she'd been gone for three days.

When she pulled up, Drew couldn't help smiling and moving down the steps to greet her. She'd only been gone for a couple of days, but a tidal wave of missing moved through him. "Hey." He wrapped his arms around her as soon as she stepped from the van and kissed her.

She giggled against his lips and kissed him back.

"I missed you," he murmured before kissing her again, his hands cradling her face and holding her in place. All at once, he remembered Dixie. He pulled away and put a couple of steps of distance between himself and Gretchen, glancing around for the girl.

Dixie stood at the front of the van, her hands on her hips. "I knew it," she said. Her chin quivered. "You lied, Mom. You said you weren't dating him."

"Dixie." Gretchen took a lunging step toward her, but the girl stomped off, then sprinted into the backyard, the dogs following her as if she was playing a game with them.

Drew felt like he'd been struck by lightning. "You told

her we weren't dating?" His voice sounded like he'd sucked in a lungful of helium. "When did she ask?"

Gretchen turned back to him, her nerves plain to see on her fair features. Seconds passed with only silence. Drew waited. And waited, his chest pinching harder with each moment where she said nothing.

17

Gretchen had wanted her beach weekend to be something fun for her and Dixie. Something relaxing after a rough couple of months with her injuries. Something rejuvenating, so she could come back to Hawthorne Harbor and make some big-girl decisions.

So when Dixie had asked her point-blank if she was dating Drew, Gretchen hadn't known how to answer. She'd said no before she'd given it any thought, mostly because at the moment she simply didn't want to think about it. She didn't want to have a hard conversation on the beach.

Dixie had seemed upset about her answer, but she'd recovered quickly. Now, though... She worried her bottom lip between her teeth as she looked at the gate Dixie had disappeared through.

Drew sighed and scrubbed his fingers through the hair on the back of his head. He was so handsome, and he'd been so patient with her all these months. He'd taken the step she'd wanted him to when he'd kissed her, and he'd simply been there whenever and wherever she'd needed him.

"I wasn't expecting her to ask," Gretchen said. "And I didn't know what to say, and I thought we should talk to her together, and..." Her voice trailed off, because she was making excuses and she knew it.

"You told her we weren't dating?" he asked again.

Gretchen nodded, horrified at what she'd done. "I'll fix this." She started toward the gate when she remembered the ice cream he wanted her to taste. She paused, torn between her daughter and Drew—exactly the spot she never wanted to be in. When Aaron died, Gretchen had vowed to herself to never put anything or anyone above her daughter. She just hadn't realized at the time that such a promise included her own happiness.

"I'll be right back." She lifted the latch on the gate and almost got mowed over by Blue. She let the dog sniff her as she tried to locate Dixie. "Where is she, huh?"

Drew had a large backyard, and she'd never been in it. But when Blue started trotting toward a huge tree in the far corner, Gretchen followed him. Dixie sat with her back against the thick trunk, tears running down her face.

Gretchen sat beside her and ripped up a fistful of grass. "I'm sorry, Dix," she said. "I should've told you the truth. Drew and I *are* dating."

Dixie hiccupped and wiped at her eyes.

"You like him, don't you?"

Dixie simply stared straight ahead, her jaw set. Gretchen had seen this exact same expression on her late husband's face, and a flash of sorrow yanked through her.

"We were going to talk to you together," Gretchen said. "That's why I didn't say anything on the beach." She looked up into the leaves of the trees, hoping she'd said enough to get Dixie talking.

She drew her knees to her chest and watched the clouds move through the sky, giving Dixie the time she needed. Sometimes she needed just a few minutes, and sometimes she'd ask to go to her room until she was ready to talk. But as they weren't at home, Gretchen hoped the conversation would get going pretty quick.

Blue and Chief scrambled up the back steps, their claws clicking against the wood. A moment later, Drew opened the door and let them in, shutting Gretchen and Dixie out.

"Are you going to marry him?" Dixie finally asked.

"I don't know, Dix." Gretchen was surprised at how much she liked the idea of being Drew's wife.

"Do you miss Dad?"

"Every day." Gretchen couldn't make her voice louder than a whisper.

"I like Drew a lot," Dixie said. "I think I've forgotten about Dad." Her tears started anew. "And I don't want to forget him."

Gretchen put her arm around her daughter and brought

her flush against her side. "I can tell you lots of stories so we don't forget."

Dixie nodded and held onto Gretchen. Her motherly emotions felt like they were about to burst. She didn't want Dixie to experience more disappointment and sadness than she already had. Her daughter deserved the very best.

"Then I think it's okay if you marry Drew." Dixie sniffled, her tears nearly gone.

Gretchen laughed, the release of tension in her chest welcome. "We're not quite to marriage yet, Dix."

"Why not?" She pulled back and peered up into Gretchen's face. Deciding to be honest, Gretchen stroked her daughter's hair and smiled.

"Adults take a while to get to know each other really well," she said. "I don't want to make any mistakes." It was too late for that, and she could only hope that Drew would be as forgiving as her daughter. "I don't want you to think he's more important than you are."

"I don't, Mom. But I'm not a baby. You can tell me the truth."

Gretchen's emotions choked her, so she only nodded. Dixie wasn't a baby, but it was hard for Gretchen to see her growing up, getting more mature, handling hard things so well.

"Let's go try Drew's ice cream." Dixie stood up, wiped her face, and brushed off her shorts.

Gretchen had no choice but to go with her, but she fell back several steps as Dixie went up to the back porch and knocked on the door. She entered and said, "Drew?" before going all the way in.

"Wow," Gretchen heard her daughter say. "This place is amazing."

Drew chuckled, which meant he couldn't be too mad. Right? Gretchen entered the house and knew immediately that he was still annoyed with her. He didn't look at her as he pulled down three paper bowls and got out plastic spoons.

He detailed to Dixie—not Gretchen—how he'd made the ice cream, and then he scooped a lovely round ball of bright baby pink ice cream into each bowl. "Try it."

Dixie didn't waste any time taking a big mouthful of ice cream. Her eyes widened and she'd barely swallowed before she said, "Drew, this is amazing." She dug back into her treat.

"You're not going to try it?" Drew finally looked at her. She wanted to apologize. Trail her fingers down his sideburns and across his bearded jaw. Kiss him until he forgave her.

She picked up her plastic spoon and pulled her bowl closer to her. "I told Dixie that we were dating, and she said she's okay with it."

Dixie slowed her ice cream consumption and watched Drew and then Gretchen while she licked her lips. "Try the ice cream, Mom. It's really good."

Gretchen focused on her bowl and scraped off the top layer of ice cream until she had a healthy mouthful on her spoon. She lifted her eyes to Drew as she put the bite in her mouth. The flavor of lavender and cranberry made a party in her mouth, and she knew instantly that Drew had found his winning ice cream.

She moved around the kitchen counter to where he stood with his arms folded, his expression as heated as it was hooded. "Delicious, Lavender King," she said with a hesitant smile. She wanted him to take her into his arms and laugh with her that he'd finally found the recipe he'd been searching for all these months.

"I'm sorry, Drew," she said. "I panicked, and I wanted you there with me when I talked to Dixie."

Dixie moved to her side. "Don't be mad at her, Drew. She says she's not going to make any more mistakes."

That got him to relax a little bit. "Everyone makes mistakes, I suppose."

He didn't seem to, but Gretchen was willing to stick around a while and see if he did and how he'd handle himself.

"Do you really like the ice cream?"

"It's a winner," Gretchen assured him.

"Do you two want to help me with the garnishes?"

"What's a garnish?" Dixie asked.

Gretchen fell back to her bowl while Drew explained what a garnish was and he and Dixie started running through possibilities. Watching him interact with Dixie, it was easy to envision herself marrying him and becoming a family. She'd been in love before, and she knew what it felt like. And she knew she was falling in that direction with Drew. He seemed to be as taken with her as she was with him, and she waited for the fear to strike right behind her lungs.

It never came.

"WE NEED TO TALK." GRETCHEN LEANED AGAINST THE doorway leading into the kitchen, where Donna sat at the table with a notebook in front of her. Gretchen recognized it as her menu plan and grocery list for the upcoming week, and she admired the older woman for being up this late on a Sunday evening, planning for the next seven days.

Donna set it aside and asked, "About what?"

Gretchen walked toward her, glad she could do so now without crutches or a walking boot. "My foot is all better." She sat across from Donna. "I have a house in town that's just sitting there."

Donna lifted her chin, determination sparking in her eyes. "It's summer, and Dixie's out of school. Who's going to watch her while you're at work?"

"I have a babysitter I've used since I came back to town."

Donna scoffed like that was the silliest thing she'd ever heard. "Joel and I are right here, and we're not a daycare."

"I can't drive her out here every day. It's too far."

Donna dropped her tough-grandma act. "We want you two to stay on the farm," she said, a slight desperate note in her voice. "Dixie is happy here. She won't have to compete with other kids for our attention, and she absolutely loves the farm. Joel can use her help as the lavender needs to be harvested, and she can earn her keep by doing chores around the farm."

Gretchen considered her words. Dixie did love it out here. She'd be happier here than at the daycare, though they had two trampolines and Sabra did a weekly field trip for the kids.

"I want to pay rent," she said.

"Don't be ridiculous."

"Dixie is earning her keep," Gretchen said evenly. "I'm not doing anything."

"Are you sure about that?" Donna asked. She gave Gretchen a knowing look, collected her notebook, and stood. "I think you're helping us out with Drew, and that's worth a lot." She left the kitchen, left Gretchen to stew over how in the world she was helping Donna and Joel with Drew.

He'd stayed at his house, opting to let Gretchen and Dixie go out to the farm alone after the ice cream tasting. She still felt stupid for how she'd handled her daughter's questions, and she tapped out a message to Drew.

Are we okay?

She wasn't sure if he'd respond or not. He had the morning shift tomorrow, and he'd said he'd be in her flower gardens by seven-thirty, same as always. But that didn't mean they were okay. She knew better than most that every conversation, every mistake, every memory rebuilt and reformed a relationship.

I'm okay, he sent back. *Are you?*

I feel foolish, but I'm okay. Next time you should come to the beach with us.

I'd like that, he said. A few moments passed before her phone vibrated again. *I wasn't lying when I said I missed you.*

She smiled at her phone, wondering how she'd gotten lucky enough to have Drew be the one to drive by when she'd had a flat tire.

Before that, she thought as she thumbed out her response. *I missed you like crazy.* She sent the message and wondered if Drew delivering Dixie had been fate. No matter what, he had a knack for coming to her rescue and fixing whatever was wrong. She wanted him by her side now and forever. She wanted to rely on him, and she decided to do what he'd done when he'd kissed her that first time.

She told him.

18

Drew lay in bed, Gretchen's messages brightening his phone screen—and his life.

I want to rely on you. Her message appeared on the backs of his eyelids even after he closed his eyes. He wasn't sure how to respond, so he let his phone drop to his chest, where he held it over his heart as it pushed love throughout his body with every pump of blood through his veins.

He didn't want to tell her he loved her in a text. That didn't feel genuine, and he wanted to see her face, breathe in her perfume, and kiss her when he told her how he felt about her.

So she'd made a mistake. After she'd explained more about what she'd wanted the weekend to be, he'd forgiven her. He understood the feeling of simply wanting a day away from everything, though he didn't seem to mind taking care of his day job, cutting flowers for her, entertaining Dixie and Jess, or working around the farm.

But he wasn't a single dad, alienated from his parents, or running his own business.

He'd forgiven her, but he hadn't gone out to the farm with them. Dixie had asked him to. She'd said she needed to start making her wish again, as it hadn't come true the first time. His curiosity burned through him as hot now as it had earlier. He didn't want the little girl to suffer, but he'd needed a few hours to himself.

Which was silly, really. He'd had most of the day to himself. But with his winning ice cream recipe now in his notebook, with ideas for garnishes in a list underneath, Drew finally felt relaxed.

And not a moment too soon. With the Lavender Festival in only a month, he needed to make the ice cream a few times and make sure it was consistent every time.

Exhaustion made his thoughts slow. Before he fell asleep, he sent *I want you to rely on me. How can I help you with that?* to Gretchen. He silenced his phone and set his alarm. Because he didn't really want to talk to her about what she needed this late at night. He also didn't believe she actually did rely on him. She *wanted* to, and that alone was a big step for her.

Big enough for now, he thought as he drifted to sleep.

He enjoyed his new reality. One where he worked with Gretchen in the flower gardens, drove into town with her, shared lunch with her, and held her hand while they wandered through the downtown park where the Lavender Festival would be held.

A week passed, each shift he worked with Russ filled with questions. Did he like this job? Why did he like it? Should he take over the farm Joel had bought? Could he dedicate his life to cultivating lavender?

He didn't know, and he didn't bring it up to anyone.

He took Dixie and Jess out to the wishing well, fed goats, and ate dinner with everyone out at the farm, getting no closer to an answer. Joel never brought it up again, but the idea of quitting his EMT job and moving out to the second farmhouse plagued Drew while he was awake and asleep.

As July dawned, he begged out of dinner one evening and went to his brother's house. He found Adam in the kitchen, pulling a frozen pizza from the oven. "That smells good. Got enough for two?"

Adam practically slammed the sheet tray on the stovetop. "Sure. Help yourself. I don't feel like eating anyway."

Drew's eyebrows rose at the same time his heart pounded. "Bad day?"

"Bad week," Adam practically growled. His jaw worked, and Drew knew it was just a matter of time before the whole story would pour from his mouth. So he got down two plates and served them both a few slices of pizza.

Adam sat at the bar, glaring at his dinner like it had done him a personal wrong. Drew joined him and ate a slice. "Okay, so I'll talk. Did you know Mom and Joel bought the farm next door hoping I'd take it over?"

Adam swung his head toward him. "They did?"

Drew swallowed and lifted one shoulder in a shrug. "Do I look like a lavender farmer to you? Be honest."

"I think you can do whatever you want," Adam said, and the words slammed into Drew's chest. It was something their father would've said, and looking at Adam's long nose and light hazel eyes, all Drew could see was their dad.

Emotion surged up his throat, where he barely managed to contain it. He nodded and said, "Thanks, Adam." He lifted another bite of pizza to his mouth. "I'm ready for the Lavender Festival. In just a couple of weeks, you're going to have to start addressing me as 'your majesty'."

Adam snorted, a slight laugh coming from his mouth. He picked up a piece of pizza, finally. "Yeah, that's not gonna happen."

Drew chuckled with his brother and finished eating. When Adam did too and still hadn't said anything, Drew asked, "So why the bad week? I haven't heard anything around the hospital." And though the police department was housed in another building, the EMTs, firefighters, and policemen often knew each other's business.

"Anita broke up with me." Adam sounded positively discouraged. Drew should've known there was something seriously wrong—more than just job problems—when he'd first seen his brother making food from a box.

"Oh, wow. I'm sorry." Drew wasn't sure if he should touch Adam. Give him a brotherly pat or something. He'd never really discussed his romantic relationships before.

Adam hadn't dated a whole lot, and it was usually Drew drowning himself in ice cream recipes and rhetorical questions when things went south with a woman.

"What happened?" he asked.

"She said she 'wasn't feeling it'. Whatever that means." Adam stood and put their plates in the sink. "I don't want to talk about it."

"All right." Drew respected his brother's privacy. "But I'm here if you want to talk."

"Nothing to talk about. Back to the job." Adam stepped over to the living room, where he sat in the middle of the couch and flicked on the TV. "I took an extra night shift tonight, so I have to go back in a little bit." He obviously wasn't focused on the television, as it blared an infomercial for a copper brownie pan that Adam already owned.

"See you later, then. Be careful." Drew let himself out, wondering what he could do to help his brother. He stopped by Andy's Anchor on his way home, an idea growing in his mind.

"Hey, Drew." Andy Parker finished wiping a table and grinned at him. "What can I get you?"

"You close at eight, right?"

"Right."

"My brother loves your giant chocolate chip cookies, and he's on the late shift tonight." Drew pulled his wallet from his back pocket. "How much for whatever you've got left to be delivered to the station on your way home?"

THE FOLLOWING DAY, GRETCHEN DROVE HERSELF AND HER VAN full of flowers—a healthy amount of lavender included—into town as it was Drew's day off. He'd promised her he'd bring Dixie for lunch, and he busied himself around the farm with the girl's help.

They fed all the animals, went out to the wishing well, and then spent hours in the fields, harvesting and pruning lavender. Gretchen had been out in the fields next door all week, clipping the wild lavender blooms and making them into beautiful arrangements for the upcoming festival. It seemed the whole town was abuzz with lavender love as the days until the town's biggest event dwindled.

And Loveland Lavender Farm was going to be ready.

"Why don't we do all the rows in the front?" Dixie asked as Drew bypassed them after bringing in their first harvest.

"Because the tourists will come next week and want to harvest their own," he said. "We save those rows for them."

"And that's when Donna and Joel will sell all that stuff they've made."

"Exactly." His mother had been making oils, soaps, and lotions for months. Joel had been in the kitchen, perfecting his lavender peanut brittle. Drew knew how to make the lavender into oils, of course, but all he did was provide the flowers for his mother. Dixie had been labeling bottles and keeping his mother company. "Joel puts up a wooden roof for her booth," he added as he saw his stepfather wrestling the structure from the storage barn. "See?"

Dixie waved, though Joel couldn't return the gesture, and Drew chuckled. "Let's get another load in, then we'll bundle everything and get it hung. Then it will be time to get over to the flower shop."

"Right. Lunch." The girl skipped up to him and put her hand in his. "Drew, do you like my mom?"

Drew swallowed and looked at Dixie. "Of course I do, Dix."

"Are you going to ask her to marry you?"

"I don't know."

Her face scrunched up. "Well, I think you should. Then we can all move into that other house." She pointed to the farmhouse next door.

"Is that what your mom says?" Drew arrived at the row of lavender where he'd left off and pulled out his shears. The already pruned lavender left little clumps of eight-inch high greenery. He thought it was as beautiful as the plants with tall lavender flowers shooting from them.

"She keeps saying she's going to ask Joel about the house, but she never does."

Drew chewed on this information as he gathered a fistful of lavender and snip-snipped it, leaving him with the perfectly pruned undergrowth and a handful of the prized plant that was bringing thousands of people to Hawthorne Harbor.

"My mom tells me stories about my dad every night," Dixie said.

Drew startled, his clippers almost slipping from his grip. "That's great."

Dixie went on, working on the plant next to him with a simple pair of scissors, the way he'd learned how. He could do three plants for every one she did, but he didn't mind. They filled their baskets and went back to the barn to bunch the plants by length, rubber band them, and hang them by paperclips in the root cellar.

"Go wash up," he told her. "And then we'll go into town."

He stepped around the side of the house to help Joel get the rooftop in place. With open sides so people could approach the lavender from any direction, the wooden legs supported the pitched roof easily.

Joel was slathering on a fresh coat of white paint, after which he'd staple fresh and dried lavender stems to decorate.

"Joel?" Drew approached slowly, his hands tucked in his back pockets.

"Yeah?" He kept the paintbrush going up and down, up and down.

"I've been thinking..." He cast a look over his shoulder to the farm next door. "I think I'd like to give lavender farming a try."

Joel froze, the brush falling to his side as he brought his eyes to Drew's. The air between them held plenty of July heat, but it was as if everything had stilled.

"All right."

Drew wasn't sure what he would do with his EMT job. He helped around the family farm, but he knew Joel worked ten-hour days even with everything Drew did. And the farm next door was wild, uncared for these past five years.

"It'll need a lot of work," Joel said. "You'll probably need help." He dipped the brush in the bucket of white paint and went back to work. "But I can have the lawyer draw up the paperwork to make it yours."

"How much do you want for it?"

"Oh, come on." Joel kept working without a single beat of hesitation.

"You bought it."

"*We* bought it for you." Joel gave him a knowing look. "It's a gift."

No mortgage. No debt. It was a huge gift, and gratitude swelled within Drew. "Thank you, Joel," he said with as much sincerity as he felt rushing through him.

He wandered over to the fence separating the properties. He'd always loved living out here, and this way, he'd be closer to his mom and Joel as they aged. He could carry on the Loveland Lavender Farm traditions.

And he couldn't help thinking about what Dixie had said—that he should ask Gretchen to marry him so they could all live in the farmhouse together.

Behind him, Joel's phone rang, and Drew started toward the house, realizing how late it had gotten. He paused when Joel said, "Oh, hello Gretchen."

He met Drew's eye with obvious surprise in his. His mouth dropped open a little, and he stammered something unintelligible. Drew edged closer, concern coursing within him.

"What's she saying?" he asked.

Joel moved the phone away from his mouth. "She just asked if I'd sell her the farm next door."

19

G retchen tried not to slam her very shatterable vases around the shop. She barely contained her anger, and she didn't want Drew or Dixie to see it. If they'd ever show up. Her stomach growled, and fury flashed through her again.

They were late. And Drew was never late.

"You should be worried, not angry," she muttered to herself. But she couldn't rid herself of this river of frustration. Joel had told her the farm wasn't for sale. No elaboration, not even when she'd asked.

"Honestly, what's he going to do with it?" She paid a pittance for the three-acre flower gardens she tended to meticulously. He obviously didn't need the money. And she didn't have the funds to buy the farm—but she was willing to do almost anything to secure them.

The need seethed within her, making her hands shake

so she couldn't work. She sat on the stool in the front of the shop, watching the sidewalk as a couple walked past. In just a few days, the streets would be flooded with people, and she'd already put her lavender arrangements front and center in her window displays. She'd done well in the past few years during the festival, as The Painted Daisy was adjacent to the downtown park where the activities were.

Maybe she should call her granddad right now, in this window of time where Drew still hadn't shown up. But she wasn't sure what she'd say to him after all these years. It felt like the chasm she'd created by moving away and not keeping the relationship going was too wide for her to cross.

She felt a scream rising through her, and tears pricked the back of her eyes. In the next moment, her beautiful blonde daughter skipped in front of the window displays and the chime on the door rang as Dixie entered. "Mom!" Her enthusiasm was infectious and Gretchen swiped at her eyes.

"What, baby?"

"Wait 'till you see the size of the cookies Drew bought!" She turned back to the door, but Drew still hadn't made an appearance. Gretchen watched for him as well, relaxing further when he appeared wearing his handsome smile, his trademark blue jeans, and a gray t-shirt. He slowed when he caught her staring at him through the glass and stopped when he filled the doorway.

"You spoiled the surprise, didn't you?" He gave Dixie a

mock frown while she giggled, and Gretchen's heart tumbled over itself to see their interactions so playful.

"I didn't tell her what kind of cookies."

"Oh, so she can guess." He entered the shop and closed the door behind him, sealing out the warm summer breeze.

Gretchen couldn't get herself to speak. Her voice was lodged somewhere beneath the teeming ball of emotions that had risen through her throat and stalled at the base of her tongue.

"Go on, Mom. Guess what kind."

Drew held up a bag from Andy's Anchor and Submarine Shop, and her choices were narrowed to two: chocolate chip or snickerdoodle. The sandwich shop only made two varieties of cookies, and if Drew had seriously thought a cookie without chocolate was worth eating, Gretchen would doubt a lot of things about him.

She finally got the ball of emotions to settle back into her stomach, where they writhed. "It better be chocolate chip."

"Yep!" Dixie danced around a display table with three huge vases on it, and it took all of Gretchen's willpower to keep herself from snapping at the child.

"Let's eat in the back," she said instead, hoping to minimize the damage. *Dixie's never broken anything*, she chided herself. *You're just in a bad mood.*

Drew passed out the food, giving Dixie her chocolate chip cookie first. "Don't eat it all," he said. "Half. Then you'll have to eat your sandwich. And don't tell my mother I let you eat your dessert first."

A memory struck Gretchen at the same time Dixie said, "Once, my dad said we could eat all our desserts first. Mom didn't even make dinner. She just put out cookies and marshmallow treats and these caramel nut things." She turned to Gretchen, who was reliving the same, sweet memory. "What were those, Mom?"

"Macadamia nut clusters," she managed to push through her throat.

"They were *soo* good. All we ate for dinner that night was dessert."

Drew met Gretchen eyes as Dixie ripped off a piece of her cookie. Something stormed in his expression, but when he said, "Sounds fun, Dix," his voice was as even as always.

Gretchen picked up her sandwich, the number eleven staring back at her. The Hawthorne harvest club. Her favorite. She wasn't sure why, but those pesky tears appeared again.

She sniffed and tried to turn away, but Drew saw.

"Dix," he said. "Run out front and get those paper towels your mom keeps under the desk."

She skipped away without an argument, and Drew closed the door behind her. "What's wrong?" He stayed by the door, pocketing his hands as he watched her.

She shrugged, which dislodged a tear, which put Drew in motion. He closed the distance between them in two strides and gathered her into his arms. "Whatever it is, it's okay."

Gretchen wanted to believe him, because when he spoke with so much kindness and so much love in his voice, it was almost impossible not to.

"There aren't any paper towels out there," Dixie said as she opened the door.

"I'll grab some from the bathroom closet." Gretchen sidestepped Drew and kept her face turned away from Dixie. She made it to the back of the shop and into the bathroom, wondering what in the world was wrong with her.

She had a roll of paper towels in her hand when Drew said, "It's about the farm, isn't it?"

Spinning to face him, Gretchen's heart beat wildly in her chest. "Did Joel say something to you?"

Something like anguish colored his expression. "About a month ago, he told me he bought the farm for me, and I've been thinking about giving up my job as an EMT and becoming a lavender farmer." His feet shuffled and he sighed. "I wasn't sure if that was what I wanted, but today, I told him I wanted it."

Gretchen had never felt so trapped. "Oh." Or so foolish. She wanted to disappear through the floor.

"You called a few minutes later." He dropped his head as if he was ashamed. "I was standing right there."

Her stomach warred against itself and she hadn't eaten anything yet. "I—I don't know what to say."

"Neither do I."

She gripped the paper towels until her fingers ached. "So when are you going to move in?"

"Joel said he'd go through the house with me. Fix up anything that needs to be repaired before I make the move." He scrubbed the back of his head in that tale-tell sign of his frustration. "I don't know what to do about my current job."

"Can you do both?" He was such a great paramedic, though she knew he'd struggled to find purpose in the job.

"Maybe for a little bit, as we head into fall," he said, inching forward. "Joel suggested I'd need a lot of help around the farm." His pinky hooked hers and he finally lifted his eyes to hers. "I was thinking you might want the job."

Her eyebrows went up. Was that a proposal? A job offer? It felt as though wild horses were thundering through her entire being.

"I'd need help with getting the lavender back into shape, and of course, you'd have to stop paying the rent on the flower garden."

"Why would I have to stop doing that?" The words barely ghosted from her mouth, because she still didn't know what "the job" was.

"Because." He chuckled. "I'm not taking rent from my girlfriend." His other hand slid around her back and he swayed with her. "Once I get the farm and house fixed up, maybe you and Dixie could move in too."

She bolted out of his arms, needing to know what he

meant by everything. Her back met the wall and panic doused her insides with icy waves. "Drew," she said. "Are you asking me to marry you?"

"It was Dixie's idea."

Gretchen felt the blood drain from her face, and Drew obviously saw it, because the softness in his face turned hard.

"I mean—"

"Excuse me." She pushed past him and turned left, exploding through the door and into the alley behind the shop. She couldn't breathe behind walls, not right now.

"Gretchen," he said, pleading in both syllables.

She held up her hand. "Don't, Drew," she said. She couldn't believe she hadn't seen this coming from a mile away. He loved Dixie more than her. She shook her head as an unhappy laugh came out of her mouth. "I'm so naïve."

"No, you're not." He closed the door behind him, locking them out though he probably didn't know that. "I'm not saying anything right today."

She faced him, her fingers balling themselves into fists. With her chin lifted, she nonverbally dared him to try again.

He pulled in a deep breath, his face ruddy and blushed. "I love the farm. I love being an EMT, but I feel...unsettled in that job. I want to see if farm life is more my style. I need time to get the house and farm operational. Then I thought maybe you'd like to get married and be a farm family with me." A small smile touched his mouth. "So yes, I guess that was a really bad marriage proposal, which happened a bit prematurely."

Gretchen couldn't move—didn't dare. She feared if she stepped, the ground would be too brittle to hold her weight.

"I'm really bad at this kind of stuff." Drew started laughing, a low sound that lifted and swelled and filled the alley, the park across the street, the very sky itself.

The joy he brought with him filled her, and she found herself laughing with him. He swept her into his arms and placed a kiss on the corner of her mouth. "Something to think about," he whispered. "I know it's a lot to take in." He kissed the opposite corner of her lips, and everything inside her melted. She folded herself into his embrace and pressed her cheek above his pulse.

Did she love him? She loved how he took care of Dixie. How easily he'd taken to her as if she were his own child. She loved how he looked after his parents. She loved his gentle spirit and kind eyes and warm hands. She loved how safe she felt with him, and the thought of not being with him brought pain like she'd experienced when Aaron had died.

She was so close to loving him, and she wouldn't let a farm get between them. "I'll help you get the farm up and running again," she whispered, tilting her head back to receive a proper kiss from the man she almost loved.

THE DAY BEFORE THE FESTIVAL, GRETCHEN SOLD THROUGH ALL her lavender sachets. She'd cleaned out all the bouquets and all the wreaths Donna had taught her to weave. Thankfully, she had another day's worth of stock in the walk-in refrigerator, and more out at the farm where she'd been living.

She paused in sprucing up her displays, the time ticking toward noon, when Janey would arrive to take her to lunch. Though they saw each other every day and they helped one another out, sometimes it was nice for the two of them to just sit and relax. Eat a meal together. Talk about their own challenges.

Gretchen's thoughts wandered down the Lavender Highway, and when her phone chimed a message from Janey saying she was at the corner, Gretchen turned the OPEN sign to CLOSED, where she'd taped a handwritten note that said, "I'll be back at 1 PM."

After making sure the front door was locked and hurrying down the sidewalk, she slid into Janey's Jeep. "Hey." She didn't mean to exhale like the weight of the world was on her shoulders.

"Oh, hey. What's up?"

"Nothing."

"Didn't sound like nothing." Janey eased onto the road. "And we're going up to Mabel's for lunch?" She cut Gretchen a glance out of the corner of her eye.

"She was kind to me when I got hurt," Gretchen said,

shrugging. "And she's having her annual lavender luncheon for her special guests. You're my plus-one."

Janey laughed, and all traces of her prior loneliness seemed to be gone. "I think Drew's your plus-one."

Gretchen lifted her chin, unable to deny her relationship or her feelings for Drew. She didn't want to either. "Not today. Just you and me, girl."

Janey aimed her Jeep along the coastal highway, and Gretchen rolled down the window, the sound and scent of the ocean calming her enough to admit, "I'm going to miss Donna and Joel."

"Why would you miss them?"

"I can't live at the farm forever," she said. "Honestly, no one but me seems to get that."

"And what about you and Drew?"

Gretchen hadn't told her about the botched marriage proposal. If what had happened in the bathroom at The Painted Daisy could even be considered a marriage proposal.

"Gretchen? You like him, right? He's good to you?" Janey pulled into the guest parking lot at the Magleby Mansion, her words rolling around in Gretchen's head.

"Why wouldn't he be good to me?" Gretchen swung her attention to her best friend.

Janey squirmed before reaching to unbuckle her seatbelt. "I'm probably worrying too much."

"Worrying about what?" Gretchen undid her seatbelt

too, but as Janey hadn't tried to get out of the Jeep, Gretchen stayed put too. "Dixie really loves Drew."

"Yeah, I know. It's not that." She gazed out the windshield, her mind obviously churning around something.

"Janey?" Gretchen reached over and put her fingertips on her friend's arm.

She startled. "It's nothing. Me just thinking about what I would do if I were in your shoes." She opened the door and got out of the Jeep.

Gretchen took a few more seconds than Janey did to find her balance in her walking boot and to come around the front of the vehicle. "And what would you do if you were me?"

Janey gazed at the ocean across the street and down the beach for an extra moment or two. Then she looked at Gretchen with all the love of a best friend. "I'd hang on to a good man like Drew."

Gretchen smiled, tucked her arm in Janey's, and said, "Let's go eat this amazing lunch."

Janey giggled as they went up the gravel drive. "I've always wanted to eat here again."

"Again?"

"Yeah, Matt and I got married here. We had a full catered dinner."

"Oh, wow." Gretchen let Janey open the door for her, and the scent of roasted meat and potatoes met her nose. "Do you think you'll come here when you get married again?"

Janey scoffed. "I'm not the one with the serious boyfriend." She quirked an eyebrow at Gretchen. "But yeah, if I could afford it. I'd totally book the Mansion again."

Gretchen glanced up to the high ceilings, seeing the brown and white stones in a whole new light—more like a customer and not a service provider.

"Gretchen." Mabel spotted her and came over as fast as her elderly body could bring her. "You made it." She held onto Gretchen's upper arms and scanned her. "You're looking well."

"Healing up nicely." Gretchen smiled and indicated Janey. "You remember Janey."

"I remember all my brides." Mabel stepped back from Gretchen and patted Janey's hand between both of hers. "Come on, girls. I have seats for you over here with the policemen."

THE MORNING OF THE LAVENDER FESTIVAL DAWNED EARLY and hot. "Come on, Dix," she called. "Drew wanted us there at eight." She picked up the jar of perfect lavender blooms she'd plucked the previous evening, and Donna handed her one final bottle of lavender scented vanilla extract.

"Take him this. It's my special blend." She grinned and Gretchen couldn't help returning the smile.

Dixie came tearing down the stairs, her flaxen hair

flying behind her, as she cradled the mint plant Drew had entrusted her with. "Ready!"

"What else is Drew garnishing his ice cream with?" she asked.

"It's a secret." Dixie looked at her with wide eyes that held the hint of deviousness.

"Like your wishes."

"Yes, exactly."

Gretchen giggled, though she still really wanted to know what Dixie had been wishing for all this time. "Well, come on. We're already late."

When they pulled up to Drew's house, he paced from the bottom of the stairs to the top. He wore a pair of dark jeans with a white polo and the anxiety right on his face. He caught sight of them as he came back down the steps.

Gretchen got out of the car and handed him the bottle of lavender vanilla extract. "From your mother."

"I'm so nervous."

"Relax," Dixe said, passing him the mint plant. "You've got this. You practiced the recipe again last night, right?"

"Yes." He bent down to her height. "The ice cream was good, right?"

She put both hands on his shoulders. "So good. You're going to win."

Drew nodded once and straightened. He kissed Gretchen quickly and said, "Well, I have to go check in by nine. Should we go?"

"You have everything loaded already, don't you?"

"Since seven this morning."

Gretchen threw her head back and laughed. "Why did we come early to help then?" She shook her head and put her arm around Drew. "You're not going to have any fun today, are you?" The competition wasn't until two o'clock that afternoon, and contestants had two hours to craft their creations and submit them for judging. The winners were announced at six, just before the annual lighting of the lavender plants that lined Main Street. After that, the big town dance started. Gretchen had never gone, because she was tired by the time they lit the lavender and Dixie had never asked to go to the dance.

"I'll be fine," he said. "Let's go."

Dixie piled into the middle of his truck and Gretchen caught sight of his premium cooler—one of the fanciest ones on the market, it claimed to keep ice frozen for seventy-two hours. He'd bought it specifically to keep his ingredients at the temperature he wanted until the competition started.

They arrived in the downtown area to swarms of cars. Luckily, she had parking at the back of the shop. Her hired help had already arrived, and she ran inside the building just to make sure the stock was holding out.

Drew held Dixie's hand on the edge of the street when she came out, and her heart stuttered at the sight.

And she knew. Like she knew the sun would rise the following morning and she knew the sky was blue and she knew she'd have her indigo daisies at her wedding.

She knew she was in love with Drew Herrin.

Gretchen couldn't stop smiling as she took Drew's other hand, and they all walked over to the Lavender Festival. Vendors worked to set up their tents and tables. Food trucks pulled in and started getting their generators set up.

The line to enter the Lavender Creation Contest stretched a couple dozen feet, and Gretchen suppressed a groan. They soon discovered that one line was for products that took longer than two hours to produce. The people in that line simply needed to drop off their bottle of lotion or bar of oatmeal-lavender soap, fill out the entry form, and leave.

Those who could create and demonstrate their use of lavender in the two-hour time period waited in another line. Foot by foot, they moved forward until it was Drew's turn to fill out the papers, pay his fee, and declare what he was making.

"Ice cream," he said with confidence.

"Ooh," Brenda squealed as she wrote the information on the single sheet she was keeping. "You know three-time champion Augustus Hammond has entered for ice cream too, right?" She looked up at him with such glee in her eyes.

Drew's countenance fell. "Yeah, I know." He handed over his twenty-dollar fee and Brenda recorded it, handed him a number and a receipt, and he stepped to the side.

"Don't worry about Augustus," Gretchen said as they faced the park. She aimed them in the direction of the petting zoo, where a small crowd of families had already gathered. The rest of the festival would be in full swing within the hour, and the scent of sunshine and lavender filled the air.

"Maybe this was a huge mistake." Drew shook his head and muttered under his breath.

"He's not going to beat you," Gretchen assured him, though a slip of nervousness tunneled through her.

"All you can do is try," Dixie said. "Mom, there's Jess and Janey. Can I go pet the goats with them?"

"Sure, go ahead."

Dixie skipped ahead, but Gretchen tugged on Drew's hand to get him to slow. "She's right, you know. All you can do is try."

He met her eyes, and the fear melted from his face. "You're right." Drew squared his shoulders. "I'm going to try."

Gretchen stretched up on her toes and kissed him. "For luck."

20

By the time Drew had wandered the festival for a few hours, he needed a dark, quiet place to gather his thoughts. He'd refused to eat anything for fear of messing up his taste buds with too much lavender, an overdose of honey, or a mouth-puckering dose of orange.

His head hurt, and all he could think about was Augustus. Of course, he'd known the man would be at the festival and would enter the contest. The man himself had told him. Yvonne too. Drew's confidence had been high at home, but now, surrounded by the dozens and dozens of contestants, he doubted every measurement, every flavor he'd prepared.

Stupid, stupid. Drew reprimanded himself for not giving Augustus as much credit as he deserved as he crossed the street, leaving Gretchen and Dixie in the park. He wouldn't see them again until after the competition. The contestants worked on their creations in a large tent, only presenting their final product to the judges and the public at the conclusion of the two-hour period.

He slipped into the back of The Painted Daisy using the key Gretchen had given him. "It's just me," he called to the girl she'd hired to sell flowers for her so she could attend the festival. Then he locked himself in the bathroom.

He splashed water on his face and looked at himself in the mirror. He barely recognized himself anymore. Sure, the beard was the same. The long nose like his father's. But now he carried something more in his eyes. Something that hadn't been there before he'd met Gretchen and Dixie on the side of the road.

"It's all going to be okay," he whispered to his reflection. Win or lose, it was just an ice cream competition. Because of the festival and the harvest and all the tourists out at the farm, he hadn't had even a moment to slip next door and look at the old farmhouse he wanted to live in with Gretchen and Dixie.

Besides, he wanted to take Gretchen with him. *Needed* her to be with him when he walked through her granddad's house and find out what she wanted in the home he hoped to make with her.

And losing this competition wouldn't cost him Gretchen. "So it's all going to be okay." Strengthened by his revelation, he collected his cooler from the cab of his truck and slung the bag of equipment he needed over his shoulder.

He arrived in the tent fifteen minutes before the competition would begin and found the ten-by-ten-foot kitchen he'd been assigned. He set his equipment and cooler down and pinned the number—sixty-two—to his chest.

His fingers itched to get things set up. Test the outlet. Flip on the burners and see how hot they got. But he couldn't. Nothing could be set up or used until the time began.

The mood in the tent thickened with every person who arrived. Tensions were high and Drew kept his back to the rest of the contestants on purpose, mentally running through his recipe one last time.

"Contestants!" A voice boomed through the tent, amplified by a megaphone, and Drew turned to find the mayor standing near the mouth of the tent, about fifty feet from him.

"We'll begin in five minutes," Mayor Lambert said, her voice warm and pleasant. "Time warnings will be given every thirty minutes, and again at fifteen minutes remaining, ten minutes, five minutes, three minutes, and one minute. All creations must be on the table, with your number, by the time the buzzer sounds to be considered. Six pieces or plates must be presented. Anything requiring to be served hot or cold will be placed in the proper place until showing."

Mayor Lambert looked around gleefully. "Are you ready?"

A cheer rose up, but Drew's voice remained silent. He hadn't prepared his ice cream in front of anyone before, and now he wished Gretchen and Dixie were here to see him work.

"And...go!" A bullhorn filled the air and people sprang into action.

Drew set up his pots and pans and plugged in his ice cream maker. He tested the power, and it seemed good. He tried the burners, and they produced a good flame.

Forcing himself to think clearly, move deliberately, and focus on what was right in front of him, he took all the ingredients out of his cooler and lined them up on the table. Whole milk, sour cream, his mother's lavender vanilla extract, cranberries—whole and raw—cranberry syrup with extra red dye, cranberry puree, sugar, eggs, vanilla, salt, and black and white pepper. He'd refined the recipe to include both, enjoying the milder flavor of the white pepper and the way it reduced the number of black flecks in the ice cream without compromising on flavor.

He had an orange so he could candy the rind for the garnish. His idea. And he had Dixie's mint plant so he could add one green leaf to the top of each bowl. Her idea. The other garnish would come from the raw cranberry itself.

He'd made the cranberry puree with water, salt, and orange juice. He'd made the cranberry syrup and reduced the amount of sugar by half. He'd taken so many steps, made so many tweaks, over the past month. He was ready for this.

He turned his attention to the base, as it would need to cool before going into the electric ice cream freezer. He worked methodically, the noise inside the tent becoming a dull roar. Drew imagined Blue barking in the backyard the way the dog so often did.

Measuring and tasting, the ice cream base came together seamlessly. He covered it, labeled it, and hurried it over to a refrigerator in the middle of the arena. Then he turned his attention to the garnishes and got sugar, lemon juice, and salt into a pan. He zested the orange right into the candy coating and cooked it for only another moment.

As he scooped the mixture onto a sheet pan, Augustus walked by. Pausing at the edge of the table, he asked, "What flavor?"

Drew lifted his chin, his first instinct to keep his flavors to himself. In the end, though, he didn't need to be so stubborn. "Lavender cranberry with pepper."

Augustus made a face and took a few steps away. "Good luck." Somehow, when he said the words, they didn't carry the same emotion as they had when Gretchen had said them.

Drew shook off the encounter and turned back to his station. He knew his flavors were spot-on. All he could do now was hope the judges agreed with him.

THE TWO HOURS PASSED IN A BLINK, BUT DREW GOT HIS SIX bowls of ice cream on the appointed table, with his number. Each held three perfectly sculpted spheres of that beautiful, black-flecked pink ice cream. The bright orange zest shone with its sugar candy coating, and the green mint leaf was a stark contrast to everything else.

They were absolutely stunning, and he suddenly didn't care if he won or not. He'd tasted the ice cream and it was fabulous. He snapped a picture with his phone, the ice cream already starting to melt. Since he'd only had thirty minutes to freeze it after he'd churned it, it wasn't all that hard yet.

An assistant whisked his bowls away to the freezer, where he hoped it would continue to set, and he thanked his lucky stars that he'd gotten number sixty-two. All the competitors filed out of the tent and into the crowd.

A wooden dance floor had been put down over the grass, with row upon row of folding chairs flanking it. The platform where the winners would be announced had been set up near the sidewalk, and the table where he'd present his ice cream had five chairs behind it where the judges would sit.

He caught Gretchen and Dixie frantically waving at him on the side closest to her flower shop, and he grinned and waved back at them. His heart bobbed in the back of his throat. He loved them both so much.

He joined them and turned to face the judges as they climbed the few steps to the top of the platform. Mayor Lambert sat on the end, her face nothing but smiles. Next to her, Mabel Magleby sat, her wrinkled face staring out at the crowd like she expected a riot to break out. Beside her sat

Gene Winthrop, who owned an essential oil company a couple of towns over. He was world-renowned for his lavender oils, and he'd built the business from his garage to a forty-thousand square foot warehouse. Beside him was Julie Spencer, the queen of botanicals at the Hawthorne Harbor Gardens. Last at the table was Yvonne Hammond.

Drew choked, his dreams of being crowned Lavender King going right down the drain.

"What's wrong?" Gretchen asked.

He hadn't spoken of Yvonne to Gretchen past that first time he'd mentioned her being his ex-girlfriend. He'd kept the texts a secret, and the one time they'd met to himself.

"See that dark-haired woman on the end?" He pointed though it wasn't necessary.

"Yeah. So?"

"That's Yvonne Hammond. Her father is Augustus, and she's—"

"The ex-girlfriend who broke your heart and sent you to Medina." Gretchen narrowed her eyes at the woman while Drew reeled with her assessment of what Yvonne had done. "How can she be a judge if her dad's in the competition? That doesn't seem fair."

"They've owned a lavender farm for six generations. Joel sat on the panel of judges a few years ago." Drew watched as the first contestant approached the judging table with a loaf of lavender honey tea bread. "There're five judges. She won't influence things singlehandedly." He would be surprised if that bread won, as the lavender honey combination had been tried and tested for decades now. But he couldn't help wondering if Yvonne had known she was going to be a judge here when she'd met him at the statue only a few weeks ago.

Yvonne's face was like a cement mask as she tasted the bread. From sachets to flower arrangements to mason jar décor, everything and anything that could be done with lavender got paraded in front of the judges.

Augustus presented at number thirty, and he put a pretty black bowl of pure white ice cream on the table in front of the judges.

"White Asian peach and lavender ice cream," he said with a flourish of his arm. The screen that had been set up on the side of the dance floor so people could see the item showed the bare spheres of ice cream. No garnishes. And the treat looked a stitch icy to Drew, but he could've been looking for the slightest flaws simply because it was Augustus.

The judges each took several bites before their bowls got whisked away and they made notes on the clipboards in front of them, the mayor smiling and nodding like she'd just found the winner. Drew relaxed after that for a bit, his nerves returning the closer to sixty-two they got.

Fifty-seven. Fifty-eight.

His leg started bouncing and he couldn't stop. When the woman before him took up her lavender cashew brittle, everything became real. He was about to serve his ice cream to the Lavender Festival judges. His stomach twisted, and he wished he'd eaten something that day besides a few quick tastes of his ice cream base.

When it was his turn, he went backstage and waited. When the assistant signaled him, he took the suddenly-there bowl of ice cream from another volunteer and started toward the platform. He placed the bowl he'd been given on the table so it could be shown to the audience, and someone else handed him a tray with the other bowls.

It seemed like fifty steps up to the judging table. He somehow made it without tripping and served a bowl of ice cream to each of the judges, carefully avoiding eye contact with Yvonne.

He stood to the side and faced the crowd on the south lawn, searching for Gretchen's beautiful face. "This is cranberry lavender ice cream, with black pepper, garnished with candied orange zest, a sugared maraschino cranberry, and mint. Enjoy."

Unable to watch them sample his ice cream, Drew opted to return the tray to the volunteer and head back out into the crowd. Dixie stood on her chair and he walked toward her and Gretchen.

"They love it," Gretchen said when he arrived.

"How can you tell?"

"Because they're still eating it!" She pointed, and Drew twisted to watch. All five judges seemed to be enjoying his ice cream, even Yvonne. But how could he really know?

As someone came forward to take the bowls, Mabel

actually pulled hers away. Her voice, though aged, could clearly be heard as she said, "I want to finish this."

The crowd laughed, and a smile sprang to his face.

"You broke Mabel!" Gretchen giggled and put her hand in his. "I just know you're going to win."

"We'll see." He squeezed onto the row with them and waited while the rest of the competition continued, his nerves over Yvonne refusing to be quieted. She seemed to look up and find him after every entry, and he couldn't figure out what game she was playing.

When the last contestant had finally presented her lavender poppy seed salad dressing, the judges stood and formed a circle. Several minutes passed before Mayor Lambert separated herself from them. "What an excellent showing of lavender products, tastings, and décor! We'll announce the winner at six, from the sidewalk, right before we light the lavender and start the dance. Thank you."

People started to disperse, and Drew's stomach roared. "After I clean up my stuff, let's find something to eat," he said. "Are you guys hungry?"

"So hungry," Dixie said. "Mom said I couldn't get a churro."

"You'd already had one," Gretchen said, shaking her head. "And I knew Drew would want to eat dinner." She smiled at him. "Go get your stuff, and we'll meet you right here."

He collected his equipment and leftover ingredients and returned them to his truck. He held Gretchen's hand as they wandered through the festival, looking at lavender sachets, toys, and recipe books before arriving at a pizza-by-the-slice food truck.

With only a few minutes to spare until six o'clock, Dixie tugged him toward the sidewalk for the big announcement. His feet itched to take him somewhere else, but he held very still. He wanted this title so badly and his ice cream had been phenomenal. He hoped.

"Your mom and Joel made it," Gretchen whispered, pointing through the crowd. He caught his mother's eye and waved, and they started weaving through the people toward them.

"You closed the farm?" Surprise touched his words. People paid to harvest their own lavender, and the profits from their farm store were impressive every year.

"Everyone's here," Joel said. "We figured we should come see you get crowned the Lavender King."

Warmth filled Drew, and a hearty dose of happiness filled him. If life could get any more perfect, he didn't want to know how.

Mayor Lambert stepped up onto a platform and took her position behind the microphone there. The woman could really go on and on, but she cut to the chase pretty quickly. "So let's light the lavender!"

She threw her hand into the air, and a moment later, beautiful tea lights filled both sides of the sidewalk. People *oohed* and *aahed* at the way the lavender made the normally yellow light more purple, and then a cheer rose into the air.

The mayor laughed along with everyone else. "And now, I'm ready to announce our eighty-ninth annual Lavender Festival Creation Contest winner." She surveyed the crowd. "But let's start with fifth place. That's a woman who presented a gorgeous, silky soap scented with lavender and pink lemonade...Georgina Watters!"

The crowd clapped and Georgina made her way up on stage, gripping her manila envelope while she beamed at the audience. His name wasn't called fourth, or third, or second. But neither was Augustus's.

Finally, it was time to announce the winner. Drew sucked in a breath and held it. And held it.

"With his delicious ice cream..." the mayor said, really drawing out something that should be quick.

Could still be Augustus.

"Andrew Herrin!"

His name bounced around inside his head before settling in his ears. Gretchen squealed and started laughing, and Dixie jumped up and down. The townspeople clapped and whooped, and everything felt like a white cyclone of noise.

"Where's Drew?" Mayor Lambert asked when he still hadn't moved.

"He's here!" Dixie practically screamed. "He's right here!"

"Go on, Drew," Gretchen said. Her face swam so close to his, and then she kissed him, and then he was walking up to the platform to be crowned Lavender King.

21

Pure joy flowed through Gretchen. She'd forgotten the magic the Lavender Festival contained, and her childhood memories seemed so close to the surface. She could practically feel the leathery, warm hand of her granddad as he'd kept her close so she wouldn't get lost in the crowds. She'd done the same to Dixie while they explored, tasted lavender caramels, and rode the Ferris wheel.

Though she'd been back in town for three festivals now, she'd worked the shop, never venturing across the street to actually partake in the festivities. She'd felt a bit of guilt that she'd kept this tradition from Dixie, but she'd stuffed it away.

Watching Drew get fitted with his gaudy, gold crown made her laugh, and Dixie's face held a glow like it was Christmas morning.

"I can't believe he won," Donna said, to which Dixie

replied, "I knew he was going to win. I wished it." She beamed at his mother, who put her arm around the girl's waist and pulled her close.

"Of course you did. I guess all those bottles you labeled are worth it now, huh?"

"Totally!"

The crowd started to wander away from the sidewalk as the music for the dance lifted into the purple-hued air. But Drew still lingered on the platform, collecting something from Mayor Lambert and shaking hands with the other judges.

"Gretchen, we'll take Dixie to get some of his ice cream, okay?" Donna held Dixie's hand so she could jump down from the folding chair. "Then we'll head back out to the farm. You and Drew stay and dance." Donna looked radiant and happy, and Gretchen couldn't help smiling at her.

"Yeah, okay." Gretchen hugged herself and watched Donna and Joel weave through the crowd with Dixie in tow. Pulling in a deep breath, she turned away from the sidewalk lined with lit lavender and took a few slow steps.

A whoop filled the air, and she spun back to the platform just in time to see Drew kissing Yvonne.

Gretchen's throat felt like she's swallowed liquid nitrogen, and everything turned to ice as she watched. The woman stepped back, smiling like she'd just won the Miss American pageant, and lifted Drew's arm into the air.

His crown had toppled to the side, and he tried to right

it with his free hand. Gretchen couldn't swallow, and though the summer was warm and wonderful, she felt frozen.

"So he won."

Gretchen tore her eyes from the tiny platform and focused on Janey. She didn't know what to say, because that liquid nitrogen had gone up to her brain too, making her thoughts sluggish.

"I sent Jess out to the farm with Donna and Joel. He's going to sleep over."

Gretchen got her throat working enough to swallow. "Okay."

"I saw him with Yvonne at the Anchor," Janey said, finally turning toward Gretchen. "A couple of months ago. He told me it was nothing." She looked like she might cry. "I'm sorry, Gretchen. I should've told you."

Gretchen shook her head and looked back to the platform. Drew had vacated it, but she couldn't quite see where he'd gone.

"Doesn't matter," she said, her dreams of arranging her indigo daisies on the tables at their wedding dinner at the Mansion shattering. Her heart hurt, and she couldn't believe she'd invited Drew inside her life. Inside Dixie's life. "I have to go."

"You're not going to talk to him?" Janey latched onto her arm as Gretchen tried to flee.

"Nothing to say." She pulled her arm away and started across the grass toward The Painted Daisy. She saw his truck parked in the alley, suddenly remembering she didn't have her van here.

She spun back to find Janey, to ask for a ride, and found her friend only paces behind her. "Come on. I'll take you home." Janey linked her arm through Gretchen's and towed her away from the flower shop, away from the dance now in full swing, away from the man who had crushed her heart.

"My van is at Drew's," Gretchen managed to say. Her phone rang, and she looked at Drew's handsome face on the screen.

"You can get everything later." Janey took Gretchen's phone and kept her moving. She drove to her house and got Gretchen situated on the back porch with a glass of lavender lemonade before Gretchen's first tears fell.

Janey let her cry for a few minutes before she said, "It's not like Drew to do something like this." She flipped Gretchen's phone over and over. "That's why I didn't say anything. And you two seemed so happy..." She looked at Gretchen's phone again. "I sent him a text."

Gretchen nearly slopped lemonade down the front of her festive lavender dress. "You did? What did it say?"

Janey held out her phone, her face a mixture of sadness and sympathy.

Gretchen looked at her text string from Drew. *I saw you kissing Yvonne. I don't want to talk tonight.*

Janey did know her really well. Gretchen didn't want to talk to Drew tonight.

He'd texted twice. *That was all her, not me.*

And I'm not with Yvonne. She knows that. Please call me.

The message was fifteen minutes old, and Gretchen inhaled and pressed the phone to her collarbone. "Do you believe him?"

"Does it matter what I believe?"

Gretchen watched the sun sink farther along the horizon, her heart still beating furiously fast in her chest, as if she were watching Drew kiss Yvonne again and again.

She needed to rely on herself. Take care of Dixie.

An image of her granddad's farm floated into her mind, and along with it came that roaring anger she'd experienced when she'd asked Joel to sell her the farm.

Drew was standing in her way.

She'd once said she'd do whatever was necessary to keep Dixie safe and provide for her. The lavender farm would do that.

So does The Painted Daisy, she thought.

And so her thoughts and her feelings rode the merry-go-round of her mind as she tried to figure things out.

"Can you take me to get my van?" she asked, setting her lemonade on the glass tabletop between them. "I need to go get my daughter and go home."

A half an hour later, Drew had called once and texted twice. Gretchen hadn't answered any of his attempts to communicate. She pulled into the driveway at Donna and

Joel's, her nerves a frayed mess. Telling Donna and Joel she had to leave the farm was going to be hard. And getting Dixie out of there was going to be a downright fight.

She steeled herself and squared her shoulders as she got out of her van. The porch swing squeaked, and a figure straightened from it.

Drew.

Her heart catapulted to the back of her throat. His truck wasn't anywhere in sight, and she felt tricked that he'd parked it somewhere else.

"I knew you'd come get Dixie," he said, his voice so quiet. But out here, everything whispered, and she heard him just fine.

"We're going back to our house," she said.

"Don't do that." Drew stepped into the light bathing the steps up to the porch in orange light. "Yvonne was mistaken. She's apologized for kissing me, and she said it won't happen again. I told her it absolutely can*not* happen again." He looked fierce and as angry as she felt.

"This isn't about Yvonne," Gretchen said, climbing the steps and moving past him. She opened the front door and called, "Dixie! We need to go."

"What's it about?" he asked.

Gretchen folded her arms and turned back to him. "My granddad's farm."

Her daughter came down the steps from the second floor bedrooms, her face filled with confusion. "Where are we going?"

"Back to our house."

"What? Why?" She held a handful of cards in her fingers. "Me and Jess are playing Hearts."

"Get in the van." Gretchen started away from Drew, no longer able to be so close to him.

"I don't want to go," Dixie said.

"Go with your mother," Drew said quietly.

"Drew—" Dixie protested.

"Come on, Dix." Gretchen spun back to her. "You don't always get to do what you want. We're leaving. Let's go."

Donna appeared in the doorway, and Gretchen's eyes heated. She didn't want to make a scene. She just wanted to take her daughter and go.

"Thank you for everything, Donna," she said, her voice breaking. "I'll come out tomorrow and get our things, get everything put back the way it was. I'm sorry." She turned away from the kindness and compassion Drew's family had offered her, unable to face them for another moment.

She climbed behind the steering wheel of the van, beyond relieved when Dixie stormed across the front lawn and joined her in the vehicle. "What is going on?" she demanded.

Gretchen couldn't answer. She put the van in reverse and set them on the Lavender Highway toward home.

"Mom, I'm not a baby. Why did we have to leave?"

"Drew kissed someone else," Gretchen said. "I—Joel won't sell me the farmhouse next door." She didn't say that it was simply too hard to be around Drew right now. Too hard to look southwest and see the land she so desperately wanted and couldn't have.

"But I wished," Dixie said, her own tears falling. "I wished that you and Drew would fall in love and be together."

"Yeah, so did I, baby." Gretchen reached over and tousled her daughter's hair. "Sometimes wishes don't come true."

"But Drew said—"

"Just because Drew says something doesn't make it true," Gretchen said with a heavy dose of harshness in her voice.

Dixie folded into herself and stared out the window. Gretchen had seen her do this exact thing after Aaron had died, and her heart shriveled to think she'd caused this sorrow for her daughter.

22

"I'm going to go to bed." Drew pushed away from the table where he sat with his mother and Joel. The kitchen light was too bright, and it hurt his head. He'd explained everything that had happened after he'd won the title Lavender King. Even his mom didn't have anything to say, and Drew was tired of the silence.

First from Gretchen, and now from his mother, and then the house. Everything felt too quiet with Dixie and Gretchen gone, with the house so empty without them. And he knew he wasn't the only one missing them, which only added to his guilt.

He could not believe Yvonne had kissed him. Kissed him right in front of everyone, on top of that platform. He couldn't believe he hadn't seen it coming. She'd been texting him for a few months now, asked to meet him, and even after her apology and the supposed closure, the communication hadn't stopped.

He hadn't responded again, but he should've known. He entered his old bedroom and found all of Dixie's things in there. His heart constricted, and he hadn't known what to tell her when she'd rounded on him, her innocent face scrunched up in confusion, and demanded, "What's going on?"

He'd told her she better hurry up and go with her mom, because Gretchen obviously wasn't taking no for an answer. Dixie had stomped away then, and his fragile heart had cracked immediately.

It struggled to beat against the sight of her clothes, her shoes, and her hairbrush. He turned and went back downstairs, avoiding the kitchen and choosing to go into the living room instead. He could sleep on the couch as easily as driving home, and he pulled a blanket and a pillow out of the hall closet and kicked off his boots.

His Lavender King crown sat on the coffee table where he'd left it, and the light from the hall glinted off the gold finish. He'd thought he'd be so happy when he won that crown, and now all it symbolized was a day he never wanted to repeat.

He couldn't sleep, and he picked up his phone and typed a message to Gretchen. *I'm so sorry. She kissed me. I didn't kiss her back. Please let me come talk to you tomorrow.*

It was Sunday, and she didn't open The Painted Daisy on Sundays. They'd been planning a day trip to the beach, and

Drew's spirits sank even further when he realized he'd probably be uninvited from that outing.

But he didn't send the text. Gretchen had said she wasn't upset about Yvonne's kiss. Though Drew knew that couldn't really be true, when he'd asked what was the problem, she'd said her granddad's farm.

Gretchen wanted the farm.

"Joel," Drew said as he swung his jean-clad legs over the side of the couch and sat up. He strode into the kitchen, where the lights still burned. His mother wasn't there, but Joel sat at the dining room table, a bowl of pickle-flavored sunflower seeds in front of him.

"What if I wanted to sell the farm to Gretchen?" Drew asked.

Joel gave him a satisfied smile, which shrank back into the man's serious face almost as fast as it had appeared. "Why do you think I'm still sitting here?"

THE NEXT MORNING, DREW WALKED THROUGH THE farmhouse with Joel, a notebook in his hand so he could write down everything the carpenter said. He'd wanted to do this walk-through with Gretchen, but he hadn't dared call her. He hadn't sent her the text he'd typed out.

Over bacon and eggs, he'd sworn his mother to secrecy after he'd shared his plans to win Gretchen back. She was currently next door, packing up all of Gretchen's and

Dixie's things, which she'd take into town later that afternoon.

"The floor's in good shape," Joel said. "We'll sand it down and refinish it."

Drew added that as the first item on his list.

"It needs appliances and furniture."

Glancing around, Drew could easily tell that the farmhouse was much bigger than the home where he lived in town. His stuff would easily fit here, and he'd have to get some new pieces as well. He pushed the bathroom door open with the eraser on his pencil. "What about in here?"

Joel stepped to his side and peered into the room. "As long as the water works, that's a functional bathroom." He shouldered his way past Drew and twisted the faucet. The water sputtered, but it came on. "Looks good."

"You don't think we need a new tub or toilet?"

"You can get them, sure. Replace it all if you want."

Drew didn't know what he wanted. He wished Gretchen were here to have an opinion about it. He put *tub?* and *toilet?* on his list and moved with Joel to the hall that led back to three bedrooms.

"Master back here," Joel said. "There's another bathroom. Honestly this all looks great. Hire a cleaning service and come get it all freshened up. Then you can repaint if you want. Maybe get new carpet in these rooms. It'll be good as new."

The carpet certainly did hold a lot of dirt, and on a farm,

in a very windy climate, the last five years had accumulated a lot of dust as well.

"Hello?" A woman called from the front of the house, and Drew's heart started tapping at twice the normal speed. He met Joel's eyes, and the older man went first, his boots clomping once they reached the hard floor.

"What are you doing here?" he asked, his voice the unfriendliest Drew had ever heard it. So it wasn't Gretchen.

Drew moved slowly, arriving at the mouth of the hallway to find Yvonne standing just inside the front door. "I came to apologize," she said. "Again."

He didn't want to hear it. "You've already done enough," he said, surprised at the icy edge in his own voice. He hadn't placed any of the blame on her last night. No, he'd directed that all at himself. He should've told Gretchen about the texts. About the meeting in the park. Everything about Yvonne. Then she'd have more background to believe that her advances toward Drew weren't welcome.

But now, faced with the woman who'd caused so much turmoil in his life, Drew's frustration grew. "You should go."

"I'm sorry," she tried again, her eyes and voice desperate.

"You've said that." Joel stepped in front of Drew, shielding him from Yvonne. "Please go."

"All right, I'll go." She shifted so she could see Drew again. "I didn't know you were dating anyone," she said. "That picture on Facebook just sounded like she was someone you'd helped once."

"She was," Drew said.

"Should I talk to her?" Yvonne asked. "I'll tell her it was all my fault, and you had nothing to do with it."

Drew almost said yes, but then he remembered that it wasn't really Yvonne that was the problem. "No, I can take care of it."

She truly looked sorry as she turned and left the farm-house. Joel faced Drew. "Why didn't you have her go talk to Gretchen?"

"I can convince Gretchen that kiss wasn't my fault," he said. "But I need to *show* her that I love her, and want her to be in my life permanently. She needs to know she can rely on me. I need her to know that I don't want this farm unless she comes with it." He drew in a big breath. "And we've got a long way to go before it'll be fit for her to live in. So let's keep going."

Joel followed him into the kitchen and deemed all the cabinetry could be sanded and painted and be good as new before he asked, "So you love Gretchen, huh?"

Drew nodded, wishing he felt happier about that fact. Wishing Joel hadn't been the first one he'd told.

"So maybe she doesn't need to wait until the farmhouse is finished to know that," he said.

Drew didn't answer. He simply followed Joel upstairs to the two bedrooms and the bathroom up there, wrote notes about the floors, the walls, and the windows. They assessed the deck off the kitchen, and the patio beyond that. And then of course, there was the yard and the gardens and the farm.

He didn't need to get all of that in tip-top shape before he approached Gretchen. Just the house. And so it wouldn't take six months or more until he could talk to her again, he needed to enlist some help.

ON SATURDAY MORNING, ALMOST A WEEK LATER, HE STOOD ON the back porch of the farmhouse and surveyed the crowd he'd invited out to lunch and a day of hard work. His brother, Adam, who had brought Trent and his five-year-old son with him. Russ, who had nothing better to do in the evenings. His mother and Joel. And Janey, who had taken the most convincing to come. Not only had Drew had to explain that he'd done nothing wrong, that that kiss wasn't his fault, and that he was trying to make things right, he had to get her to bring Dixie with her.

He'd called. He'd texted. He'd stopped by her house after work and begged.

And she'd finally relented. Dixie stood next to his mother, who kept her arm around her protectively. Jess waited only a pace away, and Janey right next to him.

"Thanks for coming," Drew said, gripping his notebook extra tight. "My mom has pizza next door, and we'll head over there and eat later." He glanced at the house behind him. "So I want to get this house fixed up fast. I had a cleaning crew come through this week, and we're ready to sand floors and cabinets, paint walls and trim, and move in a few pieces of furniture." He toed the deck, where some of the boards had come loose. "And stabilize this deck."

Drew had already explained to everyone there what he needed their help with. "So let's get started." He turned and crossed the deck to be the first to enter the house, footsteps cascading behind him. He had gone with Joel to buy the bright white trim color for the ceilings and baseboards. The gray would go on all the walls. Boxes of blinds waited in the living room, along with cans of stain for the floor, two industrial sanders Joel had rented, and every other home improvement tool Drew could think of.

He'd gone to the bank and qualified for a home equity loan to pay for everything, and Adam stepped over to the painting supplies and started handing out rollers and brushes to people. He spoke in his Chief of Police voice and sent people to different rooms to do various tasks.

Soon enough, only Drew remained near the painting supplies, which had been stacked near the back door.

"Drew?"

He turned at the innocent sound of Dixie's voice. He crouched down to her height and pulled her into a hug, hoping she hadn't felt abandoned by him this past week. Thankfully, she willingly accepted his embrace, her slight shoulders shaking as she cried.

"I'm so sorry, Dix," he said, his voice thick. "I messed up."

"I guess everyone makes mistakes," she said, pulling back.

"I'm trying to fix it. You know that's what this is, right?"

She swiped at her eyes and nodded. "Yeah, I know. Janey told me."

"And you can't tell your mom." He looked at her and wiped her eyes too. "It's a secret until I'm ready to try to win her back."

Alarm raced across her face. "She'll ask me what I did with Jess today."

"You just tell her...a version of the truth. You played, and painted some stuff, ate pizza, and had a good time."

"That's not lying?"

Drew couldn't help smiling at her. "I don't think so. And when the house is finished, I'll somehow get your mom to come out here and see it, and I'll apologize, and—" He cleared his throat, his plans for getting Gretchen back not quite as solid as they probably should be.

"I'm going to ask her to marry me," he finished, speaking as strongly as he could. "Would that be all right with you?"

Dixie nodded, a fresh set of tears tracking down her face.

"Why are you crying then?" Drew never wanted to see the girl cry again. It hurt his heart too much, and Dixie had already endured so many painful things.

"Because that was my wish," she said in a voice higher than normal. "I've wished everyday for three months that you would marry my mom, and I didn't think it was going to come true."

Surprise streamed through Drew as he hugged Dixie again. "So maybe with really big wishes that involve more than one person, it takes more than a month."

That got her to laugh, and Drew touched his forehead to hers. "All right, Miss Dixie. If you don't want to be a liar, you're going to have to get some work done around here." He straightened and handed her a paintbrush. "Go find Jess and do whatever he's doing."

Dixie saluted with the paintbrush and headed up the flight of stairs just to the right of the back door. Drew watched her go, his heart as light as it had been since the Lavender Festival.

He glanced up at the ceiling, which was a horrible shade of yellow, and sighed. There was still a long way to go before he could bring Gretchen out here to this farm and propose.

As he picked up a rotary sander and joined Joel on sanding down the cabinets, Drew started brainstorming ways he could get Gretchen to come out here. He hadn't seen her once this week in the gardens, not that he was at his parents' farm at seven-thirty anymore.

No matter what he did, he knew his first contact back with her would have to be meaningful and magnificent. Her old walls of refusing to rely on anyone else had probably been re-erected, and he'd have to find a way to break them down.

23

Gretchen yawned and it wasn't even noon yet. She finished the funeral pieces and set them in the refrigeration unit for the family to pick up. Her nerves assaulted her, because it was Augustus Hammond and his daughter Yvonne who needed the funeral arrangements. Glenny Hammond had passed away, after only a few months' battle with cancer.

Gretchen hadn't seen or spoken to Drew in almost a month. She hadn't seen or spoken to hardly anyone in that time, except Janey and the customers she had. When Augustus had come to order the flowers, Yvonne hadn't come with him, but she fully expected to see the woman today.

She'd never been so lonely as she had been this past month, not even after Aaron died. After the funeral had ended, after everyone had gone home, it had just been her and Dixie. But since Gretchen had taken Dixie from the lavender farm, the girl hardly spoke to her anymore.

Sabra said she was fine at the daycare. She talked to the other kids, got along great, and seemed to be having fun. Janey took her whenever possible, and all Gretchen could get out of her was that she and Jess had painted that day.

Gretchen had never known Dixie to like to paint so much. She still practiced her piano every day as requested, and she snuggled in bed with Gretchen most nights. She'd simply...lost her voice. Gretchen supposed she couldn't blame Dixie. She'd acted similarly after her dad had died.

But Drew wasn't her father.

As Gretchen looked at her calendar to check what the next event was, a flash of understanding hit her. Dixie had viewed Drew as her father—or at least the man she wanted to take the job.

"How did I miss that?" she asked the empty shop. The sunflowers she'd harvested that morning didn't answer. She sighed, her decision to cut Drew out of their lives wavering. It did every day, sometimes more than others. She didn't believe he'd been having a secret relationship with Yvonne behind her back. She didn't believe he'd knowingly stolen her granddad's farm from her. But sometimes she still felt betrayed. And sometimes she was angry. But most of the time she simply experienced sadness. Sadness that she didn't have someone her own age to talk with after work. Sadness that she and Dixie couldn't go out to the lavender farm anymore. Sadness that she'd lost Donna and Joel as friends. Sadness that she couldn't kiss Drew whenever she wanted.

She heaved one of those sad sighs just as the bells on the front door jangled. Mabel Magleby walked in, clutching a fistful of papers in her hand. "I hope you've been keeping your roses in bloom," she said. She smacked the papers on the desk where Gretchen sat. "Five weddings before Halloween." She beamed at the paperwork. "One of my busiest autumns."

"Five weddings?" Gretchen looked at the top paper. Shellie Blackbriar. Five years younger than Gretchen, she ran the nail salon on Wedding Row.

A single block on the other side of Main Street, Wedding Row boasted everything a bride needed: hair salon, nail artist, dress shop, shoe store, a tailor, a jeweler, and a travel agency for all the honeymoon necessities. There was a florist over there too, and from what Gretchen understood, Molly Panatier and her shop, The Blushing Bride, did absolutely fine.

Gretchen examined the paper Shellie had filled out at the Magleby Mansion. "She wants all dahlias?" One of Gretchen's favorite wedding flowers, dahlias came in all shapes and sizes. She flipped the page as Mabel confirmed. "And Nancy Allen wants thistle, lavender, and other native plants." She glanced up at Mabel. "Interesting."

"Can you do all of these, or do I need to find someone else?"

"You didn't have to bring them down," Gretchen said as

she pulled her calendar out from under the desk. "I could've come up to the Mansion."

"Yes," Mabel said, glancing around. "Seems rather slow today."

"It's Tuesday," Gretchen said defensively. She began checking the dates, writing in the weddings on the appropriate boxes. "I can do all of these," she said.

"Fabulous." Mabel set an envelope on the counter. "Here's the money for the first half of each then." She turned to leave the shop but twisted back. Gretchen had just started to reach for the money—noting how thick the envelope was—when Mabel said, "I'm so glad you weren't permanently injured earlier this year."

Gretchen switched her attention to the older woman, who so rarely showed such a human side of herself. "Thank you, Mabel."

"You're the best florist we've had in Hawthorne Harbor." She put a rickety smile on her wrinkled face. "How's that boyfriend of yours? His ice cream was so delicious. He deserved to win Lavender King."

"Oh, Drew? He's..." Gretchen lifted her chin. "We broke up."

Mabel came back to the front desk. "You did? Why?"

And Gretchen hadn't even been able to tell him congratulations for winning Lavender King. Everything had happened so fast once his name was called, and their celebration had been cut short by that silly kiss of Yvonne's.

Gretchen didn't want to explain it to Mabel. "Something

silly." She waved her hand as if swatting a fly, putting it on the envelope and sliding it toward her.

Mabel's hand landed on top of hers. "Gretchen." She spoke with such grandmotherly kindness that a punch of emotion landed in Gretchen's chest. She hadn't spoken to her mother in years, and her grandma had died when she was a teen. She really needed someone older and wiser right now, and the way Mabel was looking at her with such tenderness made Gretchen stand a little straighter and pay more attention.

"Don't let him get away over something silly," she said. "If that's really true, if it really is something silly, fix it."

"I don't know how," she said. Every day for the past month, she'd tried to think of a way she could call him and have it be normal. "I think there's something broken inside me."

"Nonsense." Mabel waved her hand. "So life has handed you a few thorns. You know what to do with those."

Did she? Gretchen tilted her head, trying to hear what Mabel was saying.

"Just take it from someone who wishes they would've fixed that silly thing all those years ago." Sadness filled her face, and Gretchen watched her walk out of The Painted Daisy, the chime on the door the only sound.

Gretchen held great respect for Mabel, but now she also knew more about the woman. And she didn't want to be seventy years old, still selling flowers for weddings, when she'd never gotten her own happily-ever-after.

She spun toward the back, fully intending to grab her purse and get herself on Lavender Highway as fast as possible. Her eye caught the red and gold arrangements she'd done for the funeral, and her adrenaline faded.

"Later," she promised herself. She'd wait until the Hammonds picked up their flowers, and then she'd close the shop and go.

Two hours later, Gretchen was about to load up the flowers herself and deliver them to the mortuary. The funeral started in an hour anyway, and she wanted to go out to the lavender farm. Why she thought Drew would be there, she wasn't sure. His days off were random, and he didn't seem to have a schedule for when he worked the morning shift versus the night shift.

She'd thought about and dismissed calling Donna at least a dozen times. The need to go, though, had her stomach clenching and her lungs in knots. Sliding open the refrigeration unit, she retrieved the largest flower arrangement, the one that went over the casket, just as the bell sounded on the door.

"Just a sec," she said, trying not to drop the heavy arrangement as she twisted to see who had come in.

"Oh, that's lovely," a woman said. "That must be my mother's. Let me help you." Another pair of hands supported the weeping blooms in the splay, and Gretchen looked up into the face of Yvonne Hammond.

"I was—uh, I was just going to deliver them," she said. "The funeral is coming up quick."

"We're running a bit behind, yes." Yvonne didn't appear to have been crying. Her makeup sat flawlessly on her face, and every piece of her seemed stitched in perfectly. Gretchen wasn't sure what Drew had liked about her if this was the woman he'd previously dated.

She felt so self-conscious as Yvonne sized her up. Her features softened, and she said, "You still haven't made up with Drew." She wasn't even asking.

Gretchen pressed her lips together and said, "Let me get the rest of the arrangements." She glanced at her planner, which lay open next to the cash register, where she'd written the amount due. "It'll be three hundred and twelve dollars."

Yvonne didn't move a muscle. Not to get out a credit card. Not to help Gretchen as she scurried to get boxes to put the arrangements in. Once ready, she stepped behind the desk and looked at Yvonne.

"You should make up with Drew," she said. "I can't live with this...this break up on my conscience."

It seemed she really wanted to have this conversation. "Did you know we were dating when you kissed him?"

Yvonne's eyes widened. "I swear I didn't." She made a little crossing motion over her heart. "I'd seen your picture on the Fire Department's Facebook page. I thought you were just the woman he'd helped all those years ago."

"I was," she whispered.

"He was not happy I'm back in town," Yvonne said. "Even when we met in the park, he was standoffish, defensive. He accepted my apology, and I tried to go to lunch with him. He disappeared while I was ordering." She gave a short burst of laughter and looked away. "I should've known then."

"Drew's very laid back," Gretchen said. "I'm sure he didn't mean to hurt your feelings." *Or mine.* And she couldn't believe she was trying to reassure this woman.

Yvonne picked up a box of flowers and bent a little under its weight. "Please promise me you'll call him. He must be so miserable."

Did she really care about Drew? Or was this about her having to live with the guilt of breaking them up? Maybe she really hadn't known about Gretchen's relationship with Drew.

"I'll call him," she heard herself promise. She lifted two more boxes and followed Yvonne out to her car. "You sure you don't need help with these?"

"My cousins are all in town," she said. "We'll get them where they need to go."

Gretchen lifted her hand in farewell as the other woman slid into the driver's seat, adjusted her sunglasses, and drove away. Then she sprinted inside the shop, flipped the OPEN sign to CLOSED, and dashed back to the workroom to get her purse and keys.

She couldn't wait to get out to the lavender farm. If Drew wasn't there, she could wander through her grand-dad's wild lavender and steal the peace from it until he showed up. She just had one stop to make, and as Duality came into view, her mouth started to water.

24

Drew worked as fast as he dared standing on a ladder. It was a miracle Gretchen hadn't noticed anything going on with the farmhouse. He noticed where she'd been in her flower gardens. He'd slept at his parents one night and stood on the porch at five-thirty in the morning, watching her prowl through the darkness to find what she needed.

He'd really hated that, and the urgency to get the farmhouse finished had doubled. Since he'd quit working for the paramedic service, he'd had more time to pour into the house. He made sure everything was cleaned up at night, but he wouldn't be able to do that today. Because today, he was giving the exterior of the house a facelift.

It was the last step he needed to accomplish before he'd be ready to bring Gretchen out to the farm. Joel worked on the opposite side of the front door, cutting in around the windows and gutters, and Janey had dropped off Jess and Dixie with explicit instructions not to get in the way.

Oh, and she'd said, "I can't keep telling Gretchen I don't have to work when I do. She knows summer is the busiest time in the park."

"Has she said anything?" Drew had asked.

"No, but if she does, I'm telling her." Janey had looked frazzled, and he didn't want to be the cause of that. So he refilled his sprayer, climbed back on the ladder, and adjusted his face mask before blasting the exposed and repaired wood with the brightest white paint he and Joel had been able to find.

The faster he got this house painted, the sooner he could get Gretchen out here. He worked through the morning, glad to be working on the east side of the house as the sun arced toward the ocean.

School started in a couple of weeks, and he'd really like to be back in her life so he could help her with Dixie. With only a quarter of the house left to paint, he started down the ladder to refill his sprayer one last time.

"Drew!" Dixie's panicked voice made him slip, and his attention went from the ladder to try to find the girl.

He stuttered down the last three rungs, his bones cracking against each other, and his momentum taking him all the way to the ground. Pure adrenaline got him back to his feet. "Dix? What is it?"

She and Jess skidded to a stop only a few feet from him. "My mom is here," she panted.

Alarms sounded in Drew's brain, and he spun as if she'd be standing right behind him. What should he do? He couldn't hide the equipment now—or the house.

"Where is she?" he asked.

"She pulled in at Donna's," Jess said. "We saw her and ran straight over here."

"So maybe my mom will stall her." And there were several tall trees separating the two houses. Maybe he had a few minutes.

Dixie frowned and stepped closer to him. He brushed his hands down his messy clothes. His jeans were smeared with paint, and his T-shirt had drips in gray and white. "I thought you wanted her to come out to the farmhouse," Dixie said.

"Yeah, but not yet." Drew ran his hands through his hair and could barely complete the action because there was so much paint. He needed to shower. And eat. And get the rest of his stuff moved in.

But a powerful, aching need had him looking toward his parents' farm and commanding him to get over there and tell Gretchen how he felt and then show her what he'd done.

He looked back at the kids. "What have you guys been wishing for this month?"

"We can't tell you—" Jess started, but Dixie blurted, "That you and my mom would get back together."

Jess stared at her like she'd just told him Santa Claus wasn't real. "Dixie," he hissed.

"You don't have to tell yours."

The boy's face colored. "Good, because I'm not going to." He folded his arms, and Drew noticed his muscles had started to fill out a little bit with all the work around the farm he'd been doing this summer.

Drew's nerves felt like someone had dropped them into a wood chipper and switched it on high. He took a slow, deliberate breath and looked at Dixie. He extended his hand toward her. "Should we go talk to your mom?"

Dixie shrieked and cheered before slipping her hand into his and practically pulling him toward the gate that Joel had put in the fence to allow easy access to both properties from the backyard.

Once they passed all the outbuildings and the house came into view, Drew's feet stalled. "You go on," he told Dixie. "I need another minute."

She didn't ask him any questions, thankfully. She broke into a run and entered the house. Drew heard his mother exclaim, "There's Miss Dixie!" in a falsely bright voice.

He breathed in and then out. In and out. He could do this. *Just go in there and talk to her.* Surely she wouldn't still be mad. And once she saw the house...

But he couldn't get his feet to move. Then he didn't have to, because Gretchen practically tore the back door of its hinges as she yanked it open.

She'd taken two stomps outside when she caught sight of him. She froze too. Shock traveled across her face, replaced quickly by that anger he'd just seen. Gretchen's fists balled and she advanced on him like a panther stalking its prey. "Tell me what my daughter is doing out here when she should be at Janey's."

"She and Jess have been helping me with the house."

"Helping you with the house." She cocked her hip and folded her arms. She scanned him from head to toe, her features softening.

"It was supposed to be a surprise," he said.

"Mom!" Dixie burst out of the back door too, slowing when she saw them. Drew thought she looked a little wheezy. "Don't be mad at him anymore. Please."

"Come on, Dix," his mom said. "Let's go find your inhaler. You're not breathing right."

"Thank you, Donna," Gretchen said, her voice much more tender when she spoke to his mother.

So maybe she was still mad at him. He hooked his thumb over his shoulder. "You want to go take a look?" He only had one thing left—the house. If that didn't win her over, Drew didn't know what would.

He moved away without waiting for her to follow. He wasn't even sure she would, so when he heard her footsteps on the gravel behind him, relief rushed through him like river rapids.

"So Joel put a gate here," he said, finding his confidence. "So we can go back and forth between the farms without having to go around to the road. That way, Dixie can—" He cleared his throat, the words suddenly gone.

Gretchen didn't help him out either, but simply watched his with curious eyes. "Dixie can what?"

"Dixie can go over to my mom's whenever she wants," he finished.

"Drew." She shook her head. "We live in town."

"Come see the house," he said, a definite note of pleading in his tone. Gates weren't that impressive, and he wasn't giving up until he was on one knee and she said no.

"So the deck was pretty unstable," he said. "But we pulled up the loose planks and found the rotted ones underneath. Joel and I did that in an afternoon. Then we got it all sanded down." He went up the five steps to the deck. "And Jess and Dixie stained it this color." He smiled at the honeyed wood they'd worked on for two solid days. "It looks good, don't you think?"

"Does Janey know you're doing this?"

"Yes." He walked across the deck. "You can't be mad at her. She's been nervous about it for a month. It's not her fault." He tossed Gretchen a look. "It's mine."

He cleared his throat. "I'm going to put my gas grill here. I bought a new storm door here, so we can open both the front and the back and get the ocean breeze blowing through in the afternoons." He stepped into the house, desperate for her to compliment the house. Say something about the efforts he'd taken to make her happy.

"This is the new kitchen. Same cabinets. We just sanded them down and painted them white. I didn't get new countertops." He ran his fingertips along the light brown ones that had been there. "I figured maybe you'd like to pick out something for the house."

She said nothing, and when Drew dared to look at her, he caught her wiping her eyes.

"Gretchen." He gathered her into his arms, happiness pouring through him when she practically wilted against him. "I love you, Gretchen," he murmured, his mouth close to her ear. "Please forgive me."

She straightened and cleared her throat. Drew's whole body ached to be close to her again. "So let me get this straight." She looked past the dining room table he'd already moved over from his place and into the empty living room. Everything was new, from the paint on the walls, to the color of the floors, to the light fixtures Adam had picked out and then installed.

"You've been fixing up this house, using *children*, to impress me."

Drew thought he detected the hint of a tease in her sparkling eyes. "Did it work?"

She giggled as she pushed her palm into his chest. He caught her arm around the wrist and tugged her close to him again. "I love you," he repeated. "I want you to marry me and bring Dixie out here to live with me." He gazed down at her, nothing but love flowing through him.

She looked up at him too, a smile gracing her beautiful mouth. "I came to talk to you," she said. "Because I didn't want something silly to keep us apart."

"That kiss meant nothing."

"I know that."

"I'd give you this farm," he said. "And me with it, if you'll have me." When she said nothing, he laced his fingers through hers and said, "Let's go see the bedrooms. Dixie chose the color for hers."

But Gretchen pulled on his hand, and he turned back to her. "I don't need to see the bedrooms."

Drew's eyebrows lifted. "No?"

She shook her head slowly, her auburn ponytail swinging. "No. I love you, Drew, and I'll take you with the farm."

Joy exploded through him, and he laughed as he caught her in a hug and swung her around. He set her on her feet, very aware that Dixie and his mother had just come up the steps and onto the deck. "I'm going to kiss her now," he called out to them.

And he did, to the chorus of a soft sigh from his mother and a whispered, "*Yesss,*" from Dixie.

An hour later, he had shown her every improvement in the house and talked her ear off about his plans for the yard and the outbuildings. Now, though, they sat on the swing on his parents' front porch, gently rocking back and forth.

Drew knew they had more to talk about, but neither of them seemed to want to start the conversation. Finally, he asked, "Why'd you come out here on a Tuesday afternoon?"

"Oh, something someone said to me."

"Who?"

"Mabel."

"Magleby?"

Gretchen snuggled further into his side. "Yeah, Mabel Magleby. And then Yvonne came by the shop to get the flowers for her mother's funeral."

Drew's chest seized. He'd forgotten about the funeral. The only reason he knew Yvonne's mother had died was because Russ had told him. He did miss his friends at work, especially Russ.

"So you talked to Yvonne?" Drew asked.

"She begged me to come talk to you." She lifted one shoulder. "I guess having two people stop by in the same day kicked me into gear."

Janey's Jeep pulled into the driveway, and she got out in her forest green park ranger uniform. Her sigh was audible as she glanced toward the other property and scanned the farm area.

"Up here," Drew called, and Janey headed for the porch. She saw Gretchen sitting next to Drew and stopped.

"He made me do it," she said.

Gretchen looked at Drew, who shrugged. "I can be pretty convincing when I have to be." He started to laugh, and Gretchen joined in.

Janey relaxed and approached the railing. "So we've made up." A brief smile appeared on her face, and she kept most of her attention on Gretchen. "Can I talk to you for a few minutes?"

"Yeah, of course." Gretchen patted Drew's knee and stood. "Does your mom still do dinner in the evenings?"

"I'll ask her and text you." He watched the two women

walk down the driveway and disappear in the direction of the other farmhouse. Drew felt more settled than he had all summer, and he went into the house to take a shower and get all the paint out of his hair. Clean and dressed, he wandered over to his farmhouse and discovered that Joel had finished the spraying.

"Thank you," Drew said, his fondness for the man stronger than ever. He stepped into him, though he wore messy, painted clothes and Drew had just showered, and gave him a quick hug. "Thank you for everything, Joel."

"Of course."

Drew may have imagined the extra hitch of emotion in his stepfather's voice, but he didn't think so.

"So you and Gretchen are good?"

"We're talking," Drew said as they walked through the gate and back to the farmhouse. "So yeah, we'll be good."

25

G retchen walked beside Janey, not sure what to say.

"I'm sorry," Janey blurted as they passed the fence and crossed from the Loveland Farm to the one Drew had been fixing up for the past month.

"I'm not mad," Gretchen said. "Well, I was." She looked up into the sky and tried to sort through her confusing feelings. "I think I just felt...I don't know. Naïve or something. I mean, how out of it am I to not even notice that my own daughter had been staining a deck and painting baseboards?"

Janey giggled and looped her arm through Gretchen's, but Gretchen didn't see anything funny about the situation.

"Drew swore us all to secrecy."

"Who else helped?"

"Oh, everyone. Adam, Trent, Russ, all the guys they

could spare from the EMT service. The kids. Me. His parents." Janey sighed. "He really loves you."

"I know he does," Gretchen whispered. She could feel Drew's love all the way down into her soul.

"I didn't want to lie to you. I told him that if you asked, I would tell you the truth."

Gretchen smiled and kept her focus on the gravel at their feet. "Thank you, Janey. You've always been such a great friend to me."

"I am pretty great." She laughed, the sound fading quickly. "Now I just need to find my roadside hero the way you did."

Gretchen giggled too. "Well, he does have a brother…"

Janey scoffed and waved her free hand. "Adam Herrin? Nah. I've known him my whole life, and there's just no spark there, you know?"

"You think there was a spark between me and Drew when he delivered Dixie on the side of the road?" Gretchen stopped walking and looked at Janey. She saw pain at the same time she saw hope.

"Of course not."

"No. But this time, there was. Things change. *People* change." She couldn't believe she was the one saying so, but she was right. She reached out and brushed Janey's hair off her face. "So maybe Russ. He's an EMT. Could be your road-side hero."

Janey rolled her eyes, but Gretchen pressed on. "Hey,

he's single. Good-looking. And he's only been in town for what? A few years?"

"Five years," Janey said. "I think." She drew in a breath and blew it out. "I don't know, Gretchen. Dixie's more easygoing than Jess. He's been moody lately, and I'm worried about him."

"He's a great kid. And he likes Drew."

"Yeah, but Drew's yours." Janey gave her a sad smile. "I'm happy for you, Gretchen." She stopped walking and hugged her friend. "I'm glad you're not mad at me."

"Nothing to be mad about." They turned around and headed back to the farmhouse in silence. But Gretchen started thinking through all the eligible bachelors in Hawthorne Harbor. After all, Janey deserved a happily-ever-after too.

Friday afternoon, Gretchen bustled around the house, looking in cupboards and under the sink for the sunscreen. She couldn't find it. "Dix! Do you have sunscreen in your bathroom?"

"No," she called back. "We're out, remember?" She entered the kitchen wearing a bright pink tank top and a pair of plaid shorts Donna had bought her. "We ran out last time we went to the beach."

Gretchen groaned and nodded. "Yeah, you're right." She

lifted her phone from the counter and tapped on Drew's name. She hesitated, as she'd already asked him to stop and get drinks and ice for the cooler.

But he'd already be at the store...

She dropped her thumb onto the call button and said, "Hey, are you still at the store?" when he picked up.

"Yeah, headed to check out now."

"So we're out of sunscreen."

"I can grab some. Just a sec." A few seconds later, he said, "Oh-kay, there's like a million different kinds. What do you want?"

"A spray, at least thirty SPF. Fifty is good for Dixie. She's so fair."

"Thirty...fifty. Got it." A beat of silence passed. "Anything else while I'm still here?"

Gretchen chuckled, and said, "I certainly hope not. We're almost ready here." She hung up, and gazed at his face on her screen for an extra moment. School started on Monday, and they were headed to the beach for the weekend—their first trip together. Gretchen's nerves fired strangely from time to time.

She wasn't sure why she was nervous, probably because she and Drew had been talking a lot about marriage, when they should have the wedding, and if she should invite her parents or not. He wanted to. She didn't.

And he hadn't even proposed yet. Until he did, she wasn't making any plans.

She took a big breath. So this was just another trip to

the beach with the people she loved. She'd booked a beach-front cottage on Whidbey Island, with three bedrooms and three bathrooms, and she did not want to make any adult decisions this weekend.

Drew knocked at the same time he entered the front door, plastic shopping bags in his hands. "Sunscreen and drinks."

Gretchen went to help him, and told Dixie to unload the drink pouches into the cooler. Working together, she caught a glimpse of what family life would be like once she and Drew did get married.

She paused, drinking in the moment and committing it to memory. She hadn't done much of that with Aaron, and like Dixie, she'd started to forget.

Drew dumped ice over the drinks and Gretchen put the cold cuts and cheese on top so it wouldn't get waterlogged. He caught her eye, and she saw something in his. Something that said he wanted to say something but didn't know how.

"Dix, go grab your beach bag. It's on your bed." Gretchen smiled at her daughter. "And make sure you have your inhaler."

Once she'd flounced away, Gretchen leaned into Drew and kissed him. "Tell me what you're thinking about."

His hands snaked around her waist and he leaned his forehead against hers. "I'm glad you called and asked me to get the stuff at the store."

Gretchen hadn't known what he was going to say, but that wasn't it. "Oh."

He inched back and looked into her eyes. "I like it when you need help. I like that you're relying on me to provide that help."

"It was a sugary drink and some ice."

"And before, you'd have had to go get it yourself." He released her and stepped back to resume packing the cooler. "I'll put this in the back of the truck and come help with the bags."

"We can get those," Gretchen said, unsure of why she couldn't just let go and rely on him to do the heavy lifting, the errands, all of it. She took the bags out to the driveway, and she let Drew lift them into the bed. Maybe that was all she needed. Someone to meet her halfway.

By the time they arrived at their cottage and checked in, the afternoon was fading into evening. Dixie changed into her swimming suit anyway and went running across the patio, down a few steps and onto the sand. Gretchen watched her go, the joy flying off of her so infectious that Gretchen had to smile.

Drew wrapped his arm around her shoulders and pulled her into his body. "Chief and Blue would've loved this beach."

"Next time we'll book somewhere that's pet friendly."

Several beats of perfection passed, and Gretchen couldn't believe that she was standing here, with Drew. It seemed surreal almost.

"So I stopped by Engagements the other day," he said, and Gretchen flinched.

"No." She shook her head. "We agreed that this weekend —the *last* weekend before Dixie has to go back to school— would be non-serious."

He chuckled and swept his lips across her temple. "Right. No talking about weddings, or parents, or venues."

"Or engagement rings." She nudged him with her hip. "It's nothing but two days of sand castles and sleeping in and eating dessert for breakfast."

"All right," he said in a higher voice than normal. "If that's what you want."

"It's what I *need*," she said. "Remember how I have five weddings in the next six weeks?"

"I remember," he murmured. "No ladders, okay?"

She laughed and snuggled closer to him. "Oh, I don't know. The last time I used a ladder, you came to my rescue. Again. Without that, maybe we wouldn't be here now."

"Oh, we'd be here," he said.

Surprise shot through Gretchen. "You think so?"

He gazed at her with the same golden warmth that the sun was casting over the water. "Do you even know how much your spare tire was?"

She blinked, his conversation topics full of surprises today. "Well, no."

He grinned and lightly touched his mouth to hers. "That's because I paid for it. I was doing everything I could to make sure I'd see you again."

She wrapped her arms around him and laid her cheek against his chest, happier than she thought she could ever be in a world without her first husband.

26

Drew got out the cold cuts and the jar of mayo and set them on the counter in the beach rental. He checked out the huge wall of windows that faced the water just to make sure Dixie and Gretchen were still knee-deep in the ocean.

Of course they were. He'd been in the house for less than sixty seconds. He could count on Dixie to beg and whine to stay in the water until Gretchen dragged her in to eat. So he had plenty of time to get the diamond out, get it set right in the middle of the table, right where Gretchen couldn't miss it.

But he wasn't sure if he *should*.

Gretchen had expressly said she didn't want to even talk about engagement rings. He hadn't told her he'd gone to Wedding Row and bought her a ring. Hadn't told her that he'd talked to Mabel about a spring wedding. Hadn't told her that he'd called her granddad and asked for her hand in marriage.

And what a conversation that had been. Drew smiled at the way Will Ryder had said, "You should definitely marry her, Drew. You actually know lavender from a daisy."

Drew had chuckled, glad he did—now. Gretchen still hadn't shown him her cross-pollinated indigo daisies. She claimed they weren't ready to show to anyone yet, and though Drew had helped her cut the flowers she'd needed for a couple of months, he'd never seen the indigo daisies in her garden.

The doorbell rang, and Drew nearly jumped out of his skin. He hurried to answer it, taking the vase full of yellow and white daisies from the man on the doorstep. He couldn't speak much more than "Thanks," and the glass and water and flowers felt so heavy in his hands.

He turned slowly, trying to decide what to do. He could say the owner of the cottage had dropped them by. He didn't have to get out the ring this weekend.

Dixie's voice filtered to him and his muscles seized. They'd come in already? He ducked around the corner and sure enough, they'd come in already.

"Drew?" Gretchen called, and her eyes locked onto him a moment later. He had no choice but to continue into the kitchen, and set the vase of daisies on the counter.

"What are those?" She eyed the flowers as she toweled her hair.

"Daisies," he said as if she didn't know.

"What's this?" Dixie held the ring box in her hand, her eyes round. She looked up at Drew, and he wasn't sure if he should lunge for the box and hide it behind his back or drop to one knee.

Gretchen had frozen too, and Dixie danced between them. The black velvet box seemed like a spotlight, and Drew didn't know how to turn it off.

"Drew," Gretchen said, drawing out his name in a way that said, *Tell me what's going on right now.*

"Can I have that, please?" Drew glanced at Dixie. And then the flowers. And finally that velvet box. Everything inside him settled, even though all his plans hadn't worked out.

"Drew," Gretchen said again, this time with more snap to her tone.

"Okay, so I know you didn't want to talk about anything serious this weekend. But I'd sort of already made a few plans, and well, I was trying to decide what to do about them."

Gretchen reached out and trailed her fingers along the petals of one of the white daisies. She didn't say anything, and Drew's emotions surged up his throat.

"So I got these daisies, and I was going to have everything all set out...I don't know. Nicely." He set the ring box on the counter and got out a stack of plates. He got out the cheese, the head of lettuce, and a bottle of mustard. He kept talking as he worked.

"So I was going to have everything out." He spun and

grabbed the macaroni salad she'd made that morning. "And set this right here." He put the ring box on the plates. "Where you'd see it. And then wait for you on the deck, and I don't know…"

Drew stopped talking and moving, realizing that both Dixie and Gretchen were frozen.

"So what's in the box?" Dixie finally asked.

"Dix." Gretchen drew her into her side. "It's a ring."

"How do you know that?" Dixie looked up at her mother.

She giggled and looked down at her. "I just do. Rings come in boxes like that, Dix. Expensive rings." She met Drew's eyes again, and he was struck breathless. "Expensive rings from Engagements." She cocked her eyebrow.

Drew shrugged. "I told you I'd stopped by." He shook his head, none of this going how he'd planned. He wasn't sure what the next step was, because so much depended on her reaction.

He grabbed the ring box, cracked it open, and dropped to one knee. "I love you, Gretchen Samuels. Will you marry me?"

Dixie squealed, and Gretchen gasped.

"Mom!" Dixie danced in front of her. "You're going to say yes, right?"

"Yes," Gretchen said, a smile blooming on her beautiful face. She looked at Dixie and then right into Drew's eyes. "Yes."

Want to read Adam's love story? Read on for a sneak peek of chapter one of **THE DAY HE STOPPED IN, available in Kindle Unlimited.**

Or if you like to save money, you can **get the WHOLE SERIES for only $9.99 - and the boxed set is available in Kindle Unlimited!** You'll save 40% rather than buying the books individually.

Yay for Drew and Gretchen! I'm so glad they made their relationship work! **Please tap here to leave a review for this book.**

Join Elana's newsletter to get your next sweet romance - a Bride in THE HELICOPTER PILOT'S BRIDE.

Hawthorne Harbor
SECOND CHANCE ROMANCE
the end

SNEAK PEEK! THE DAY HE STOPPED IN CHAPTER ONE

"I don't want to go," Adam Herrin said, but his best friend would not be deterred.

"Come on," Matt said, that perpetual smile still stuck to his face. "You like the Fall Festival." He nudged him, making Adam slop milk over the side of his cereal bowl. "Besides, you can pretend like you're already on the force. You know, scan for vandals and all that while I find the prettiest girl there and ask her to dance."

Adam grunted and wiped the spilled milk from the countertop of the apartment they shared. He'd been back in Hawthorne Harbor for just over a month, and he'd just finished his final round of police interviews.

"I'm starting work on Monday," he told Matt.

His friend whooped and sent his spoon clattering into his cereal. "You got on? They hired you?"

Adam let a smile spread across his face. "Yeah. I found out last night."

"And you're just now telling me?"

"You were out really late with Bea."

The joy on Matt's face disappeared as if Adam had flipped a switch. "Yeah, well, not tonight."

"You mean we won't be out late?" Adam's heart lifted, as he preferred the early-to-bed, early-to-rise method of living.

"Of course we'll be out late," Matt said. "I just meant not with Bea."

"You don't like her?"

"She's not my type."

Adam pictured the tall, beautiful blonde that he and Matt had grown up with. Both men had gone away to college and then returned to their hometown, and they were both settling back into the social scene of the small, beach-side town of Hawthorne Harbor. Bea Arnold had gone to college too, but only for a couple of years. Just long enough to get an accounting certificate so she could handle the finances of her father's hardware store.

"Well, if she's not, good luck finding someone here," Adam said, picking up his bowl and rinsing it out in the sink.

"There are lots of women here," Matt said, his blue eyes taking on that glint that said Adam wouldn't like was about to come out of his mouth. But he said nothing. Just refocused on his breakfast.

Adam didn't need a lot of women; he had his eye on one:

Janey Burns. He'd known her for as long as he could remember, as she was his younger brother's age. Just a couple of years younger than him, and still single. She'd been back in town for a few months, and she was already putting her Natural Resource Management degree to use at Olympic National Park, just a few minutes away from Hawthorne Harbor.

He'd had a crush on Janey since his junior year of high school. She was beautiful and kind and smart. But she'd had a boyfriend on the football team, and Adam had graduated before her and left town while she still had two years of high school to finish.

But tonight....

He banished the treacherous thought and said, "I'm going to go running."

"Again?" Matt lifted his eyebrows and Adam shook his head and started down the hall to his bedroom to change. "You already got the job!" Matt yelled after him, with a loud bit of laughter coming with it.

Sure, Adam had gotten the entry-level policeman job with the Hawthorne Harbor Police Department. But he wouldn't stay there for long. Oh, no. Adam had plans to climb that ladder until he stood at the top of the department, and that meant he had to maintain his top physical condition.

So he ran. His favored route took him right past Janey's house, which sat near the beach. He told himself it wasn't stalking, because she didn't even live there anymore. Her parents did though, and he waved to her mother as she worked in the rose garden to prepare it for the winter ahead. Though it didn't snow in Hawthorne Harbor, because the town sat right on the northwest edge of the North American continent, it got plenty cold.

Adam loved the cool sea spray in his face as he ran, the homes eventually fading behind him and the cliffs coming into view. High above the water sat the Magleby Mansion, where he'd worked mowing lawns and raking leaves as a teenager.

Without a job to fill his time, Adam spent his time working out and making plans for his first day on the job. When Matt knocked on his door and said, "Are you coming?" Adam couldn't wait to get out of the house.

They arrived at the Fall Festival, which took place in the square in downtown Hawthorne Harbor. The shops on Main Street seemed to glow among the twilight as dusk came quicker now that fall was upon them.

He hunched his broad shoulders and stuck his hands in his pockets, his eyes constantly scanning for danger. Okay, fine. He wasn't looking for danger. Not tonight, at least. He let his mind have a brief fantasy of this time next year, and if he'd be on duty like the two officers he spotted hanging out near the face-painting booth.

The scent of freshly juiced apples hung in the air, along with a heavy dose of cinnamon. Matt brought him a cup of hot apple cider, and Adam wrapped both hands around it, back to searching the crowd for the one woman he wanted to see.

Janey Burns.

Tonight was the night. He was going to ask her to dance, and not just because they'd been old friends. His pulse picked up, and he couldn't make sense of what Matt had said. His friend handed him his plastic cup of cider and pressed through the crowd to an auburn-haired woman Adam couldn't quite remember.

Her name sat on the tip of his tongue, and he watched as Matt smiled and laughed and somehow knew exactly how to causally touch Nina—aha! Nina Goodwin—on the back as they walked out to the dance floor that had been laid over the grass in the park.

A band sat down on the other end, where a temporary stage had been erected. The slow warblings of a ballad filled the air, and Adam turned away from the blissful couples swaying together.

Carved pumpkins glittered with candlelight, and he smiled at their garish faces as he passed. Families were finishing up with the pony rides and petting zoo, and he leaned against a fence post as the day crowd thinned and the evening festivities took over.

A flash of brilliant brown hair the color of unroasted coffee beans caught his eye, and he finally saw Janey squeezing between two people as she headed toward the food booths. A jolt shot through Adam's bones and muscles, somehow kickstarting him into following her.

She was with one of her sisters, and he kept his eye on Anabelle's head, as she stood quite a bit taller than Janey. They stopped for funnel cakes, and he paused as if he were going to get a hot dog.

This is stupid, he told himself as the two women turned. Anabelle looked right at him and so did Janey.

"Hey, Adam," she said, a brilliant smile lighting up her whole face. Adam wanted to bask in the warmth of it for the rest of his life.

He managed to say, "Hey, Janey. Anabelle," but his voice sounded like he was suffering from a bad chest cold. He tried to clear the nerves from his throat and he almost ended up choking.

"Are you heading over to the dance?" he asked.

"Yes," Anabelle said, her eyes sliding down him in an appraising way. "Are you?"

He shrugged as if he wasn't really sure what his evening plans were.

"Why do you have two cups of cider?" Janey asked.

Adam looked dumbly at the red plastic cups he held. "Oh, one's for Matt."

"Matt Germaine?" Anabelle asked, her interest obviously piqued. "I didn't know Matt was back in town." She looked at Adam as if he'd deliberately kept the information from her.

"He's dancin' with...someone," he said.

Anabelle hooked her arm through Janey's and bent her

head toward her sister's. They moved away, pressing back through the crowd to the dance floor.

Adam followed, because he didn't have much else to do and well, he wanted to dance with Janey. If he could get her sister off with Matt, Adam might have a chance at more than friendship with the girl he'd been thinking about for eight years.

"See? There he is." Adam gestured with Matt's apple cider toward where he stood on the dance floor, this time a blonde in his arms. Adam once again marveled at the easiness with which Matt did everything. He'd studied mechanical engineering at school while Adam had done a year in the police academy and then three years to get his criminal justice degree.

"What's he doing back?" Anabelle asked.

"He's working for the ferry system," Adam said. "He's their lead engineer. Started last week." He wanted to blurt out that he'd be starting with the police department on Monday, but neither Anabelle nor Janey asked.

They both couldn't seem to tear their eyes from Matt, and Adam frowned. He lifted his drink to his lips and in that brief flash of time, both women slipped away from him and out onto the dance floor.

Janey danced with a man named Clint that Adam recognized from the automotive shop on the edge of town. His mood darkened by the moment as she laughed and spun, her dark locks spraying out behind her when her fourth dance of the night twirled her.

He finished his cider and threw both cups in the trash.

It was his turn.

No more sitting on the sidelines, watching.

He'd taken two steps onto the dance floor when the people parted to give him an unobstructed view of Janey. Her face was flushed and her smile captivated him.

A man stepped up to her and half-bowed to her, his hand extended as he asked her to dance. She ducked her head, the flush turning into a full-blown blush as she put her hand in his and they situated themselves for the next slow dance of the evening.

Adam stared, sure he'd be able to ask Janey to dance after Matt finished with her. After all, neither of them had danced more than one song with the same partner.

But the song ended, and Matt kept his hands on Janey's waist. They danced another song, and then one that wasn't even meant for couples as the beat took the music into the rock category.

Adam's feet seemed to have grown roots. He couldn't move them though he desperately wanted to. He couldn't look away either.

So he saw Matt lead Janey off the dance floor, her hand tucked securely into his, and watched them disappear into the night.

SNEAK PEEK! THE DAY HE STOPPED IN: FOURTEEN YEARS LATER

J aney Germaine stood in front of her mirror, wondering when the lines around her eyes had gotten so deep. Or when the bags underneath had become some dark.

"Mom!" Her twelve-year-old son yelled from the kitchen, and Janey startled away from her reflection. So much had happened over the past decade and a half, and each line probably had a dozen stories to tell.

So don't be embarrassed by them, she told herself as she exited her bedroom and found Jess standing in the kitchen, the pantry door flung wide in front of him.

"Do we have any blueberry Pop-Tarts?"

"If we do, they'll be in there."

"I don't see them."

"Then we don't have any."

Jess grumbled and frowned and slammed the pantry

door, shaking the old house. She'd bought it the first summer she'd returned to Hawthorne Harbor, fresh out of college and with a job she'd been lucky to get.

She still had the job at Olympic National Park, something she was grateful for every day. She filled a coffee mug as she kept one eye on Jess. He'd started complaining that she watched him too much, so she'd been trying to do it on the sly these days.

"What are you doing after school today?" she asked.

"Don't know," he mumbled.

"I'm off today, and we can get Dixie when the elementary kids get out and go out to the lavender farm." She lifted her mug to her lips and took a sip of the bitter liquid. "I mean, if you want." She didn't want Jess to think she really cared about what he did or who he spent time with. She hoped he wouldn't veto the idea just because she'd suggested it, something that had been happening a lot since he started at the junior high a few weeks ago.

He picked up his backpack and threaded his arms through the straps. "Sure, whatever." He stomped on the end of his skateboard and caught the front of it as it popped up. "Bye."

"Bye," she called after him. "Have a good day!"

She used to drive him to school every day, or her best friend Gretchen would stop by. Both single moms, they'd been watching out for each other for years. But with Gretchen engaged now, and to be married by Christmas,

Janey stared out the window and wondered if she should get back into the dating pool.

Problem was, she didn't even own an appropriate swimming suit for such things. She had no idea who was available in town, or how Jess would take the news of her dating again, or why anyone would be interested in a thirty-seven-year-old woman with a twelve-year-old son and a husband who'd died thirteen years ago.

Everyone had loved Matt. It was always "Matt and Janey," never "Janey and Matt." He had a laugh that could fill the sky with fun, fill her heart with joy, fill anything that needed filling.

She saw so much of him in Jess and she stepped into the living room and ran her fingertips along the top edge of a gold frame. The picture inside showed Matt, with his trademark smile on his face. He sat with a very pregnant Janey at the Silver Lake Lodge, a commercial venue inside the National Park where she worked.

She got one free night at the lodge every year, and that year, she and Matt had used it for their anniversary getaway. Little did anyone know that he'd be dead within four months, drowned and presumed lost at sea after the ferry he'd been on had caught on fire and simultaneously gone up in flames and sank into the bay.

Janey turned away from the picture, wondering if it was time to purge the house of them. She'd lived in this space with Matt for exactly thirteen months before he'd left for work and never came home.

She hadn't been able to move, because the scent of his skin was still in some of his shirts. At least back then. She'd brought Jess home to this house. She loved the neighborhood, and everything about the small cottage spoke of home to her.

Carefully, so she wouldn't break the glass, she pushed the frame face-down. Matt's face no longer watched over the happenings in the house, and Janey paused, trying to find her feelings.

One breath in, and everything was okay. Just fine. Two breaths and a sense of...strangeness flowed over her. By the third breath, she could barely get her lungs to expand from the guilt crushing them.

She lifted the picture frame and stared into the handsome face of her husband, the man who had captivated her that night at the Fall Festival all those years ago. Boy, had her older sister been *maaad*.

Anabelle had apparently had a crush on Matt Germaine for a couple of years, and when he'd barely looked her way, Janey wanted to leave the dance with her sister. After all, she and Anabelle had always been close.

Matt had put a wedge between them for the first six months, and then Anabelle had come to terms with the relationship. Meeting her own husband had certainly helped, and she'd gotten married only two months before Matt's accident. Anabelle had been Janey's biggest support during that time, and then her life had moved on. She had three kids now, and while she stopped by often and called or texted Janey everyday, Janey had learned to rely more on Gretchen if she needed help with rides, homework, or babysitting for Jess.

She stared at the picture, the all-too familiar questions flowing through her mind. Do I have to grieve for him forever? Can I ever love someone else again? Should I start dating again?

Sometimes her life felt absolutely unfair. So unfair that it would be hard to breathe and she'd press her hand against her heart to feel it firing against her ribs. Other times, she existed in the world without a care. The taste of butterscotch in her mouth as she hiked, or the scent of pines as she helped junior rangers earn their badges, as easy as anything.

Most days, she oscillated between the two feelings, and the worst part was she never knew when one would strike or how long it would stay.

She listened to the analog clock in the kitchen tick, waiting waiting waiting for something to happen. What, she wasn't sure, and she turned away from the pictures neatly lined up on the mantle and returned to the kitchen.

Janey got a couple of days off each week, but it usually wasn't Saturday and Sunday. Wednesday seemed to be one of the slowest days at the park, so she had that day off. And usually Mondays as well. Jess didn't seem to mind going out to the Loveland's Lavender Farm, but he'd become surlier and surlier in the past couple of months.

On her days off, she usually went back to bed with her cat, Princess, as she had a hard-to-break habit of staying up until all hours of the morning reading. With a bowl of chocolate chips and pretzels nearby, no less.

Surprisingly, it wasn't nighttime that haunted her, but the early morning hours just before the sun rose. She imagined the ferries getting prepped and ready for the day and wondered why her mechanical engineer husband had to be on the only ferry that had malfunctioned in the past two decades.

With a piece of toast and a banana in her hand, she retreated to her bedroom to eat and enjoy her second sleep. As she drifted from consciousness to unconsciousness, she wondered how she could meet a man in this town who didn't know everything about her.

Impossible, her hazy mind thought.

Might be easier anyway, she told herself. *Then you won't have to explain everything about Matt.*

THAT AFTERNOON, FRESH FROM HER MORNING NAP, AND showered, and done with the yard work for the season, Janey sat on the front steps, waiting for her son to come home. When he didn't show up by three-ten—his usual arrival time—she started flipping her phone over and over.

Worry ate at her, first in small bites and then in huge, sweeping waves. But she didn't call. Jess didn't like it when she "babied him" by calling if he was ten seconds late. Sure, they'd had a talk about why it was important to be on time, and that he should send a text, even if it was only five minutes.

Five minutes could mean a lot. So many things could happen in five minutes.

Janey glanced both ways down the street, her heart catapulting to the back of her throat when the police cruiser eased around the corner and headed her way. She knew it was Adam Herrin—the Chief of Police himself—just by the way the car stayed right in the middle of the street and came to a simple stop at the end of her driveway.

With the tinted windows, Janey couldn't see into the backseat, and she didn't want to rush the car anyway. If it was an emergency, Adam wouldn't have driven four miles an hour down the street and he wouldn't have gotten out so slowly a moment ago and be stretching his back like he'd been driving for days now.

She'd known Adam Herrin for almost four decades. Her whole life. They'd been friends in elementary school, a relationship which had lasted all the way through high school and into adulthood. Matt had been his best friend, and Adam had been the best man at their wedding.

He opened the back door of the cruiser and Jess got out, his face set into an angry scowl. Adam said something to him and Jess nodded before he marched up the driveway to where Janey sat on the porch.

"What's going on?" she asked.

"He took my board," Jess said, taking the steps two at a

time and disappearing into the house with a slam of the front door.

Janey flinched, a sigh leaking from her body as Adam popped the trunk on his cruiser and extracted Jess's skateboard. He came up the driveway and sidewalk too, his broad shoulders and mirrored sunglasses so police-like Janey stood and straightened her hair.

Don't be ridiculous, she thought. This was Adam. He'd seen her at her worst, all red-eyed and leaking from everywhere after Matt had died. It had been Adam who'd come to get her, to tell her about the fire. Adam who'd driven her to the dock. Adam who'd held her hand, and kept her close, and helped her stand when it was declared the ferry was a total loss.

Adam who'd stayed on her couch that night, listening to her sob and then dealing with a three-month-old Jess when he screamed and fussed in the middle of the night.

"Afternoon, Janey," he said in that deep, delicious voice of his. He'd sang in the high school choir, and now she imagined that no one dared to disobey a voice as powerful as his.

She sighed as she looked at him, something...odd firing in her. *What was that?* Her stomach felt like it had been flipped over and she had the strangest urge to reach up and trace her fingers along Adam's three-thirty shadow. He'd no doubt shaved that morning, but he'd started shaving when he was fourteen and it was a constant battle to have smooth skin.

She marveled at the maturity of him and a realization hit her square in the chest. *He's your age. And single.*

Her heart started beating irregularly, and she wasn't sure if it was because of the attractive silver she saw in his beard and hair, or if the sunglasses he wore made him so attractive, or if she was losing her mind.

Because Adam Herrin?

He'd never been on her romantic radar.

But it sure was screaming a warning at her right now.

"You okay, Janey?" he asked.

She pressed one hand over her heart, willing it to calm down, while she shoved her phone in her back pocket. "Yeah, fine." She took the skateboard from him and sank back to the steps. "Why'd you bring Jess home?"

"Oh, there was a little trouble at the skate park." He exhaled like he carried the weight of the world and Janey glanced at him, the word *trouble* bouncing around between her eardrums.

"Sit down," she said. "Rough day?"

"Sort of." He positioned himself next to her, and she got blasted with the scent of his cologne. Fresh, and beachy, and minty, she wondered if she could sprinkle some on her sheets and fall asleep with such a delectable smell in her nose.

"Is Jess in trouble?" She focused on her son, trying to figure out where all these traitorous thoughts about Adam were coming from. Jess was who mattered. Jess who'd been brought home by the Chief of Police himself.

"I know he didn't do it, but he's not sayin' who did." Adam gazed out across the front yard she'd just finished mowing and getting ready for the winter. She hoped she wouldn't have to do much more before the spring. Though she loved being and working outdoors, sometimes shouldering everything alone took its toll.

"What happened?" she asked, wishing she were as even and calm as Adam always was. She'd literally never seen the man get upset.

"There was some vandalism on the back of the building that borders the skate park," Adam said, finally swinging his attention to her. He took off his sunglasses, and wow, had his eyes always been that particular shade of brown? One step above black, liquid, and deep. Janey lost herself for a moment, quickly coming back to attention when he continued with, "And Jess was there, a spray paint can only a few feet from his backpack."

"He—he didn't say he wasn't going to skate park today." She wondered who he'd been with. "I was going to take him and Dix out to your brother's farm."

Adam looked at her steadily, and dang if that didn't make her pulse riot a little harder. "It looked like they'd been there a while, Janey."

"But school just got out, and—oh." She let her hands fall between her knees. "You think he skipped school."

"At least fourth period," Adam said. "He wouldn't say anything to me." He cast a glance over his shoulder. "Which isn't normal for him. Everything okay here, at home? You're not...." He cleared his throat and for the first time, Janey saw a blip of discomfort steal across his face. "Datin' anyone new or switching jobs or anything that could disrupt his normal schedule?"

Dating anyone new. Dating anyone new?

Janey threw her head back and laughed.

SNEAK PEEK! THE DAY HE STOPPED IN CHAPTER TWO

Adam had no idea what he'd said that was so darn funny. But Janey couldn't stop laughing. Just when she started to quiet, she'd look at him again and dissolve into more giggles. After several seconds, Adam smiled, the infectious nature of her laughter too much to ignore.

Oh, how he loved the sound of her voice. He wished he could erase the stiffness in her shoulders and the worry from her eyes. If she'd ever given him any indication that his presence in her life as more than a friend would be welcome, he'd do it. But she'd been as closed off to men since Matt died as anyone he'd ever known.

"Nothing's changed," she finally said when she could stop laughing. "I have the same schedule I've had for five years, since I was promoted." She added a smile to the statement that left Adam concentrating on what should be an involuntary function: breathing.

"And I'm not dating anyone."

Do you want to start dating? He swallowed the thought and said, "Maybe it's just the hormones," instead.

Janey moaned and swatted his bicep. Was that flirting? The sign he'd been hoping for? The touch was so light and so quick, he had no idea.

"Don't tell me I have to deal with that already," she said.

"He's in seventh grade," Adam said. "I guarantee his brain's already fallen out of his head. It's probably rollin' around under his bed."

She laughed again, and this time Adam joined his chuckle to hers. "He's a good kid," he said. "I told him he needs to be careful who he chooses to hang around with. Even if he's not the one doin' anything, people can get the wrong idea about him just by who he's with."

Janey cut him a nervous look. "Who was he with?"

"A couple of older boys I couldn't see as they ran off. The Fenniman twins, who are also in seventh grade and not bad kids." Adam shrugged, not wanting to alarm Janey too badly. He knew she was a huge worrywart already, and while he would like to thump Jess on the noggin for causing worry for his mom, the boy hadn't actually done anything yet.

"Will you keep an eye on him?" Janey asked, peering at him now with those intoxicating eyes. He was a sucker for those big brown eyes of hers, and he found himself nodding. While technically, it was his job to keep an eye on everything, he could spare a few minutes every day for Jess. For Janey.

"So are you excited about the planning weekend?" she asked.

Adam blinked at her. "The what?"

She gazed right back at him. "You're the best man for Drew and Gretchen's wedding, right?"

Adam's mind whirred, trying to find the missing piece of the puzzle for this line of questioning. "Yes," he said slowly.

"I'm the matron of honor. Gretchen and Drew are taking everyone in the wedding party for a weekend at the beach, but we all know it's just to help them plan." She flashed one of her brilliant smiles. In her tan face, the contrast of her white teeth really stood out. "I'm thinking I won't even bring my bathing suit. Gretchen will have me poring over magazines and then patterns to find her perfect dress."

Adam got stuck on "bathing suit" and what that might entail for Janey. "When is this weekend?"

"End of September. Cutting it really close, if you ask me." She stood like she'd go inside and see what Jess had gotten up to. "I mean, if they want a Christmas wedding, that only leaves three months for all the preparations."

"As I recall, you and Matt got married after a short engagement." He stood too, not quite sure why he'd said anything about Matt. Though it had been almost twelve years since his death, the way Janey's face blanked, and the way she swallowed, meant his fantasies of asking her out would remain exactly that: a figment of his imagination.

"Just three months from him asking to you saying 'I do', same as Gretchen, right?" Why was he still talking? And who would remember that? He cleared his throat. "I'll keep an eye out for Jess." He started to walk away, unable to look at Janey's beautiful, horrified face for another moment.

He flipped his sunglasses back into place, a shield between him and the rest of the world. Once behind the safety of his tinted windows, and with the air conditioner running, he dared to glance back to Janey's porch. She still stood there, watching him, a peculiar look on her face. He couldn't place what it was, but he stared at her too, memorizing the confusion and the...hope? Was that hope?

She turned and climbed the stairs, and Adam headed back to his office at the police station. He pulled down the current Rubix cube he worked whenever his thoughts got too wrinkled and he needed to iron them flat.

While his fingers worked the rows and columns, and his mind sorted through the colors and what needed to go where, he freed up other important brain waves that could focus on the things that eluded him.

He had nineteen solved Rubix cubes in a variety of sizes and colorations, all in a row on the shelf behind his desk. Ten of them had been solved while he worked on particularly difficult cases as a beat cop and then a detective. A few while he debated whether he should leave Hawthorne Harbor and complete the FBI training—which he'd ultimately done. And a few more over the four years he'd been Chief of Police.

One after Anita had left him and he didn't leave the office for days on end. This one, he suspected, would be devoted to Janey and his rotating thoughts as he tried to figure out what to do about her.

And a beach weekend? How in the world had he missed that?

All the green squares lined up and he turned the Rubix cube over to find the other side a complete array of colors. He set the puzzle down and picked up his phone to call his brother.

"Drew," he said when he answered. "I just talked to Janey and she mentioned something about a beach weekend? How come I don't know anything about this?"

His brother started laughing, and Adam didn't appreciate the gesture for the second time that day. "I told you about this weeks ago," Drew said. "You said you'd clear your schedule."

Adam looked down at his desk calendar. He flipped the calendar from August to September, and sure enough, he'd reserved the third weekend in September for "personal vacation."

He sighed. "I swear I don't remember talking about it."

"That's because I brought over a half dozen of those cookies you like. You'd have agreed to anything."

Adam scoffed while Drew chuckled. "I do remember the cookies." And the four miles he'd put on the beach the next morning to get rid of the cookies. At least he still enjoyed running to the sound of the ocean waves coming ashore.

"Has something come up?" Drew asked. "You can make it, can't you?"

"Janey made it sound like you guys had disguised a weekend of work by taking us to the beach."

The silence on the other end of the line confirmed it, and Adam glanced up as his lieutenant poked his head into the office. "I have to go." He hung up before Drew could say anything else and asked, "What's up, Jason?"

Lieutenant Zimmerman came in and sat on the couch in front of Adam's windows. "Kristin wants you to come for dinner on Friday night." He wore a placid look, but Adam knew what a dinner invitation at the Zimmerman's house meant. On the weekend, no less.

"Who else did she invite?" he asked.

"She wouldn't say."

Adam swiped the Rubix cube from his desk and started twisting like he could wring Jason's neck the same way. "I don't need to be set up."

"It's been months since Anita."

He gave Jason a dark look. "I know how long it's been."

"You're grouchy when you're not dating."

Adam didn't know what to say to that, especially since Jason probably took the most flack from Adam's bad moods. He minded the least though, if the twinkle in his eyes was any indication.

"So just come." He stood and knocked twice on the doorjamb. "She's making that Brazilian steak you like." He walked out of the office, and Adam decided he couldn't spend the next hour doing paperwork or sitting at his desk. He rarely could contain himself behind walls if it wasn't absolutely necessary, which was why he'd been driving by the skate park at the exact right moment that afternoon.

He stopped at his secretary's desk when she lifted her hand to get his attention. Sarah held the phone receiver to her ear and said, "Yes, thank you, Beth."

Adam's heart skipped a beat. Beth Yardley was the director of the Fall Festival, and he'd been after her to find out the topic for this year's cook-off. "It better not be chili again," he said, the anticipation of what the culinary topic would be making his muscles tight.

Sarah sighed as she replaced the receiver and met Adam's glare head-on. She'd been a familiar face at the station for two decades—longer than him—and he appreciated her candor when he needed it, the fresh flowers on her desk in the summer, and the poinsettias at Christmastime.

She brought pastries for birthdays, and kept everything in the department running.

"Soups," she finally said.

Adam growled and smashed his hat on his head. "I'm going to patrol something." He stalked out, his mind ping-ponging from Janey and the upcoming beach weekend and the half-dozen soup recipes he could try before entering the Fall Festival with something that could win.

After last year's chili debacle, he needed something to re-establish his street cred as the tough, no-nonsense Chief of Police—who also happened to be a genius in the kitchen.

BOOKS IN THE HAWTHORNE HARBOR ROMANCE SERIES

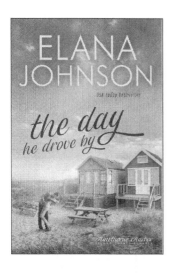

The Day He Drove By (Hawthorne Harbor Second Chance Romance, Book 1): A widowed florist, her ten-year-old daughter, and the paramedic who delivered the girl a decade earlier...

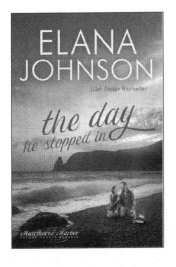

The Day He Stopped In (Hawthorne Harbor Second Chance Romance, Book 2): Janey Germaine is tired of entertaining tourists in Olympic National Park all day and trying to keep her twelve-year-old son occupied at night. When long-time friend and the Chief of Police, Adam Herrin, offers to take the boy on a ride-along one fall evening, Janey starts to see him in a different light. Do they have the courage to take their relationship out of the friend zone?

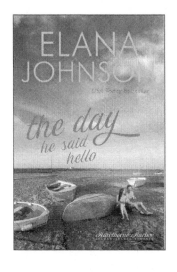

The Day He Said Hello (Hawthorne Harbor Second Chance Romance, Book 3): Bennett Patterson is content with his boring firefighting job and his big great dane...until he comes face-toface with his high school girlfriend, Jennie Zimmerman, who swore she'd never return to Hawthorne Harbor. Can they rekindle their old flame? Or will their opposite personalities keep them apart?

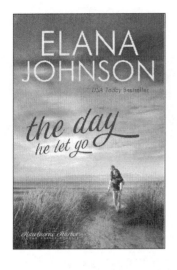

The Day He Let Go (Hawthorne Harbor Second Chance Romance, Book 4): Trent Baker is ready for another relationship, and he's hopeful he can find someone who wants him and to be a mother to his son. Lauren Michaels runs her own general contract company, and she's never thought she has a maternal bone in her body. But when she gets a second chance with the handsome K9 cop who blew her off when she first came to town, she can't say no... Can Trent and Lauren make their differences into strengths and build a family?

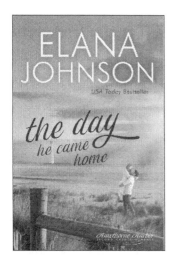

The Day He Came Home (Hawthorne Harbor Second Chance Romance, Book 5): A wounded Marine returns to Hawthorne Harbor years after the woman he was married to for exactly one week before she got an annulment...and then a baby nine months later. Can Hunter and Alice make a family out of past heartache?

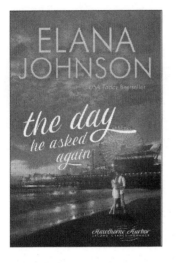

The Day He Asked Again (Hawthorne Harbor Second Chance Romance, Book 6): A Coast Guard captain would rather spend his time on the sea...unless he's with the woman he's been crushing on for months. Can Brooklynn and Dave make their second chance stick?

BOOKS IN THE GETAWAY BAY BILLIONAIRE ROMANCE SERIES

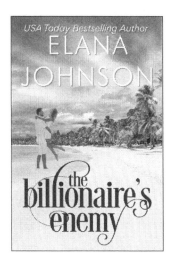

The Billionaire's Enemy (Book 1): A local island B&B owner hates the swanky highrise hotel down the beach...but not the billionaire who owns it. Can she deal with strange summer weather, tourists, and falling in love?

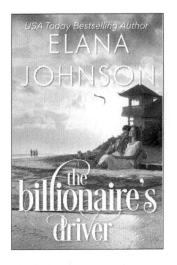

The Billionaire's Driver (Book 2): A car service owner who's been driving the billionaire pineapple plantation owner for years finally gives him a birthday gift that opens his eyes to see her, the woman who's literally been right in front of him all this time. Can he open his heart to the possibility of true love?

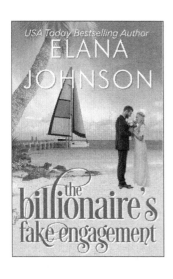

The Billionaire's Fake Engagement (Book 3): A former poker player turned beach bum billionaire needs a date to a hospital gala, so he asks the beach yoga instructor his dog can't seem to stay away from. At the event, they get "engaged" to deter her former boyfriend from pursuing her. Can he move his fake fiancée into a real relationship?

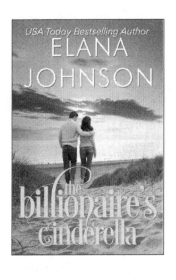

The Billionaire's Cinderella (Book 4): The owner of a beachside drink stand has taken more bad advice from rich men than humanly possible, which requires her to take a second job cleaning the home of a billionaire and global diamond mine owner. Can she put aside her preconceptions about rich men and make a relationship with him work?

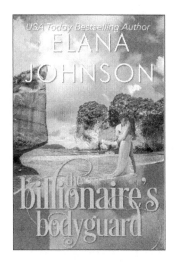

The Billionaire's Bodyguard (Book 5): Women can be rich too...and this female billionaire can usually take care of herself just fine, thank you very much. But she has no defense against her past...or the gorgeous man she hires to protect her from it. He's her bodyguard, not her boyfriend. Will she be able to keep those two B-words separate or will she take her second chance to get her tropical happily-ever-after?

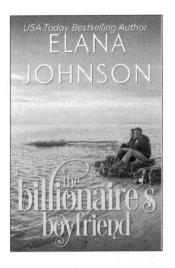

The Billionaire's Boyfriend (Book 6): Can a closet organizer fit herself into a single father's hectic life? Or will this female billionaire choose work over love...again?

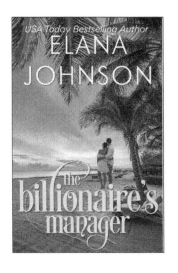

The Billionaire's Manager (Book 7): A billionaire who has a love affair with his job, his new bank manager, and how they bravely navigate the island of Getaway Bay...and their own ideas about each other.

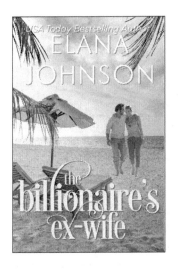

The Billionaire's Ex-Wife (Book 8): A silver fox, a dating app, and the mistaken identity that brings this billionaire faceto-face with his ex-wife...

BOOKS IN THE BRIDES & BEACHES ROMANCE SERIES

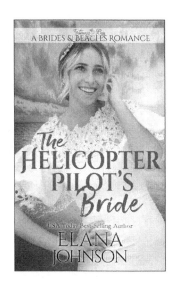

The Helicopter Pilot's Bride (Book 1): Charlotte Madsen's whole world came crashing down six months ago with the words, "I met someone else." Her marriage of eleven years dissolved, and she left one island on the east coast for the island of Getaway Bay. She was not expecting a tall, handsome man to be flat on his back under the kitchen sink when she arrives at the supposedly abandoned house. But former Air Force pilot, Dawson Dane, has a charming devil-may-care personality, and Charlotte could use some happiness in her life.

Can Charlotte navigate the healing process to find love again?

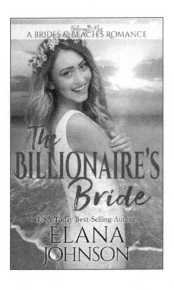

The Billionaire's Bride (Book 2): Two best friends, their hasty agreement, and the fake engagement that has the island of Getaway Bay in a tailspin...

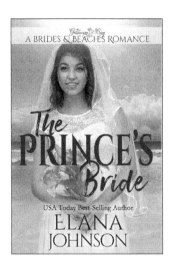

The Prince's Bride (Book 3):
She's a synchronized swimmer
looking to make some extra
cash. He's a prince in hiding.
When they meet in the "empty"
mansion she's supposed to be
housesitting, sparks fly. Can
Noah and Zara stop arguing
long enough to realize their
feelings for each other might be
romantic?

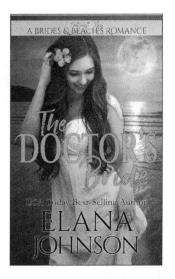

The Doctor's Bride (Book 4): A doctor, a wedding planner, and a flat tire... Can Shannon and Jeremiah make a love connection when they work next door to each other?

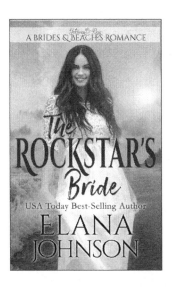

The Rockstar's Bride (Book 5): Riley finds a watch and contacts the owner, only to learn he's the lead singer and guitarist for a hugely popular band. Evan is only on the island of Getaway Bay for a friend's wedding, but he's intrigued by the gorgeous woman who returns his watch. Can they make a relationship work when they're from two different worlds?

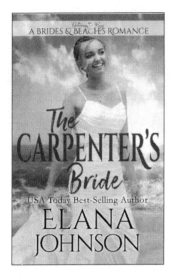

The Carpenter's Bride (Book 6): A wedding planner and the carpenter who's lost his wife... Can Lisa and Cal navigate the mishaps of a relationship in order to find themselves standing at the altar?

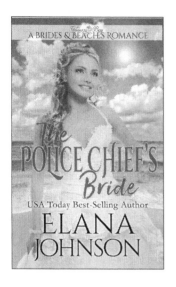

The Police Chief's Bride (Book 7): The Chief of Police and a woman with a restraining order against her... Can Wyatt and Deirdre try for their second chance at love? Or will their pasts keep them apart forever?

BOOKS IN THE STRANDED IN GETAWAY BAY ROMANCE SERIES

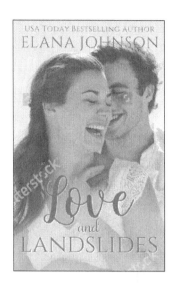

Love and Landslides (Book 1): A freak storm has her sliding down the mountain...right into the arms of her ex. As Eden and Holden spend time out in the wilds of Hawaii trying to survive, their old flame is rekindled. But with secrets and old feelings in the way, will Holden be able to take all the broken pieces of his life and put them back together in a way that makes sense? Or will he lose his heart and the reputation of his company because of a single landslide?

Kisses and Killer Whales (Book 2): Friends who ditch her. A pod of killer whales. A limping cruise ship. All reasons Iris finds herself stranded on an deserted island with the handsome Navy SEAL...

Storms and Sentiments (Book 3): He can throw a precision pass, but he's dead in the water in matters of the heart...

USA TODAY BESTSELLING AUTHOR
ELANA JOHNSON

Crushes and Cowboys (Book 4): Tired of the dating scene, a cowboy billionaire puts up an Internet ad to find a woman to come out to a deserted island with him to see if they can make a love connection...

ABOUT ELANA

Elana Johnson is the USA Today bestselling author of dozens of clean and wholesome contemporary romance novels. She lives in Utah, where she mothers two fur babies, taxis her daughter to theater several times a week, and eats a lot of Ferrero Rocher while writing. Find her on her website at elanajohnson.com.

63028359R00221